THE LAST ENEMY

THE LAST ENEMY

RHODA KAELLIS

PULP PRESS

THE LAST ENEMY
Copyright © 1989 by Rhoda Kaellis

Published By:
PULP PRESS BOOK PUBLISHERS
100-1062 Homer Street
Vancouver, B.C. Canada
V6B 2W9
A Division of Arsenal Pulp Press Book Publishers Ltd.

The publisher gratefully acknowledges the financial assistance of The Canada Council.

COVER ILLUSTRATION AND DESIGN: Michael Bender
EDITOR FOR THE PRESS: Linda Field
PRINTING: Hignell Printing
TYPESETTING: Vancouver Desktop Publishing Centre
PRINTED AND BOUND IN CANADA

CANADIAN CATALOGUING IN PUBLICATION DATA:
Kaellis, Rhoda, 1928-
    The last enemy

    ISBN 0-88978-214-8

    I. Title.
PS8571.A34L3 1989   C813'.54   C89-091387-0
PR9199.3.K33L3 1989

This book is dedicated to the fifteen survivors
whose experiences in the Holocaust
inspired the story of Sarah and Lilly.

FOREWORD

IN 1987 RABBI VICTOR REINSTEIN, OF CONGREGATION TEMPLE Emanu-El in Victoria, British Columbia, suggested that the personal recollections of the community's Holocaust survivors be recorded. I volunteered my services to interview everyone I could find. I located fifteen survivors, and, over a period of nine months, recorded their histories.

I allotted a couple of months for the task. After all, as an experienced interviewer, I assumed I could estimate the time I needed. But I found it impossible to proceed in the usual way. I allowed more and more time to elapse between interviews, and at the end had to force myself to complete the work.

The records I collected were from men and women who at the time of the Holocaust had been anywhere from five years old to their early twenties. They had been nationals of Germany, Poland, France, Holland, and Belgium, and had experienced starvation, beatings, torture, and slave labor. They had been under threat of murder and had been witnesses to the murders of neighbors and relatives.

One man who had done slave labor building the Autobahn, termed it "a Jewish graveyard." When people dropped from exhaustion and starvation, they were paved into the road. He saw his brother's body incorporated into the cement.

After I had collected all the data I needed and was about to compile a written record, the idea for a novel about the Holocaust occurred to me so forcefully, almost violently, that I set aside everything else and began the first draft of what was to become *The Last Enemy*.

While many of the incidents in the novel are based on the accounts I collected from the survivors, they also reflect my own life's experience as a Jewish child growing up in New York during the Second World War and after.

The Holocaust holds a weird fascination that is difficult to analyze. There is such a sense of profound unreality about these experiences, that accepting them became, for me, almost a feat of will. The survivors seemed to have a similar problem. Again and again they told me, "It happened to me but it's still hard for me to believe."

I have mulled and puzzled over why this should be so, as I shook my head in disbelief, not about the truth of what I was told, but over the fact that one human being could do these things to another. I finally decided that no sane person is capable of understanding how men and women could methodically and repeatedly—even within the context of a program of annihilation—gratuitously engage in such prolonged cruelty towards defenseless men, women, old people, infants, and children. There is no way a rational mind can ever understand why or how the Final Solution could be carried out.

In spite of this, or because of it, the fear remains that it could happen again.

The Last Enemy deals with one of the most painful periods in history. For many North Americans the Holocaust was another horror story, heard at a distance, intruding into a post-war environment of victory and hope for the future.

Some who personally did not experience the loss, pain, fear, anger and degradation of the Holocaust feel that now, nearly a half-century later, is a time to forgive and forget. Others insists that it never happened. If the poisons of the Holocaust are repressed and permitted to fester, the plague may once again break out, not only in acute mass deliberate violence, but in chronic cynicism, alienation, and despair.

The Holocaust left awful scars. Even those who survived the death camps paid the full price. Their families, neighbors, friends, towns, and culture had been irremediably destroyed. Their universe had perished, leaving them in a state of limbo.

Some attitudes did change after the Holocaust. Among believing Jews there was and is a continuing quest for answers about where God was in Auschwitz. Among Christians, there has been a re-examination of traditional attitudes toward Jews which periodically gave rise to hatred and violence. More Jews and Christians have begun to form lasting friendships. However, these changes are occurring in a matrix of a thousand years of prejudice which underlines the enormity of what has yet to be accomplished. Perhaps this is one reason that stories of the Holocaust do not seem to lose their importance and meaning.

CHAPTER ONE

THE NIGHT BEFORE LILLY CAME TO LIVE WITH US I DIDN'T SLEEP at all. I know I was excited but I can't really remember any other feeling. I might have been frightened too, or at least apprehensive. Then again, it's hard to tell. I'm probably only projecting my present feelings onto the past. What I did though—at intervals all through that night—was put on the new bedside lamp that my mother had allowed me to choose, to look at my refurbished bedroom; a twin bed matching mine, with all its gold and orange ruffles made painstakingly by Mama of new cotton then dipped in liquid starch and when still damp pressed smooth and shiny with a hot iron. The faint odor of crisp cleanness sat in the room all ready for Lilly, who was going to be my best friend, and the sister I never had.

She was my first cousin, the nearest thing to a sister, and needy. A little less than a year after the war was over my family was doing a *mitzvah*, a good deed according to the commandments, taking in a relative made an orphan by the Holocaust.

I'll never forget that spring of 1945 and V-E Day, not if I live to be a hundred. On May 8, the war in Europe ended. The armies of West and East had met, American and Russian soldiers running toward each other across no-man's-land, to throw themselves into each other's arms. The Movietone News ran it in all the local theaters. White flecks spotted the film which went out of focus a couple of times. It was so real, my heart swelled and thumped hard against my ribs as I looked at the overjoyed faces of the soldiers. Amazingly, some of them were crying; the tears shone wet on their cheeks.

When President Truman announced the Allied victory over fascism, I was eleven years old. It was an unseasonably warm spring and along with all the other people half-crazed with joy, I ran and danced in the streets of Brooklyn, streets closed off to traffic and hastily strung with lights that blazed through the night of celebration. The long, frightening war in Europe was over. Millions had died in shocking ways, but the rest of us were safe and now the damaged and wounded could start to heal themselves. The Nazi threat that might, God forbid, invade America was gone. The most depraved horde of monsters ever known had been defeated and put to rout. We could feel secure again.

My mother and father were observant Jews and I was their only child. Talk of the scourge that had crushed Europe and specifically the Jews was common at our table. Along with my parents, I agonized over the invasion of eastern Europe and Holland, had nightmares over the reports of round-ups, cattle cars, reprisals, burnings, gassings, extermination, and concentration camps.

My parents didn't even try to shield me from information and news as commonplace as the weather reports. They believed I had to know what was happening. But I couldn't understand why people were doing these things and my parents couldn't explain it. All they could do was comfort me, hold me close to them when I got frightened.

At night I would lie awake in my safe pleasant room surrounded by my books and favourite dolls, and fantasize. I was a giant standing astride Europe. I reached down to scoop up handfuls of Nazis, squeezing them to a pulp in my hands. I lifted my colossal boot and brought it down on battalions, whole armies of Nazi troops. Single-handed I saved the Jews of Europe and at the same time, other victims of the horror. My fantasies were normal enough—all we talked about with relatives, neighbors, and friends, was the war, the Nazis, the events in Europe. Most of the school curriculum was devoted to it. Every class, from English to art, reflected it.

I first heard of Lilly six months after the war ended. My father had asked me to say the blessing for bread before we started to eat, and while my mother dished out carrots and green beans, he said, "I've been in touch with Yankel. They're pretty sure they've found Esther's girl. She was in a Catholic orphanage near Brussels."

My father was the youngest of thirteen children and Esther was his oldest sister. He and his two youngest brothers had emigrated to New York in 1915. The rest of the family lived in London. But in 1919, in Belgium, Esther had met a Polish Jewish refugee at a friend's wedding, fell in love and married him. There she stayed because her new husband had no papers and she couldn't get him admitted to England.

I found it hard to keep track of, or sort out, all my father's brothers and sisters, and all the photographs looked the same to me. Stiff men, stiffly dressed, standing like cardboard cutouts behind broad, solid women, rigidly upright in ornate chairs, covered from neck to toe in heavy, ornate clothes. I felt suffocated just looking at them.

I vaguely recalled talk of Aunt Esther being trapped in Belgium with her husband, but the first I heard of a child was that day when my father spoke of having located Esther's daughter.

"How old is she now?" my mother asked.

"A little younger than Sarah, I think. Let's see . . . Lilly was born in the spring or early summer of '35 . . . . "

"That's not a little, Papa," I said, "I'm a whole year older."

I remember my father's smile. Often he looked solemn, almost sad, but his smile lit up his entire face. Toward me he was always indulgent and humorous, as if I amused and pleased him at the same time. I have never met a man handsomer than my father.

"Of course, Saraleh, a whole year is a lot when you're only twelve. I think Lilly is eleven."

"I never knew Auntie Esther had a child, Papa."

"Well, she did. And one of your uncles has been looking for the girl. The Red Cross helped him. Her name was changed to keep her safe, but her papers, and the neighbors who kept track of her after . . . after your aunt and uncle were killed . . . it looks like it's really your cousin Lilly."

There was more talk about papers of release, but I was already busy imagining this unknown and newly-discovered cousin, almost my age but younger. She would be thin and weak, all eyes, like the pictures I saw of people liberated from concentration camps, cheated of her childhood and school, dolls and pretty clothes. If we ever met, I would take her under my wing, become her teacher, showing and sharing with her all the things she'd missed. I would do this *mitzvah* so well, she would be filled with gratitude, and love and admire me. We would become inseparable. I would always protect her, so the terrible memories would fade away.

I was young and naive like most of the people I knew in those days. We thought we were hardened by the carnage of modern warfare and the disclosure of Holocaust evidence at the Nuremberg trials, so nothing could shock us anymore. But no one had any idea how future generations would continue to suffer from the thirteen year tide of deadly malignant hatred released by the Nazis, tainting everything it touched.

I can't remember how long it was, some weeks, perhaps a month or two, before the subject of Lilly came up again. This time the setting was more formal.

Mama and Papa called me into the living room from the kitchen where I always did my homework, and sat me between them on the sofa. Papa folded my hand into his large warm one. It looked very brown and thin compared to my pudgy, white fist. His dark eyes were bright as he looked down at me.

"Saraleh, remember we were talking about Auntie Esther's girl, Lilly?" I nodded. "Well they took her to London and she's been staying with Auntie Fanny. But Fanny's family is very large and things are still very bad in Europe. It's even hard for them to take care of their own children. We want to bring Lilly here, to live with us. And we hope you'll be happy about the idea. It's a very great *mitzvah* to raise an orphan, especially one who has survived the Catastrophe."

I could hardly believe my ears. It was like a dream come true. "Really Papa?!" I squealed. "Lilly can live with us?! That'll be like having my very own sister!"

Papa smiled and Mama stroked my hair. She smiled too, though her eyes were sad, and she said very solemnly, "You'll have to be patient and kind, Sarah. They say that Lilly is a nervous girl and often not very happy. She's been damaged by her experience. You'll really have to be the big sister and it may not always be easy.''

To this day the word 'damaged' sticks in my head. The image that popped into my mind when my mother spoke the word was of a label I had seen on a chair in a furniture store which read, 'Damaged. Reduced to $12.95.'

I was bouncing on the sofa. "When is she coming, Papa?"

"They're making the arrangements now. In a couple of weeks they should be able to get her on a ship. By the end of the month, the latest.''

I was breathless with excitement, but before I could spend time marvelling over this new development, my mother and I were in a flurry of redecorating my room. My parents thought it would be a good idea for us to share my room at first so Lilly would not feel too much alone and like a stranger. Later, if we wanted, Lilly could move into the spare room next to mine.

Papa rearranged my closet with extra shelves and rods to accommodate two wardrobes. With great satisfaction, I emptied half of my bookcase to make room for Lilly's things. Mama let me choose my favorite colors for the new bedspreads and curtains.

I looked at my familiar, comfortable home with new eyes, seeing it as Lilly would. The downstairs entrance hall led to the living room on the right and the dining room on the left. Through the dining room arch, a short hallway led to the kitchen at the back of the house, and gave onto the back porch and yard. Papa's little study was also off the dining room hall, in the front of the house. The entrance hall led to the upstairs bedrooms—Mama and Papa's, mine, a spare room, and the four-piece bath.

It was a modest house. I loved every inch of it. Mama's taste in decorating was ahead of her time. The hall, dining and living rooms were painted white, the kitchen lemon yellow with white trim and fixtures. Our fruitwood furniture had clean, uncluttered lines, and was upholstered in brown and beige tweeds, golds, and Jefferson blue. We had good prints on the walls—Cezanne, Chagall, Van Gogh. The feeling was of peace and order: warm in winter, cool in summer.

It was very different from my friends' and aunties' homes which were dark and overflowing with furnishings and somber wallpapers and brocaded upholstery, heavy drapery, and elaborately patterned carpets. The atmosphere was stuffy and dusty, and going back to my own pretty house was always a pleasure. I would be proud to show Lilly around her new home.

As my excitement grew, I saw myself more and more like a fairy godmother. My fantasy of rescuing Jews was becoming a reality.

I could hardly wait for the first Friday night after I learned Lilly was coming to live with us. My cousin Yosuf, his kid brother Duvid, and his mother and father—Papa's brother Chaim, and Chaim's wife, my Auntie Aviva, were coming for Friday, *erev Shabbat* supper.

Papa's brothers lived only a few blocks away, and we shared many occasions like the Sabbath with them. Yosuf, my favorite cousin, was sixteen and someone I counted on for information, advice, and general support. Now I had something really important to talk about. Overnight I was going from being a kid to a mature person with a grown up job to do.

As soon as I had helped Mama and Auntie clear the table and stack the dirty dishes, I invited Yosuf to come up to my room to see how we had prepared for Lilly's arrival.

"This is Lilly's bed, and her own dresser. We'll share the closet. Oh Yosuf! It's going to be such fun, having a sort of sister."

Yosuf laughed, scoffing at the idea. "You can say that because you've never had one. It's not all fun you know. Besides, don't count on too much. Lilly's had an awful time and lost her parents. A lot of those people don't get along with other people."

"I *know*, Yosuf. Mama told me I'd have to be patient. I know that doing a *mitzvah* isn't always easy, but I'm gonna make her so happy she'll feel better very soon."

Yosuf shrugged his narrow, bony shoulders and we went down to have our tea and honey cake.

It was going to be my last Friday without Lilly and I spent time doing my memory trick. No Friday after this would be the same, and so I etched the details of that evening into my mind. Our living room was warm and bright, and Papa's profile was silhouetted against the lamp shade as he read aloud from the *Morgen Journal.* Everybody sipped comfortably from glasses of tea. Duvid lay on the rug reading a comic book. My mother and aunt sat side by side, occasionally murmuring something to each other. I sat on the sofa next to Yosuf admiring my Baby Jane patent leather shoes, and after the heavy meal, growing drowsy in the quiet warmth of the room.

To this day, I can evoke the picture in its every detail anytime I want, and I often do, like a touchstone of peace and safety. It soothes me, and sometimes when I can't sleep, remembering that evening helps me drop off.

My father was born in London, England, but his ancestors had lived for centuries in Spain, part of the Sephardic or Mediterranean Jewish *diaspora*. They considered themselves the elite or the aristocracy of Jews and claimed the Hebrew they spoke was purer than the adulterated versions of the Eastern European Jews.

The Sephardi were often wealthy, generally well-educated, and until the Spanish Inquisition, led cultured, active lives in the country they considered their home. The church Inquisition ended that phase of their existence and those who could, fled, while others were broken on the rack, and as a consequence, embraced Christian mercy and love to escape further torture. Still others died in agony, refusing to relinquish their stiff-necked adherence to their God regardless of all the persuasion used on them to rid them of their mistaken ideas.

My father's great, great, great, etc., grandfather, Eliahu Cardozo, was rich enough and smart enough to get out when he could, taking his liquid assets, his aged mother, and his wife and four children. He made his way up the west coast of Spain to Bilbao where he and his entourage found a ship that delivered them eventually to Bordeaux in France. There are no details of how he effected this passage or how long it took, or how long the family remained in various cities in France as they made their way northward to Holland and finally, Rotterdam. The Cardozos remained in Holland until the 17th Century, when a branch that became my father's ancestors moved to England and settled in London. The Dutch line of the family was destroyed in the Holocaust. The survivors were from the English line.

My father was fourteen when he came to New York in 1915 with his brothers Chaim and Shmuel, who were nineteen and twenty-one at the time. My father's parents did not strenuously object to this fractioning of the family. With ten children left, many grandchildren and more promised, it must have been something of a relief when Shmuel, a talented goldsmith, got himself sponsored to America by a visiting diamond merchant and entrepreneur.

Maybe my father grew up faster in New York without a mother and with two brothers as surrogate fathers than he might have at home in London. The brothers did well. Chaim went into the expanding garment industry, and Mikhel, my father, who was the 'brains', went on to graduate from the College of the City of New York's school of business.

It was here he met my mother, Molly, a native-born first generation American, whose parents had come from an eastern European city on the ever-changing Polish-Austrian frontier.

Molly Sokolov was learning office skills and bookkeeping: Mikhel Cardozo was in his last year of accountancy. I don't know if there was a great romance, or love at first sight. My parents didn't talk about these things, but they married soon after my father graduated, and there are several sepia-colored photos on cardboard backing from that time.

My mother is almost ethereal in her wedding dress of white satin: her mass of wavy hair which spins out around her head like a dark cloud is held in check by a circlet of blossoms on a short veil. Her eyes are large and dark and the little smile on her mouth seems tremulous to me. My father looks out at me proudly, almost defiantly, his arm around my mother, hand firm on her elbow as if to say, "See, look what I got. This is *my* Malkah." He is handsomely dark, Turk-like, a throw-back to the Spanish blood running in the family veins.

The date on the back of this picture is 1930, when the Great Depression was digging its talons into the economic body of America and Europe. They were courageous or foolish or both, to embark on the venture of marriage in such uncertain times. But then, what times are not uncertain, especially for Jews? In any case, the Cardozo brothers were doing well on a small scale and Mikhel was keeping accounts for his brothers' enterprises. He was also connected with a small but solid firm of accountants and would stay with them for the next fifteen years.

I was born four years after their marriage, a long-awaited, much longed-for child, and for reasons not discussed with me, remained an only child. My parents started their life together in a small apartment, which I remember fairly well because I was six when we moved to our house in Bensonhurst.

It was a middle-middle class neighborhood. The house was red brick with white trim, on a city lot. The small yard was a mix of grass and weeds, with a few flowers near the fence. My mother wasn't much of a gardener, but the trees in front of the house and the two in our yard, an apple and a maple, made up for the lack of shrubs and blossoms.

There were two or three styles of houses in the neighborhood—one-family detached brick like ours, one-family semi-detached stucco, and two-storey apartment houses with eight to ten units. The houses were neat, the tree-lined streets were clean. It was a good place for children to grow up.

With no brothers or sisters I made do with cousins. Deborah and Murray, Uncle Shmuel's children, were much older and so more like another aunt and uncle, but Yosuf, Uncle Chaim's older boy, was my closest, dearest friend and confidant. When Yosuf's brother Duvid came along, he was already outside my interests or concerns, he was just my baby cousin.

I had my own girl friends, the kids in the neighborhood with whom I played on the street or in the playground, while our mothers sat together overseeing us, knitting and talking. Anne, Rebecca, and I remained friends when we started school, clustering together in kindergarten, and as we went through the grades, meeting after school to do homework and share experiences and dreams, or spending *Shabbat* morning together in the women's section of the synagogue.

Our synagogue served about three hundred orthodox families. It was a red brick building with no pretensions to anything but serviceability. The interior had white-painted plaster walls, and a wooden women's balcony at the front of the building under a large Star-of-David window. A blue curtain separated the women's section from the rest of the room. The wood floors were creaky, the wooden pews were worn. The *bima* was a raised platform behind a fence which held two electric-lit candelabras at either end. It was reached by three steps on both sides of the platform. Behind the *bima* was the Ark which held the scrolls, with a plain blue curtain drawn in front of it. Above the Ark were the Ten Commandments, inscribed on two tablets with a Lion of

Judah guarding them on either side. Three lights in round frosted globes hung from brass chains down the center of the room.

Shul was as familiar and homey as my own kitchen and just as much a part of my life. This was also true for Anne who lived in the house next to ours, and Rebecca, whose house was on the other side of the synagogue.

Anne, the oldest child in her family, had a younger brother and sister, much to my envy. She was a roly-poly girl, a small replica of her mother, with a wide grin, a happy laugh and a zany sense of humor. Rebecca, the third of the Three Musketeers, as our mothers referred to us, was taller than either of us and squarish, not fat, but without an indication of hips or waist. She was the solemn one, tending to moodiness. I loved both my friends, but slightly favored Anne. It was a bias I fought and occasionally lost. Then I'd be attacked by guilt.

The three of us were together as much as we could be. We started school the same year, and I went off to kindergarten eagerly with no qualms. Each new school year was more exciting than the one before.

We were in the same class throughout grade school and junior high school, separated only when I chose French as my first language and they German, and when I chose an academic program and they, commercial. I went on to algebra, while they took typing and business maths.

New York had wonderful teachers in those days because teaching was a good profession which paid well and was regarded with respect. Among Jewish families, respect for education went hand-in-hand with religion, and my teachers got the best I could give. My grades were good and I shone in English, History and Art.

When I was twelve, we had just begun to admit to an interest in boys, and Anne confessed she thought my cousin Yosuf was 'cute.'

Every once in a while the three of us would get dressed up in stockings and our best clothes and go into Manhattan to the Metropolitan Museum of Art or the Museum of Natural History. We would eat in the museum cafeteria and spend hours looking at objects in glass cases or paintings in elaborate frames and armless statues of nude men and women in heroic poses. We would start out at nine in the morning, arriving just as the buildings were opening their doors, and in winter, return in the late afternoon when the streets grew dark by four-thirty. In those days there was never any problem about being out. The worst a young girl could expect in a crowded subway car during rush hour was some strange man pressing up against her and rubbing a surreptitious hand along her buttocks. The subways were dreary but clean, the rare grafitti taking the form of tiny initials scratched into the olive-drab paint of the subway cars. For us, these excursions created a pleasant cadence of high points interspersing the even, predictable tenor of school and home.

Anne and I always waited to walk home with each other, but Rebecca lived in the other direction, so we had to leave her at the school gate. When we didn't do our homework together after school, the three of us would dally in the street exchanging important information that couldn't wait for the next day.

There were other children of course. Regularly we would go to birthday parties or be the star attraction at our own, and sometimes our little nucleus would expand to four or five, but the three of us were all important to each other. What we shared was special.

Aside from school, a lot of our talk was about our families and what our mothers or fathers did and said. Anne and Rebecca talked about their sisters and brother. Rebecca had an older sister, and she thought I was lucky to be an only child. She would scoff at my yearning for a sibling, pointing out advantages such as not having to share anything.

But Anne sympathized with my lack and avoided bragging about her status, because she knew I was really unhappy about being an only child. Each time her mother came home from the hospital with a new infant, she minimized the importance of the event, holding out hope that my mother would one day do the same.

I had long since given up such expectations, until the wonderful, incredible day when I knew I would be acquiring a surrogate sister, actually as good as a sister, because Lilly was a blood relation. I could hardly wait to see Anne and Rebecca together, and almost burst my seams while Anne and I dashed over to Rebecca's house. To have told Anne before Rebecca would have been undiplomatic, straining the friendship more than resisting the urge to tell Anne was straining me.

Once at Rebecca's house, I milked my secret for all it was worth, giving them three guesses each, laughing smugly as each guess got further from the soon-to-be-revealed facts. When they learned I was to be sister to a survivor of the Holocaust, the respect that shone in their faces was well worth the deprivation I had suffered up to then. I had what they never would—romance, adventure, and good deed rolled into one. All they had were biological siblings, no big deal, given the seeming ease with which most families added to their numbers.

They insisted I tell them when they would meet Lilly and although I didn't know any more than they did, I promised that as soon as she arrived, I would arrange for an immediate meeting, or at least one that would come as soon as humanly possible. I realized that my mother and father might have conflicting plans for Lilly, though I couldn't imagine anything more important than for her to have ready-made friends in the neighborhood and at school.

After that, whenever Anne, Rebecca, and I met, our first order of business was an up-date on Lilly. When I told them Lilly was to arrive the next day, they squealed as loudly and jumped as high as I had when I'd heard the good news. Now I was the one to be envied as we talked about what I would wear. Something plain so Lilly would not be embarrassed. We talked about what I would say, how I would make her feel at home and at ease, how I would share my favorite dolls and books and secrets.

I was not at all restrained, in either my imaginings or my ramblings. This was the stage I set, out of ignorance and desire to lay claim to my acquired sister. Nothing could have tempered my headlong exposition of the future or stopped me from fantasizing with my friends. From the very beginning, where Lilly was concerned, I threw caution to the winds.

Dealing with real ambivalence for the first time, I couldn't wait to tell my friends, but I also wanted Lilly all to myself. The idea she might find someone else more important or more interesting made me jealous even before I knew what she looked like. But my twelve-year old drive to brag was stronger, and every step of the way, not only did Anne and Rebecca get a blow-by-blow description of how 'Operation Lilly' was proceeding, but so did my entire seventh grade class. Most of my English compositions had at least a mention of her, she was a regular topic of conversation in my French class, and history was a natural place to discuss her story and the recent events in Europe.

Lilly came along like a gift when I had already given up any hope for the good fortune of ever having a sibling.

CHAPTER TWO

THE DAY OF LILLY'S ARRIVAL, WE TOOK THE BMT SUBWAY TO 49TH Street, and then a taxi to the piers on the west side where all the Trans-Atlantic liners docked. Until the war in Japan ended, uniformed men and women soldiers and sailors were a common sight all over New York. Down at the piers that day, they were in the majority. It was fascinating and exciting to listen to the gabble of foreign languages and identify French and British uniforms.

As we made our way to the arrivals area to meet Lilly, I gawked at ship's bows still painted in war-time camouflage, towering ten stories overhead. The luxury liners converted to troop ships carried refugees, fashionable passengers, and military personnel in a hodge-podge mixture. I couldn't look fast enough to take in the spectacle, the ceaseless flow of humanity with its noisy, vibrant sounds and colors. My mother insisted on holding my hand, pulling me along. Like a baby, I looked where I had been, not where I was going, so I paid no attention to how we got to the reception lounge. My father had the papers we needed to claim Lilly in his briefcase. I could hardly wait for the moment we would meet and I could put into practice all my plans for helping her.

I had already formed a picture of Lilly in my mind when I looked up the flower in the encyclopedia. I decided she would have the whitest skin, and a delicate face, small and thin. Her hair would be darker than mine but straight and long, like the stem of a lily. Then I saw her for the first time.

She was standing by herself near a bench with her feet neatly side-by-side and her hands clasped together in front of her. She was half-a-head shorter than I was, and had a smooth, round face with high, wide cheek bones. My first shocking thought was, she doesn't look Jewish! She looked like some of the Polish girls in my class at school. Her hair was pale brown and straight, parted in the center and braided into two plaits on either side of her head. Her nose was round and small like a button, and her eyes were large and round, like brown buttons—so different from my own long, narrow face with its sharp bones and nose and my hard-to-manage, curling, dark brown hair.

Lilly was staring blankly ahead of her, not looking around anxiously as we were, but even before my father said, "There she is!" I knew it was Lilly.

I suppose what we did was swoop down on her. I know I could hardly wait to tell her I was her cousin Sarah, so we must all have been talking at once. I remember Lilly's oblique glance at me before her eyes traveled upward to Mama and Papa who were bending down toward her.

Lilly's face didn't change, but she seemed to shrink into herself, growing somehow more compact as Papa took her hand and Mama bent to kiss her cheek.

Papa was saying, "Let's get the paper work done," and Mama herded Lilly and me before her, the three of us following in Papa's wake as he cleaved through the crowd toward Customs.

Lilly kept her eyes straight forward. I wanted her to look at me and smile so we could talk, but when she didn't, I had a chance to study her. She was wearing a navy blue boater hat on the back of her head, decorated with a two-inch wide grosgrain ribbon that hung down over the brim. Her coat was navy blue with embossed brass buttons and a tiny brown fur collar. She was wearing real stockings and black leather pumps with a little purse to match hanging from her shoulder on a narrow strap.

The way she was dressed was another surprise, and my tweed coat, saddle shoes and ankle socks from which my long, skinny legs extended, made me feel clumsy and foreign while Lilly looked as if she was one of the fashionable travelers.

We stopped at some kind of a counter and while adult conversation went on over our heads, I said to Lilly, "My name is Sarah."

She didn't answer or turn to me, so I assumed she couldn't understand my English. Papa said Lilly's native language was French, but her mother, Auntie Esther, had spoken English to her until the time Lilly went into the orphanage when she was five years old. The London relatives told us that Lilly was learning English very fast and understood everything.

I figured I had to get Lilly to look at me, so without touching her I walked around to face her. We were looking directly at each other for the first time. I smiled. "My name is Sarah, Lilly. I'm your cousin."

I was startled and confused by what happened next. Lilly's lips compressed and her eyes seemed to become opaque, so hard in fact they reflected the light and I could see myself in them. It was a look I never saw before and I was so surprised I dropped my eyes and turned away, wondering if I had offended the cousin so eagerly anticipated and awaited. While I wondered if what I said might have meant something else, something bad in her language, Lilly stood in the same spot, not moving, looking, it seemed to me, at nothing at all.

The joyful excitement drained away. Now I wanted Mama and Papa to be done with the officials and act as intermediaries between Lilly and me. After all, I was still only a kid needing guidance from older people who knew what to do. It probably didn't take too long but the wait seemed endless. At last my parents turned back to us.

"We're done, girls," Papa said triumphantly. "Let's go home."

In the taxi we all sat on the back seat, Lilly and me between Mama and Papa. Lilly sat next to Papa and the little valise that held her things rested on the floor at her feet.

"Did you have a good trip, Lilly?" Papa spoke slower than usual and more clearly.

Lilly turned her head to look at him, and for a moment I thought she would treat him the way she had me. But in a moment she looked down at her lap where her hands were folded neatly · together and said, barely audibly, "Yes, *merci*."

"That's good," Papa said.

I was thrilled. Lilly had actually said 'thank you' in a genuine foreign language. I had just started to learn French in junior high school and I imagined the advantage it would be to us when we would rattle away together fluent in both languages, she teaching me French, I teaching her English. I would be the envy of my friends and the best French student in my class, thanks to Lilly.

The bewilderment I experienced in the ship terminal was gone. I was sure I had read bad things into what was only shyness and confusion. I had to remember that everything was new and strange for Lilly, including a language she was just beginning to learn again. Mama had told me I would need a lot of patience. The word 'damaged' flashed into my head. Of course, Lilly was damaged by her experience. I was behaving like a silly little girl when what was needed was maturity and a grownup understanding attitude.

I had expected friendship based on *my* experience. In New York, making friends was uncomplicated and direct; kids introduced themselves and decided to play together. But Lilly was an orphan, and not just an ordinary orphan whose family had died of some sickness or a car accident. Lilly's parents had been taken away to be killed in an extermination camp. I was going to have to learn a whole new set of rules to suit her.

By the time we reached the subway and piled out of the taxi while Papa paid the driver, my fantasy of guiding Lilly into a happy, wholesome life as an American girl was renewed.

On my mother's side I was second generation American and very proud of it, even as a child. My mother was educated, a college graduate, who, before I was born, had been an executive secretary during the first few years of her married life.

During the Nazi years, being an American living in America had the advantage of safety in a very threatening world and the privilege of abundance in an economy burgeoning with war-work. We had a lot to be grateful for and we didn't want to forget it.

When Papa read the headlines from the newspaper for us after supper, Mama would exclaim with shock and sorrow, "Oh those poor people!" and "God help them!" or "Why must they suffer like that!"

Papa would read a story from the front page, shake his head in disbelief and sigh, "Thank God for America."

When London was being bombed and news from his parents
and sisters and brothers and their families was slow in coming,
Papa's face would crease with anxiety and he would mutter, "Who
am I to be so lucky, when so many have such troubles?"

Then Mama would click her tongue and shush him. "Mikhel,
don't question God's purpose for you. Be grateful and do what
you can to help."

I very soon absorbed a sense of guilt for being so lucky to be
safe and warm, healthy and well-fed, and felt even guiltier when I
was glad to be me and not one of the unfortunates caught in the
bombings or the terror of roundups for shipment to the death
and slave labor camps, or in an occupied country suffering short-
ages of food and goods. There were times when I caught myself
praying the war would stay 'over there' so we would never have to
endure any of those misfortunes. Then I would be overcome by
shame for my selfishness.

It was better after America entered the war. Our soldiers and
sailors filled the streets. I took pride in the uniforms and the trim
look of our fighting men and women. Flags with blue stars were
displayed in house windows to show that a family member was in
the armed forces. Women filled the factories to do war work and
replace men in essential industries. My favorite song was 'Rosie
the Riveter.' I learned all the words and sang them off-key until I
drove Mama to desperation.

Before the war no women I knew smoked or drove a car, and
once or twice I heard some man in the street yelling abuse after
the rare woman driver. I couldn't understand what they were so
angry about. But then, almost overnight, women became drivers
of their own cars, and of public buses and street cars. The first
time I saw a woman driving a ten-ton Mack truck, and wearing
overalls as well, my eyes popped and my mouth fell open.

Things were changing so fast for everyone, there was a feeling
of breathlessness as we rushed along. My friends and I did our part
for the war effort. We collected tin cans and cigarette foil door-to-
door, then flattened the tins, rolled the foil, and carried boxes of
it to the collection depots. We spent several periods a week in
school crocheting squares for war blankets. I bought packages of
vegetable seeds and sweated and fumed in our backyard, scratch-
ing in the hard dirt, clearing weeds, trying to get radishes and

carrots to grow for my Victory Garden. Anne, Rebecca, and I found an old kiddie wagon and used it to collect discarded newspapers. At last we could do more than talk and when I thought about my life as an American girl, my future seemed boundless. I could be anything I chose, and as good as it was, I wasn't going to be just an ordinary secretary like my mother.

For Lilly the future was also unlimited. With the advantage of my having been born an American, I would be able to advise and guide her so she would reach her full and absolute potential, no matter what that was.

CHAPTER THREE

ALTHOUGH THE FIRST DAYS WITH LILLY IN THE HOUSE RAN TO-
gether, they were different because Papa took some time off from
work to help Mama register Lilly at school. It was long and
complicated to decide her grade level. Then she had to be
examined and vaccinated and taken to the dentist, and clothes
had to be bought to fill out her skimpy wardrobe, after Mama
altered some of my outgrown things to fit her.

Mama and Papa asked me not to bring my friends home during
the first week, since there was so much that Lilly had to get used
to. I didn't like putting Anne and Rebecca off—they were longing
to meet my cousin—but then again I wasn't unhappy at the
thought of having Lilly all to myself. I admit that when I told them
I had to get right home after school to "help out with Lilly", I
didn't try to hide the new feeling of self-importance motivating
me.

I practically flew through the streets, bursting into the house
with a breathless "hello" to Mama, who insisted I sit quietly and
have my milk and cookies like a lady before I changed from my
school clothes into play things, and turned my attention to Lilly.

She was always in our bedroom when I got home and when I
pounded up the stairs, I would find her standing at the window
looking down at the front yard and the street. When I came in she

didn't turn around the way I would have, but I sang out, "Hi, Lilly," anyway, and as soon as I'd changed my clothes would set about entertaining her.

I'd choose a book with nice pictures, or I'd show her one of my dolls and its clothes, or I'd tell her about school and what happened there, even though for all I knew she didn't understand a word I was saying. She'd stand with her head hanging, looking at me in flashes out of the corner of her eye. When I'd urge her to touch or hold one of my things, she'd put her hands behind her back, or move away.

I never had trouble talking. Mama said I unraveled at the mouth, but after ten minutes or so of this, I'd start to run down, wondering what to say next. After the first three days, I spent a lot of my time in school thinking of things that might entertain her. One lunchtime, I skipped eating in order to go to the public library and find some picture books I thought she'd like. That day rushing home from school, I stopped at the gate to the front yard and looked up toward my bedroom window, a thing I had never done before. Lilly was there looking out and down at me. Her forehead and one hand were pressed to the pane, as if she were a prisoner trying to get out. She looked so lost and sad, my heart wrenched with fear. I don't think she saw me or anything else in the street, but I couldn't understand why I was scared. Lilly spoke hardly at all to any of us and what she said was in whispered monosyllables. She ate almost nothing. Right away Mama and Papa were worried, especially Mama, who at first over-filled Lilly's plate and watched anxiously as this unhappy little girl sat tensely over her dish, picking up a tiny morsel on her fork or spoon to put gingerly into her mouth. I marvelled at the length of time she was able to chew a bit of food that lasted barely a moment in my mouth. No matter how I tried, cooked carrot disappeared with five or six good chews, and when I was hungry, which was almost always, less than that. Mama said nothing, but at each meal put smaller amounts on Lilly's plate, trying, I suppose, to encourage her appetite. But at the end of every meal, because the food had been moved around, the plate looked fuller than in the beginning.

When I was in the kitchen doing my homework and Lilly was sitting across from me looking at a picture book, Mama and Papa

began to talk to each other in Yiddish. Of course I understood
every word they said; I knew they didn't want Lilly to realize they
were talking about her.

Papa would urge Mama not to worry; loss of appetite, silence,
and shyness were to be expected until Lilly got used to us and her
new home. Mama would sigh and ask how long a child could go
without food before becoming sick. Papa would remind her Lilly
had been checked by the doctor and the dentist and was in
remarkably good health. Besides, she didn't seem to be losing
weight, or to be fading away.

"Maybe she's not used to my cooking and I should ask her
what she would like to eat," Mama wondered.

On and on they murmured those first few days, and somehow
their doubts and uneasiness comforted me because I was beginning to wonder myself whether I was up to the job of making Lilly
feel at home and happy. I remember an entire week had gone by
and Lilly had not spoken to me or looked at me directly.

I had taken my French book and tried to patch together a few
simple sentences including, '*Je m'appelle Sarah. Je suis ta cousine*,"
and had gotten no response. Instead, Lilly turned away to hide
her face from me.

Each night that first week, after we were in bed and Mama and
Papa had kissed us and said goodnight, as soon as they left our
room I would say softly toward the back that lay humped under
the quilt, "*Bonne nuit, ma petite cousine*," getting of course, the
usual no-response.

If I hadn't heard Mama and Papa's worried conversations, I
would have been in despair. As it was, I was becoming uncomfortable in my own room, afraid to move too much, or open
drawers too loudly or turn on a light, things I used to do without
a thought. I began to sleep badly, having strange dreams which
woke me in the middle of the night, but which I couldn't remember.

One night at the beginning of Lilly's second week with us, I
had awakened and was lying on my back looking at the dark ceiling
when I heard a sound that raised the hair on my head. It started
as a low snuffling, sucking, which went on interminably.

Cautiously I raised myself on an elbow and peered through the
dark toward Lilly's bed hoping to be able to see something, and

as I did, a moaning, groaning wail punctuated the snuffling and died off to a grunt. Then started a jumble of whispered or spoken sounds that was neither English nor French nor any language I could recognize. The sounds were eerie and so disturbed, I knew with certainty they could be made only by someone undergoing a kind of deep personal torture.

I was very frightened and didn't know whether to try to wake Lilly or call my mother, when suddenly there was an agitated stirring in Lilly's bed and a subdued shriek. I snapped on the bedside lamp, unable anymore to contain my fear of the dark and the noise.

Lilly was sitting straight up in bed with her eyes wide open.

I jumped up and ran to her, saying softly, "Lilly, what is it? Are you sick? Should I call Mama?"

Then I realized that Lilly was totally unconscious. Her eyes were not only unseeing but inward-looking, the eyes of someone in a deep sleep. I reached out and pushed gently on her shoulder, touching her for the first time, feeling the warm, moist skin under her nightgown. As I pushed her down, she yielded easily, closing her eyes with a sigh and burrowing her face in the pillow. I covered her and stood there for a moment or two, oblivious to the cold floor under my bare feet. Somehow I knew that Lilly would sleep peacefully now.

I returned to my bed, switched off the lamp and lay for a long time thinking about what had happened. For the time being I wouldn't tell my parents. This must be what Mama meant by damaged. I shivered under my quilt, thinking of all that Lilly had suffered, and she a year younger than I. What would I do if I had no mother or father or friends? If I could barely speak the language that everyone around me was using? If I suddenly found myself in a strange country, with nothing I knew, no familiar streets or places?

I was overwhelmed by two feelings: gratitude that I was so lucky to be me and not Lilly, and guilt that I was so lucky, and Lilly, through no fault of her own, so unlucky.

I woke up the next morning with a bright idea. Hurrying into my bathrobe, I went to Mama and Papa's bedroom door. Papa was looking in the mirror putting on his tie. Mama was all dressed and making their bed. They had been talking quietly and when they saw me, stopped in the middle of a sentence.

Papa said, "Come in, Saraleh, and give your Papa a kiss."

I stood on tiptoe to reach his face and he leaned down toward me while he finished knotting his tie. I loved to kiss his cleanly-shaven cheek. It was smooth and firm and smelled like fresh laundry.

I said, "Mama and Papa, I have a swell idea. Today after school, what if I take Lilly out for a walk around and show her where the grocery is and the library and the school?"

Mama and Papa exchanged a look, then Mama said, "That *is* a good idea. It'll help if she knows her way around. She'll be starting school next week, or the latest, the week after."

Papa was smiling his fond look at me. "You're being a good friend to Lilly, Saraleh, we're proud of you. Now you'd better go get ready for breakfast, it's getting late."

I went happily, a bounce and skip in my feet. I was sure this would help get Lilly's attention onto something pleasant. I entered my room cautiously; she was still an immobile, small bump in the bed. She never got up before I left for school and I tiptoed around getting dressed and making my bed. But next week, she'd be getting up with me to go to school.

The day sped by. Whenever I had the chance, I rehearsed in my mind just what I would say to Lilly when I got home. As it turned out, she was in the kitchen playing with a glass of milk when I came into the house. I watched her as I drank my milk and ate two chocolate chip cookies. She had a white mustache which made her look kind of cute and funny, but she was sticking her lip in the glass without really drinking any milk. I finished and Mama sent me upstairs to change. When I got down, Lilly's mustache was gone. So was her glass of milk and the plate of cookies.

Mama said, "Okay girls, you can go out now. Sarah, be back no later than four-thirty."

I was excited. "C'mon, Lilly, there's a lot to see."

She got up from the chair really slowly and she wouldn't look at me. I felt like heaving a big sigh, but I controlled myself. "Wait'll you see the library. If we hurry, we can get a card for you and you can take out your own books."

In the street I kept talking and showing her things. "That's my friend Anne's house, you'll meet her soon. My friend Rebecca lives the other way." I pointed to show her.

"School is over there, three blocks. See, you can see the top of the building once we pass that house."

She didn't really look where I pointed, but I kept on anyway. "Let's go to the library first. Then you can take out your own books whenever you want."

We were half a block from the library when Lilly stopped in front of a house and looked down the walk with a little smile on her face. She made a kissing sound with her lips and a fluffy gray cat came running up to her and rubbed its head against her ankles. Lilly leaned over to scratch behind its ear. The cat rolled onto its back, and Lilly crouched down to rub its belly. I stood and watched. She must've forgotten all about me. She was grinning at how the cat was rolling all over and stretching itself out and purring. She was talking in French very softly and I could tell she was saying sweet things to it. I hated to interfere because it was the first time I ever saw her look happy. But after awhile I went and touched her on the shoulder. She looked up as if she was surprised to see me.

"Lilly, we have to go or we won't be home in time."

The light went out of her face and she stood up and began walking. The cat followed us, but Lilly didn't look at it or touch it again. By the time we reached the corner it turned around and went back.

We went to the librarian and I explained everything. While she typed out a card, Lilly and I went to the shelf with the picture books for younger kids, and I showed her a few about cats and dogs and horses. I said she could take six books at a time and take them home for two weeks. She looked puzzled and I told her again, using the few French words I knew and nodding a lot and making gestures with my hands.

Finally she knew what I meant and said in English, "I take theese to the house?"

"Yes. Not to keep, but to read for two weeks." I held up two fingers, pointed to the books, then to Lilly and nodded hard.

She gave me a little smile, held the books tight against her chest, and we went to check them out. That night she ate a little bit more supper than usual.

My father's mother and father had followed the orthodox religious practices of many working class European Jews. The New World's opportunities could be an ocean of secular temptations in which religion could easily drown. That my father, so many years and miles away from the parental influence, and my mother, a native-born American, should have chosen to maintain a religiously observant lifestyle is now, to me, a matter of wonder. But when I was a child it was perfectly normal and easy to accept the benign restrictions of not working, traveling or writing on the Sabbath. Buying and eating kosher foods posed no problem. Pork was not only no temptation, it was a non-food, a sort of poison that made you sick.

Living in a predominately Jewish neighborhood and going to schools with a ninety percent Jewish population supported our orthodox home-life. I went to synagogue with my parents almost every Saturday morning and rarely missed a special holiday.

September and October were the busy times because school began right after Labor Day and the most important Jewish holidays fell together in those two months—first *Rosh Hashanah*, the New Year, then *Yom Kippur*, the Day of Atonement, *Simhat Torah* next, and finally *Sukkot*. My yearly clock was set to function in good order by the clustering of these significant events.

Shul was mostly fun. We kids had almost unlimited opportunity to talk and move around, and the toddlers were given even more freedom, so that while I occasionally got bored when the service was particularly long, I never felt it was oppressive.

I was registered in Hebrew school the same year I began kindergarten, and by the time I was ten, could read well enough to follow the service even though I didn't always follow the meaning. I looked forward to the holidays and occasions I loved with happy anticipation and enjoyed them with youthful wholeheartedness. Each year, my father built a *sukkah*, a kind of lean-to, roofed with dried grasses and decorated with fruit and vegetables, against the back of our house in the yard, and here we would eat all our meals during the week of *Sukkot*, the celebration of the harvest. It was a family 'camp out' in the middle of the city. And

Simhat Torah—no Jewish child could resist the appeal of the little blue and white flags with the Star of David, lit candles attached to the flagstaffs. We waved these vigorously as the entire congregation sang and danced around the Torahs. All the scrolls, little ones and big ones, were removed from the Ark and paraded around the synagogue to be kissed and venerated.

And there were special occasions like Yosuf's Bar Mitzvah, for which he prepared and studied for a year and the family planned and plotted for months. My mother and the aunties talked about the *kiddush* menu for weeks. Days were devoted to scouring the shops for the right dresses and shoes and undergarments. The day before the big event we helped Yosuf's mother prepare the bags of candies and nuts to distribute to all the children in the synagogue, to be hurled at Yosuf the moment he finished reading his *Haftorah.* I was so keyed up with excitement, I couldn't eat or sleep. With a background like this I found it difficult to understand why Jews in Europe were being attacked and destroyed for their Jewishness.

I had never experienced antisemitism directly because I had little to do with non-Jews, and that only at a distance. The ten percent or so in my school who were Gentiles were a small and to me, amorphous group. I knew of no distinct classifications among Christians, knew in fact only that these people believed in someone they called Jesus Christ who, for unexplained and unexplored reasons, was a mortal enemy of the Jews, and whose very name, if uttered, was associated with bad luck and vague presentiments of danger.

Christmas, so strong and pervasive it invaded even our secure enclave, was associated with Jesus. It was his birthday, and cause for great rejoicing among Christians, especially in all the department stores. I had never entered a church, had no idea what transpired in one, and only through the rare movie I was permitted to attend with my friends did I see a church interior, when hero and heroine were married to the strains of the wedding march played on an organ.

We had a *mezuzah* on the outside door jamb of our house and each time we entered the house, touched it with our fingertips, then kissed our fingers. I loved our *mezuzah*. It was a beautiful silver filigree with a delicate, intricate design, and I felt particularly protected and looked after because it reminded me of God's presence in our house.

I saw Lilly watching us out of the corners of her eyes when we kissed the *mezuzah*, but when Papa explained that it held the *Sh'ma* and began to say why it was there, Lilly looked so frightened, Papa told her not to worry about it just then. I didn't say anything but I didn't know why Lilly should be scared. The *Sh'ma* was so beautiful, like poetry. When I read it out loud in English, I loved to roll the "thou's" and "thy's" around on my tongue. "Hear, O Israel, the Lord, our God, the Lord is One . . . Thou shalt love the Lord thy God with all thy heart, with all thy soul, and with all thy might. Thou shalt teach . . . thy children . . . when thou sittest in thy house . . . walkest by the way . . . liest down . . . and risest up . . . and thou shalt write them upon the doorposts of thy house and upon thy gates." I wished I could read it to Lilly like a story, so she could see how wonderful the *mezuzah* was, but I figured I'd better wait until she knew us better. Later I heard Papa talking to Mama in Yiddish about how Lilly had spent her formative years with Catholics, and who knew what they had taught her about Jews and Jewish ritual. Mama said there was plenty of time. Lilly would be with us for the rest of her life.

On the first Friday we were all going to have a regular *Shabbat* supper with Auntie and Uncle and Yosuf and Duvid, I could hardly wait to get home from school. Lilly and I would get all dressed up and ready. It was going to be so much fun!

I hung my coat away and put my books on the hall table. Then I went into the kitchen for my after-school milk and cookies. Mama was doing the last minute things for *Shabbat* supper and Lilly was sitting at the table with a plate of cookies and a glass of milk in front of her. My full glass was already waiting for me, so I kissed Mama, said hello to Lilly and sat down.

I watched Lilly as I drank and ate and answered Mama's questions about what I had done in school and listened to her tell me about things that had happened at home. Lilly was breaking her cookie apart, picking out the chocolate chips, eating them and dropping the rest of the cookie into her glass of milk which already had a layer of crumbs covering its surface. She was not drinking the milk and I was amazed not only at what she was doing, but that Mama was ignoring it. I had been taught never to waste food.

After I finished my milk and two cookies, Mama told me to wash my glass and take Lilly upstairs to get ready for *Shabbat*. Going up I told Lilly about the beautiful *challah*s and candles and wine and prayers and the songs we'd sing and how Papa read from the paper while we had our tea and cake afterward.

I'd learned not to expect Lilly to answer and found it easier to talk if I didn't look at her, because most of the time her expression startled, puzzled, or frightened me.

I showed her what I was going to wear and told her I was going to wash my hands, arms, face and neck, and brush my teeth before I put on my good clothes, and she should do the same. Finally I looked at her. Her head was down and she seemed to be examining a spot on the floor near her left foot.

"Lilly," I said, "did you understand what I said?" Then in halting French, "*Comprends-tu ce que j'ai dit?*"

I saw her lips compress and felt something impatient rising in me. It was taking much longer to make Lilly happy than I had imagined. I reached out and touched her hand. She pulled away as if stung, and without thinking I said, "Oh do what you want. I'm getting dressed. I'm not gonna be late for *Shabbat* because of you!" and flounced away.

No matter how I tried I couldn't seem to reach her. The less success I had the more guilty I felt, but I was finding it harder and harder to be patient with her. I spent a lot of time scolding myself for being selfish and mean about someone who had suffered so much, but it didn't matter how long and hard and often I scolded, the feelings still kept popping up. Sometimes I even caught myself thinking of the nice parts of being an only child before Lilly came to live with us.

I finished dressing and brushed my hair in front of the mirror over my bureau. Lilly was lying on her bed with her back to me, dressed exactly as she had been when I left her to go to the bathroom and wash.

"Lilly, you'll make the whole family late for *Shabbat*." I said to her back, "You can't do that."

"I will not come downstairs tonight." She spoke clearly and firmly.

Well at least she's talking, I thought. "Are you sick?"

No answer.

I turned off the light and went down to Mama with a report on what had happened. Papa came home as I was talking, so I started all over again. It was no longer a consolation to me to see how upset they looked.

"Why is she like that?" I asked. "Will she ever get better? Is she always going to be like this?"

"We will do the best we can, Saraleh," Papa said. "We'll be as kind and patient and thoughtful as we can and maybe after a while Lilly will feel less lonely and more at home and come to enjoy all the things we like. Meanwhile all we can do is wait and help her however we can."

Somehow that *Shabbat* wasn't the same with Lilly upstairs on her bed while we ate and drank and sang. Mama took a tray of food up to her and Auntie Aviva said something about spoiling her and not helping Lilly or ourselves. Yosuf reminded me that he had warned me it's not all fun to have a sister or a brother and I said, "Yes, but is it as hard as this?"

"Harder," he said. "At least Lilly leaves you alone. What if she were on your neck all the time?" And he looked pointedly at Duvid.

It seemed to me that I would be thrilled to have Lilly "on my neck" but I said nothing. By the time everybody went home and I was going up to bed, Mama had taken away the tray which had not been touched and Lilly seemed to be asleep. As quickly and quietly as I could I got undressed and into bed, glad to let my uneasy thoughts about Lilly drift away as I fell asleep.

In the States, in the early thirties when I was born, families with ten or thirteen children were no longer usual and were associated with outmoded times and ideas. But having an only child was not considered desirable. In fact it was looked upon as an impediment, perhaps a little shameful, though not as bad as having no children at all, this being a matter for pity. It was assumed that when a married couple had no children, they were physically incapable of doing so.

It was believed that an only child faced untold dangers in the course of growing to maturity. The greatest of these was being spoiled. Although the only child did not literally rot away, turning green and pulpy and filling the air with vile odors, it was understood that something similar happened inside. Putrefaction occurred in the heart or the mind or the spirit, and forever burdened with a rotten personality, the spoiled child was a disappointment to himself, an encumbrance to his parents, and a trial to mate, neighbors, and co-workers.

Compliments were dangerous, and so rarely given. They could spoil a child, or worse, attract the evil eye to a child's good fortune if he were nice-looking, or smart, or even-tempered. These were the guidelines my relatives applied diligently, while my parents avoided the blatant expressions of love which might harm my personality.

When I was a young woman several years out of college, my Aunt Aviva revealed to me at last that my mother's pregnancy had been difficult and the delivery dangerous, and somehow in the course of it her fallopian tubes had been mutilated so that she could never expect to have another child. My parents had kept this information from me because they hadn't wanted me to feel even by implication that I was in any way responsible for the situation that caused them so much sorrow. I realized then how painful it must have been for them to have me beg for a brother or sister.

Someone once said, "Don't wish for what you want, you might be unlucky enough to get it." Well here I was, in the years before Lilly came to live with us, envying all my friends and cousins for having siblings, and wishing, even praying, for a brother or sister. Many times after Lilly came, I wondered what it would have been like to start off fresh with my own, born-to-my-family sister, instead of someone whose past and experiences were so alien to mine.

I was always up early on *Shabbat*, and got all dressed before I went over to look at Lilly still lying the same way as when I went to shower. As I came around the bed she closed her eyes, so I knew she was awake.

"Lilly, you'll be late for *shul*. You'd better get up."

"I'm not going," she said.

I was shocked. "If you're not sick, you've got to go."

"Yes, I'm sick."

"I'd better tell Mama you're sick. Maybe you need a doctor."

"Why do you not leave me alone?" she hissed.

"How can we leave you alone when you live here?"

"I did not ask to come here." Her voice was full of hostility.

I didn't know what to say so I left and went to find Mama. I finished my account feeling by now like a snitch and bearer of bad news.

Mama said, "I'll stay home with her today. Maybe by next week she'll be ready to share *Shabbat* with everybody."

"But what if she's not, Mama? Does that mean you'll never go to *shul* again?"

"Hush, Sarah, don't be silly. There's no point in talking, 'what if.' Now get ready to go with Papa."

I didn't mind for my sake that Mama wouldn't be going, but for hers. I would have my friends to sit with in the women's section and we always had plenty to talk about. They had been waiting eagerly for this Saturday when they expected to see Lilly in *shul.* Now I would have to tell them some story about how hard it was for Lilly to adjust to all the new and different things around her, and try to answer their questions about when they'd be able to meet her. Life was certainly getting more complicated for me, full of surprises I hadn't expected, and I didn't think I liked any of them very much.

Three weeks from the time she had arrived Lilly started school. Mama packed lunch for both of us. We each carried a paper bag containing an egg salad sandwich on rye bread with mayonnaise and lettuce, an apple, and a cookie. We had a nickel apiece to buy milk. I carried my books and looseleaf notebook, but Lilly had only some pencils and a pen, and a little pad for notes.

As we walked along I chattered away trying to use easy words to allow for her limited understanding. "You'll really love our school, Lilly, the teachers are so nice. The kids are nice too. I'll introduce you to all my friends. Until you make your own friends you can play with us. We aren't in the same class but I'll see you in the halls and we can eat lunch together. I'll take you to the lunchroom. Don't worry, you won't be lonely, everybody knows you're coming and that you're my cousin, so they'll be nice to you."

I was so intent on telling her all this that I didn't realize we were walking more and more rapidly. It took me several blocks to see it was Lilly who had speeded up while I tried to keep up with her. Just as I finished reassuring her that she would be treated well because she was my cousin, she turned to me for the first time and hissed something that sounded like, "*Ferme ta gulle!*"

It left me mystified. I knew only that it must be French, and spent the next few minutes memorizing the sounds so I could ask my French teacher to translate for me. This kept me busy until we reached school, so I had no time to think about Lilly's attitude. It was just as well since things at home had not gone much better than during the first days of Lilly's stay. She still looked at me only obliquely. She rarely responded to anything I said to her and never started a conversation or spoke to me except when absolutely necessary. To my questions she would answer in a mumble, with one word if possible and only if I repeated myself.

We reached the school yard with me several paces behind Lilly. I saw a cluster of my friends at the entrance gate watching our progress closely. If we kept on as we were going I knew Lilly would sail right past everybody waiting to be introduced to her. I hadn't dreamed of a problem like this. I had seen myself leading a tremulous, frightened Lilly who would be grateful for any smoothing of the way I could arrange. Now my problem was how to stop her. I could see the whites of my friends' eyes. A decision had to be made. I was desperate and more embarrassed over what they would think than afraid about any reaction from Lilly. Just as we drew alongside the target, I reached out and clutched Lilly at the elbow, hard. At the same time I said very firmly and overly loud, "Lilly, here are my friends; they want to meet you."

Lilly turned to me with a look of sheer astonishment. In that moment of weakness, I hastily introduced her, still holding her elbow, and then with the same momentum pushed ahead, saying we had to get Lilly to her class and I would see everybody later.

I felt the pull of Lilly's arm trying to release itself from my grip and as soon as I could, let her go. We raced into the building with Lilly setting the pace. I don't know which of us was more relieved to see the other go when I left her at the door of her home room.

French was my second subject of the morning. After class I stayed to ask my teacher if she could translate my verbal imitation of what Lilly had said. I explained to Miss Sondheim that my cousin had said something I couldn't understand and to me it sounded like, "*Ferme ta gulle.*"

Miss Sondheim was an old maid of perhaps thirty with straight black hair, nice skin and thick glasses. Her forehead puckered between her brows and she said, "You couldn't have heard your cousin correctly, Sarah."

"Why not, Miss Sondheim, doesn't it mean anything?"

"Maybe she meant *gueule* but a polite little girl wouldn't use that expression, and certainly not to someone who's being nice to her."

My heart speeded up. "I guess I was wrong about what she said, but what does it mean?"

Miss Sondheim looked at me for a moment. "It means, 'shut up,' and it's a very rude way of saying it."

I felt my lips going numb and the hot color coming into my face. "Thank you," I said and left as fast as I could. I knew then that I had heard correctly. What I couldn't fathom was why Lilly seemed to dislike me so much. It was luck that my next class was art where I wouldn't have to concentrate or answer questions.

I was absolutely miserable. No one had ever openly expressed disgust toward me and I was having a hard time coping with it. In an agonized moment I wished I had never even heard of Lilly and wished she would disappear from my life as suddenly and unexpectedly as she had come into it. My thoughts and feelings were so disagreeably muddled I couldn't listen to what was happening in class. I asked for permission to leave the room and, holding the eight-inch wooden slab that was the passport through the halls, I sped to the toilet where I locked myself into a stall and pressed my burning face against the cool metal door.

I'm only a little girl, I kept thinking, I don't know how to help a damaged person. I remembered Yosuf telling me that it might not be so easy and how lightly I had taken his warning. Now I was stuck with Lilly for the rest of my life and we were just getting started! I thought of explaining everything to Mama and Papa who would as always comfort and rescue me. But how disappointed they would be that I was giving up, being a crybaby over nothing, being spoiled, wanting everything to go my way. After all, the only thing Lilly had done was not live up to my expectations. I thought about Lilly's really awful problems. I was selfish and mean. So what if she told me to shut up, and didn't want to walk with me or meet my friends. It hurt but I knew it couldn't kill me. I was embarrassed because I had bragged to my friends and acquaintances. It would teach me to be more modest. I unlocked the stall door, washed my face with cold water and went back to my class, having talked myself into feeling a little better.

I decided to go straight to the lunchroom instead of looking for Lilly to escort her there. Anne and Rebecca assumed Lilly would eat with us, so I was forced to join them in searching for her instead of going right to our table after we'd bought our milk. Rebecca carried our tray while Anne scanned the tables, with me pretending to be looking as hard as she was.

Just as I said, "Maybe she hasn't gotten here yet. Let's sit down, it's getting late," Anne pointed.

"Look, isn't that your cousin?"

My heart sank as I followed the direction of Anne's finger. Lilly was sitting where the Polish girls always sat, all the grades together, a small Gentile enclave in the predominately Jewish school.

"What's she doing sitting there? Let's get her," Anne went on.

My response was automatic. "No, I don't want to embarrass her. Besides, maybe she's making some friends. I'll see her later and find out what's happening."

I felt Anne's reluctance and Rebecca said, "Oh gee, I thought we'd get to talk to her." But my instinct told me I was doing what I should for my own protection if nothing else.

We turned and went back to our table. I was relieved that the only other thing I had to face that day was meeting Lilly to walk home with her.

The afternoon had never gone by faster and I managed to urge Anne to go home without waiting for me. When I got to Lilly's home room, all the kids were gone. Lilly was standing at the teacher's desk getting instruction and when I opened the door, Mrs. Greenberg, who had been my sixth grade teacher and one of my favorites, looked up and invited me inside.

"We'll be only another few minutes, Sarah," she said. "I'm just bringing Lilly up-to-date on some work assignments. You can help her, but Lilly will catch on soon. She's a smart girl, like you."

Mrs. Greenberg's smile made me feel good. Maybe things would start to work out after all. I sat down in a front seat and watched Lilly. She was listening intently but was standing so that the corner of the desk was between her and Mrs. Greenberg. She had to tilt her head at an uncomfortable angle to see the book. Mrs. Greenberg put her hand on Lilly's arm, and I saw Lilly pull away, as she did with me. Mrs. Greenberg felt it, looked up startled from her book, and removed her hand.

So it wasn't just me, I thought. Maybe she doesn't like anyone. Maybe she can't stand to have people touch her. How awful, I thought, when it was so nice to be hugged and stroked and cuddled. I couldn't imagine being without Mama stroking my hair and kissing me goodnight, and Papa putting his arm around me and holding me against his side when we sat together on the sofa.

"Okay, Sarah," Mrs. Greenberg said, "you can take Lilly home now. She understands English really well. Soon she'll be talking as fast and as much as you."

I smiled back at Mrs. Greenberg, and said bravely, "C'mon Lilly, let's go."

We left more or less together and once we reached the street, I said, "Did you have a good time today, Lilly?"

She shrugged but didn't say anything. "Did you make any friends?" I went on doggedly. No answer.

"Hey, Lilly," I said, "I know everything's strange, but I want to help. Mama and Papa want you to be like their own girl and I just want you to be happy. Please talk to me even if you don't want to be friends."

We went on for half a block and just when I'd given up on her, she said, "I am making friends. If you will leave me alone I will be okay."

It was the most she'd ever said to me, and I found her accent thrilling and romantic, though she'd said "okay" just the way everybody else did. It took a few moments for me to really absorb what she had said.

"Do you mean you don't want me to talk to you or meet you for lunch or walk with you?"

She gave me one of her oblique looks and then nodded emphatically.

"Never?" I asked, anguished.

For a moment she looked at me directly and whispered, "Yes, leave me alone."

I couldn't keep the lump out of my throat, or my eyes from filling with tears. She gave me a look of pure disgust, then lengthening her stride, moved away from me toward our house. I didn't have the heart to follow her and I didn't want Mama to see me crying, so I leaned against a tree with my forehead pressed against the rough bark.

I'd never felt so alone or so much in need of a brother or sister as at that moment. This kind of failure was new to me. My parents loved me, and I always sensed that love like a deep strong current whose energy never fails even when its presence can't be seen. I had friends who never spurned or rejected me; our mutual regard was as dependable as the sunrise. I was popular with my teachers and a good student. With someone who 'had it made,' as I did, a single failure shouldn't be devastating, could even be shrugged off philosophically. Yet I felt I was somehow at fault—as though there was some lack on my part that made Lilly treat me as if she loathed me.

Strangely enough, all my feelings of self-worth evaporated. I couldn't think of any reason why *anyone* should like or want me. Lilly, one little orphan girl, survivor of the Holocaust, was able to do this to me, and I know now it was because she was in no way ambivalent about her feelings and what she wanted. There was no uncertainty in her attitude toward me. There was no doubt, no wavering, she never hesitated. I was defenseless because I wasn't used to this kind of contempt. I was not conditioned to protect my feelings from such an attack, since there had never been a need for it in my life. So the only conclusion I could come to was that Lilly was right; she saw into the true degenerative depths of me. I was managing to fool everybody else who knew me. But the horrible thing was, what if all the people I was fooling began to see me as Lilly did?

At supper I worked as hard at avoiding looking at Lilly as she did me. I felt exposed, as if Mama and Papa could read me like a written page and know all about my failure with Lilly. There were now two of us pushing food around on our plates.

Mama felt first my forehead, then Lilly's, saying to Papa, "I don't know what's wrong with these girls. They don't have fevers. Saraleh, do you feel sick? Why aren't you eating?"

"Now, Malkah," Papa said, "stop fussing. They're not going to starve. You *shtup* too much food. Maybe their stomachs need a rest. Let them leave the table if they want."

Over Mama's mild protest, Papa sent us out of the dining room to do our homework. Lilly and I sat across from each other at the kitchen table with our heads buried in books. I knew she didn't want me to talk to her and I didn't even feel like it anymore. I had trouble getting down to work and could hear Mama and Papa in the dining room talking Yiddish, but this time I could catch only a word or two, so I guessed they didn't want me to hear what they were saying. At one point I caught my own name and realized that I too was the subject of their conversation.

Bitterly I imagined their saying how badly Lilly was reacting to me and holding me responsible. I didn't know then that people could be destroyed by being told often and strongly enough that they were worthless, or contemptible, or disgusting. I didn't know that Jewish children in Germany during Hitler's rise to power had committed suicide, unable to face the contempt and rage of their teachers and school mates.

My head had begun to ache from a combination of hunger, circular thinking, and being in the grim atmosphere of Lilly's dislike for me. I stood up abruptly, closed my books with a slam, and gathered them together, ignoring the movement across the table which I supposed was Lilly raising her head in surprise, and walked out of the kitchen.

My parents stopped talking as soon as I entered the dining room. "Mama and Papa, I'm tired. I'm going to bed now. I'll get up early and finish my homework in the morning."

"You see, Mikhel, there's something wrong," Mama said.

Papa called me over to him and with a hand on my shoulder, looked into my face and said softly, "Saraleh, is something wrong? Is everything all right in school?"

The safe, familiar scent of starch in Papa's shirt, the faint fragrance of his shaving lotion, almost broke my resolve.

"School is fine, Papa."

There was a long pause. I felt his eyes resting on the top of my head while I kept mine fixed on the knot in his tie.

"Is anything wrong between you and Lilly?"

I couldn't look at him. I knew if I did I would burst into tears and expose myself and all the horrible things that had been happening. "No Papa, I'm just tired, so I'll go to bed . . . I'll be okay Papa, honest."

He held onto me for a long moment while I refused to raise my head to meet his eyes.

Finally he sighed and let me go. "Okay, Sarah, go and have a good rest."

I went to my room thinking how wonderful it would be to be alone again, dreading the moment when Lilly would come up and invade my space like some prickly, poisonous creature whose tentacles reached out to sting or inflict wounds. I was off-balance and couldn't figure out how to get back to the predictable life I'd had only a month ago. I felt as if there were two of me existing side-by-side; one who was patient, kind, and understanding and could love Lilly no matter what she said or did, and the other who couldn't tolerate the rebuffs and reacted with hatred or an angry desire to hit out. I never knew which me would be stronger, or why I would feel first one way, then the other. In fact I hardly knew what was happening to me, or why.

Rapidly I undressed, washed my face and teeth, got into bed turning my back to Lilly's side, and pulled the quilt over my head.

The next I remember was waking up to a dark, sleeping house with a gnawing emptiness in my stomach. I'd never before gone to bed without supper. In those days, Jewish families did not withhold food from children as a form of punishment. Food was necessary and God's sacred gift. Using it for lessons in behavior or to exact obedience from a child would have been a sin against everything holy. The order, 'Eat! Eat!' used by Jewish mothers was more profound than the simple word implied. So when you were lucky and had plenty to eat you never left anything on your plate, if only because the children in Europe were starving.

Warily, so as not to disturb Lilly, I turned back the quilt, sat up and slid my feet into my slippers. Moving slowly in the dark, feeling my way over the familiar terrain, I tiptoed past Mama and Papa's closed door and cautiously down the stairs toward the kitchen.

Then my heart popped into my mouth. A weird glow and strange sounds were coming from the kitchen. I froze and stood shaking, wondering what sort of beast or thief was in our kitchen. Then I heard clinking, like bowls being moved around, and forced myself forward until I was able to peek around the dining room doorway into the kitchen. The door of the new refrigerator stood wide open and in the light from the bulb inside, Lilly was stuffing herself on leftover chicken.

She was tearing off great bites, and after a few chews, swallowing noisily. I watched fascinated as she ate the chicken, licked her fingers, then plunged her hand into another bowl and brought out a roast potato, which disappeared down her throat faster than the chicken. I had never seen anyone eat so much so fast. She ate everything with her fingers, licking each one before reaching into another bowl for something else.

At last she finished, rinsed her hands under a trickle of water from the tap, then dried them on a dish towel. She gave a long rolling belch and closed the refrigerator door, plunging the room into darkness. I flattened myself against the dining room wall and waited. After what seemed a long time my eyes had begun to get used to the dark, and I heard the cautious shuffle of Lilly's feet as she felt her way toward the dining room.

I held my breath as she passed inches from where I was standing. Had she turned toward me or brushed me, I would have had a heart attack. My thoughts were tumbling over each other with this new discovery. Was this the first time Lilly had come down to raid the refrigerator? Or did she do it all the time, which would explain why she was never hungry?

It made me sick to think about her fingers covered with spit touching all our left-over food. I wondered what to do about all the things I was finding out about Lilly and her habits. I didn't know how to tell Mama and Papa because I couldn't make any sense out of what I knew, but I had a terrible need to talk to someone and decided to see Yosuf as soon as I could.

My hunger was gone, wiped away by the fright I had suffered, and I was chilled to the bone from standing in the cold darkness. I crept back to bed and lay in the frigid space under my quilt, shivering until I fell asleep.

Mama was shaking me. "Saraleh, wake up. I'm not going to call you again, you'll be late for school. If you're sick you can stay home today, but Lilly is all dressed and wants to go early."

My eyelids and limbs were heavy with the need for sleep, but I forced my eyes open and said, "Let Lilly go. I'll get up in a minute. I'm okay, I just didn't sleep too well."

I heard Mama walk to the door of my room and call Lilly. Then I heard the outside door slam and Mama murmuring, "She left already. What's the matter with everybody?"

I sped through dressing, devoured a thick slice of rye bread with butter and jam, and grabbed my lunchbag from the kitchen counter and my books from the hall steps. I hadn't done my homework assignments for half my classes, but I was happy to have Lilly off my hands for that morning.

On the run, I kissed Mama as she said, "Well I'm glad to see you seem to be feeling better," and made it to school as the last group of kids was pouring through the big double doors. I did a lot of thinking on the way, and decided if Lilly didn't like me it was part of her problem and might clear up as time passed, so for now I resolved to stay away from her. As embarrassing as it would be to tell my friends Lilly and I weren't getting along too well and she had to get used to me and her new life, it was much better than trying to force the issue, something I didn't know how to do anyway.

Lunchtime I headed straight for our table and when Rebecca pointed out that Lilly was sitting with the Polish girls again, I shrugged and said, "It won't kill her, and anyway that's her business. Maybe she's used to them. She lived in a Catholic orphanage more than half her life."

Rebecca was shocked. "Do your parents know she's friendly with the *goyim*?"

I was getting angry with her. "How could they know? This is only her second day at school."

"But she's your *cousin*! You can't let her sit with them!"

"And what should I do, Becky? Tie her up and drag her here?" I said sarcastically.

I felt really good. I was just an ordinary kid. I would go my way and let Lilly go hers. What's more, I was going to let Lilly come home on her own and if my parents complained, I would handle that when the time came.

It was Wednesday and I always stayed after school for extra-curricular activity, to work on the school newsletter. This afternoon I planned to go to Yosuf's house instead. I'd be home at my usual time and Mama and Papa wouldn't know I went to see him in the middle of the week. Wednesdays Yosuf generally came right home from high school, and spent an hour or so on Hebrew lessons before doing his regular homework. I was counting on his regularity. I had my books piled up and my coat on before the bell rang, and was out of the door like a shot as soon as Mrs. Trask dismissed the class. I heard Anne calling me, and turned to wave but didn't stop.

I yelled back to her, "See you tomorrow."

I could see how puzzled and annoyed she was and thought that before everything with Lilly got straightened out, I would lose all my friends.

Yosuf lived seven blocks from my school, and as I rushed along I thought of all the things I would tell him. Then, ahead of me, I saw Lilly walking as fast as I was. Was she confused and lost? Or running away from home? I abandoned my plan to go straight to Yosuf and began to follow Lilly instead. No matter what, she was my cousin; I had to make sure she was all right.

I kept her in sight, hoping she wouldn't turn around and see me. Two blocks before Yosuf's house she turned off and headed up a busy street. She walked like someone familiar with the neighborhood, which was a border between the Gentile and the Jewish sections. I had never walked here alone, having no reason to and being fearful as well, from the stories I had heard about Jewish kids getting attacked and beaten up by Gentile hoodlums.

After we'd gone three long blocks, I was scared because I didn't know where she was going and where I'd end up. I considered abandoning Lilly. If she didn't show up at home by evening I could tell Papa and take the blame for whatever horrible thing had happened to her.

We were approaching a huge building. I knew it was a church, though I had never been in one, God forbid! It took up the full block, with broad steps running right across the front and leading to four heavy, carved wooden doors.

I felt sick when Lilly ran up the steps and, struggling with the weight of the center door, pulled it open to disappear inside. I was horrified, overwhelmed with indecision, fear and a longing for an older, wiser head to tell me what to do. I was too terrified to follow her, having no idea what existed on the other side of those massive doors and fearful of being confronted by priests in their frightening black suits or by nuns in their ominous black and white outfits.

In those days, New York nuns were seen in public only in pairs or groups. They were covered from head to toe and belted with chains on the ends of which hung enormous crosses. Their shoes were black oxfords like the ones worn by old ladies with bad feet. They strode along very purposefully, their ground-length skirts swinging around their ankles as though weighted with lead pellets.

I never dared look directly at them—all these details were acquired from the corners of my eyes. In the summer when I wore sleeveless dresses or shorts, I'd see these women bound up like mummies and wonder why they didn't pass out with the heat.

My friends and I were frightened of nuns. When we would sight a couple at a distance, we would cross our fingers in order to dispel the evil associated with them. If they were approaching on the side we occupied, we'd cross the street to avoid passing near them. The thought that they might touch us accidentally or deliberately was terrifying.

Priests were not quite as bad. At least they looked almost like ordinary men. But I had never been closer than ten yards to any and would have bitten out my tongue rather than speak to them. This was all the preparation I had on the day I saw my Jewish cousin run into the church.

If Lilly were in trouble shouldn't I go and rescue her? But if Lilly *were* in trouble and I went into that formidable building, wouldn't I be in trouble too? To what avail if we were both to disappear off the face of the earth? If on the other hand, I went to tell Yosuf right away and there was any rescuing to be done, he would know better than I what to do and how to get help.

Retracing my steps as fast as I could, I ran all the way to my Auntie and Uncle's house, arriving within five minutes, breathless and agitated. Panting to the second floor, I leaned on the bell of their apartment. I was lucky for a change. Yosuf answered, an annoyed look on his face until he saw me.

I burst through the door, dropped my books on a hall chair and began to babble. "Yosuf, we've got to help Lilly. She's in the big church on Avenue M, maybe she'll never come out. I was scared to go in. I followed her from school. Everything is terrible, she hates me and won't talk to me or walk with me and she doesn't eat at the table but steals food from the refrigerator in the middle of the night. I don't know what to do. You've got to help me," and I burst into tears.

Yosuf pulled me into the living room and sat me down on the chesterfield. "Saraleh," he said, "have you gone crazy? I can't understand a word when you talk so fast. What are you doing here at this hour? Why aren't you at home? And where is Lilly? What's going on?"

"I'm trying to tell you," I gulped.

I finished crying and answered Yosuf's questions. Finally he understood all the things that had been happening in the month or so since Lilly had come to live with us. When I stopped talking and was blowing my nose and wiping my eyes on a tissue, Yosuf just stood in front of me with his arms folded on his chest. I knew he was thinking, because when he did his left eyebrow went down and straight across, but I wanted him to hurry.

"Yosuf, don't just stand there. We have to save Lilly. What are you going to do? Where is Auntie Aviva?"

Yosuf made a face and shook his head. "My mother's shopping, thank God . . . if she heard all this . . . who knows? Listen Saraleh, I'm going to tell you a few things, but you'd better keep it to yourself."

I nodded and sat waiting.

"You know what *really* happened to Lilly . . . she was saved because they concealed her identity when she was in that Catholic orphanage, or the Nazis would have come and gassed her just the way they did Aunt Esther and her husband. They treated her like a Catholic. Even her name was changed. When the relatives found her and took her to London, she had this little box of beads and crosses and pictures of saints. They took it from her and she made an awful fuss. The neighbors who kept track of Lilly after the Germans took her mother and father away wanted to adopt her, and the nuns at the orphanage wanted to keep her and take her into their order. But Aunt Esther made the family promise to get Lilly and raise her in England in case she didn't come back. So if Lilly is going to church, Sarah, she knows all about it. You can't rescue her, and if she sits with the Gentile girls it's what she's used to, so you can stop thinking there's something wrong with you and what you're doing."

I felt strange, almost lightheaded, piecing together what had been happening with Lilly and what Yosuf had just told me. Finally I said, "Why didn't anybody tell me?"

Yosuf shrugged. "I don't know."

"So is Lilly always going to be like this? And why does she hate me? I didn't do anything to her, so what has she got against me? Or Mama, or Papa? How can she hate us for wanting to help her?"

"Who knows? A lot of the people who survived are very peculiar. Who wouldn't be after all that? As for what's going to be with Lilly . . . . ?" Again Yosuf shrugged. "Leave her alone the way she wants you to. Maybe after a while she'll feel better and forget all that other stuff. And you can stop blaming yourself. You're not doing anything wrong. You weren't the one who hurt her and her family. It was the Nazis and the other antisemites. Just remember that."

I felt better but at the same time I felt very disappointed. In the face of the reality, my childish fantasies of Lilly and our lives together were absurd and shameful. The scope of the problem was beyond not only my ability to cope with it, but even my understanding. While I felt better knowing I'd expected too much of myself, I also felt hopeless. Could the terrible harm inflicted on Lilly ever be alleviated? And what about the other survivors? How would they ever fit into the world again?

I stood up. "Thanks, Yosuf. I'd better go home before Mama starts to worry."

Yosuf walked me to the door and I picked up my books from the chair. "If you want," he said, "I'll try to find out more about other people like Lilly. Maybe it'll help."

I nodded.

Yosuf patted my head as I pulled the door open and went out.

CHAPTER FOUR

THERE WAS A VERY STRANGE SMELL IN MY BEDROOM. AS I WALKED around, the smell faded or got stronger. It reminded me of the Canarsie mudflats, where seaweed and other slimy things lay rotting in the sun. Mama had told me I wasn't keeping things clean. But the only thing different was Lilly and though she kept her stuff neat, I didn't know how well she cleaned her part of the room. Anyway, she hadn't come home after school again, and I suspected she'd gone to the church, which would give me some time to look around.

I went sniffing around the room. The trail led to Lilly's bureau. If it was from one of the drawers what was I supposed to do? Go through all her stuff? I balked at the idea because I was afraid of what I'd find and that she'd find out I went through her things.

By now everybody in our house was pretty tense. Mama had actually yelled at me a few times for things she'd never made a fuss over before. She looked tired and worried and I heard her sighing to herself a lot. Papa was getting stricter with me about helping in the house and being up-to-date with my Hebrew lessons and things like that. I figured it all had to be because of Lilly, so I didn't want to tell them my problems with her if I could help it.

I closed the bedroom door for the few extra seconds it would give me to hide what I was doing if Lilly came home while I was at it. Then taking a deep breath, I pulled open the top drawer of her bureau. There was a jumble of panties and socks and undershirts. With my index finger I poked a few things gingerly, but whatever was causing the smell wasn't there. Same with the middle drawer.

When I opened the third drawer I almost fell over. It smelled like our outside garbage pail before the men came to empty it at the end of the week, only a hundred times worse. I hated to put my hand into the mess of loose socks, pieces of ribbon, handkerchiefs and scarves, but I forced myself, taking things out and putting them on the floor. At the back of the drawer, jammed into a corner was a lump of what I thought were more unmatched socks, but when I pulled the mess forward the stink was so bad I had to hold my breath. There were three separate socks, each had something in it and the 'something' was making the smell.

I didn't even care anymore if Lilly came in on me. Holding the socks by the cuffs at arm's length, I carried them into the bathroom and turned them out into the tub. A rainbow of molds was growing on something that might have been a hunk of salami. I thought I recognized the remains of a hardboiled egg under the rot that covered it. A crust of bread was still distinguishable. My stomach flipped and I gagged. I tore off a long strip of toilet paper and used it to pick the garbage out of the tub, then flushed everything down the toilet. Then I took the socks outside to the garbage pail and threw them in. I washed the tub with scouring powder, and took the drawer into the bathroom and scrubbed it with hot water and scouring powder. I took it back into the room and put it against the wall to dry. I piled Lilly's things on her chair. Then I sat down to think and wait for her.

Was she saving food to make a getaway? Had she been eating in our room and forgotten some food? How come she didn't smell it? And did she think we wouldn't notice? I couldn't figure it out. Anyway, I didn't want her doing it again and ruining my room with germs and bugs and smells.

It was growing dark when I heard her coming up the stairs. I kept on reading my book, not really reading anymore, just waiting for her to come in. She walked right by me and turned on her lamp. Then she saw her bureau and turned around to look at me. Her usual look of dislike was mixed with indignation, so I expected this time she would be the one to start to talk. I just looked right back at her and if she expected me to start as usual, she was wrong.

In a minute or two she said, "Why do you look into my things?"

Something mean in me took advantage of this new situation. I just stared back waiting for her to ask me again, the way she made me do all the time. She walked right up to me with her eyes blazing hatred.

Through clenched teeth she said, "Why do you look in my things?"

I was scared. She looked as if she'd kill me if she could, but I stood up and put my face close to hers. "Why did you turn your bureau into a garbage pail? You had filthy, rotting food hidden in the drawer. You were stinking up my room. If you couldn't smell it everybody else could. So—don't—do—it—again!"

A flicker of surprise crossed Lilly's face, and for a moment, a look that was free of contempt or disgust. Then her eyes grew opaque and her face expressionless. She turned, walked to the bureau drawer, and picked it up.

I registered that flicker of attention because all of a sudden I was sure of how to act. "Put that down," I said, "and don't put it back until it's dry. And if I catch you at it again, I'll throw all your things out."

She hesitated, then dropped the drawer and went to her bed and lay down with her back to me and her shoes on the bedspread. I went over to her, grabbed her ankle and pulled off her shoe without opening the lace. She began to kick at me as I reached for the other foot and we struggled silently, panting and scuffling until she rolled off the bed and hit the floor with a thump.

I heard Mama coming up the stairs. So did Lilly. Hastily we both straightened out ourselves and Lilly's bed and were standing together facing the door when Mama appeared. She had the worry lines between her eyebrows. It seemed a long time since I had heard her laugh.

"What's going on, girls? It sounds like bowling balls up here."

"Nothing, Mama," I said. "We're just cleaning out our bureau drawers and the drawer slipped out of my hand."

"Well, be careful, Sarah. And make sure you put everything back neatly. Both of you be ready to eat in half an hour."

As soon as Mama was out of hearing, I bent down to Lilly and whispered, "If you put your dirty shoes on that nice spread again and I catch you, I'll make you sorry."

Then I walked away from her and went to the bathroom. I was amazed at myself. I couldn't believe I had said and done what I had, and even better, felt so good about it. I had given up on love, admiration, or friendship; all I wanted now was protection from Lilly for me and my things.

At supper that evening, Lilly ate slightly more than usual although there was still a lot of food left on her plate. I could see Mama's look of relief as another spoonful went into Lilly's mouth, and I felt pleased thinking I might have had something to do with her improved appetite.

We were eating baked apple for dessert when Mama said to Papa, "The service man was here about the refrigerator. He said there's nothing wrong with it. I asked him why the freezer frosts up so fast and why it uses so much electricity. He said I'm opening it up too often or leaving it open too long. What's the good of a refrigerator if you can't open it? My old fridge worked better. He said if we still had trouble call him again. That's the kind of service you get now-a-days." And Mama shook her head in exasperation, as she reached over to stack some plates.

Papa said, "Malkah, you wanted a big refrigerator and now you complain it uses too much power. Just enjoy." Papa shook his folded his napkin neatly and put it next to his empty dessert dish.

Meanwhile I sat staring at Lilly, willing her to look up at me. I saw her moving uneasily in her chair and sure enough, she gave me a glance. I made my face tell her I knew about her raiding the refrigerator at night, and when she dropped her eyes, I could bet she understood what I meant.

After the incident of the bureau drawer, a sort of undeclared truce existed between Lilly and me. I stopped offering her advice or help, and she understood there were basic ground rules she had to follow to keep me out of her way. Lilly began to eat more at meals, which pleased Mama and Papa. I guessed she'd given up night raids on the fridge and other secret snacking.

Everything else stayed the same, except that during the third month of Lilly's stay, she began to come downstairs for Friday night suppers, though she didn't talk and ate less than at regular meals. But she wouldn't go to synagogue either on *Shabbat* or other occasions. At Papa's insistence, Mama reluctantly agreed to leave Lilly by herself in the house on Saturday mornings. And she was the first one to leave *shul* after services, rushing home to make sure Lilly had not hurt herself or burned the house down.

Lilly was with us about a month when Mama told me I could invite Anne and Rebecca for lunch on Saturday after *Shabbat* services. They were excited and I was nervous. Mama left *shul* early. Rebecca, Anne, and I followed about ten minutes later. Papa stayed for the *kiddush* and to talk to some of the other men.

When we got to my house, Mama was in the kitchen preparing lunch. "Saraleh, go call Lilly down," she said.

I ran up to our room, but Lilly wasn't anywhere upstairs. I told Mama, who frowned and asked me to look outside for her. I left Anne and Rebecca setting the kitchen table.

I was worried, but when I got to the sidewalk, I saw Lilly running up the street toward our house from the direction of the school. "Where've you been, Lilly?" I called. "Mama has lunch for us. My friends Anne and Rebecca are here."

Lilly slowed to a walk and we went into the house together. "She's here." I yelled.

Mama came out of the kitchen wiping her hands on a dish towel, looking pretty grim. "Lilly, I don't want you wandering around on your own. If you won't come to *shul,* I expect you to stay near the house. Where were you?"

Lilly just hung her head and didn't say anything. Mama heaved a sigh and said, "All right. Go wash your hands and come right down. Lunch is ready."

When Lilly came back, my friends and I were sitting, waiting. Mama was ladling out vegetable soup. Lilly sat down in her regular place and I said, "Lilly, you remember Rebecca and Anne? They were at the gate your first day of school."

The girls said, "Hi, Lilly. Nice to meet you," using their best manners.

Lilly nodded and looked at them from under her eyebrows, keeping her chin down on her chest.

"How d'you like school, Lilly?" Anne asked.

I held my breath. Was she going to answer? Lilly was pleating the paper napkin next to her bowl. We all waited expectantly. Even the kitchen clock held its breath and stopped ticking.

Action! I saw Lilly shrug. "It is okay," she whispered.

There was a collective sigh of relief. I heard the clock ticking away. Mama put bowls of soup in front of each of us. We picked up our spoons and dug in eagerly. Rebecca said she always hated the first day of school. Mama said the first day was hard but exciting. Anne said her baby sister Yentl screamed and kicked every inch of the way when she first went to kindergarten. The ice was broken. We were all chattering as usual, so Mama had to remind us to eat. I sneaked a couple of looks at Lilly, who'd raised her head and was looking from Anne to Rebecca as they talked.

When we were eating chicken sandwiches and cole slaw, Anne asked Lilly, "What's your favorite subject, Lilly?"

Lilly had really forgotten herself. She looked puzzled. "*Quoi?*" she said.

Anne looked at me. I giggled. "That means 'what' in French."

"Oh." Anne thought for a minute. "What do you like the most in school?" She said it slowly, rounding her lips for each word. She looked cute and I felt like hugging her for being so nice to Lilly.

"French is easy. And arithmetic I like too."

Anne smiled. Rebecca covered her mouth with her hand and giggled. I glared at her, afraid Lilly would be insulted, but Lilly looked pleased with herself and laughed. I took a huge bite of my sandwich. Mama was watching us and smiling.

"Children, when you're done, you can go to Sarah and Lilly's room to play."

My friends stayed until five o'clock talking about all the things we always talked about. Lilly listened. Sometimes she asked a question, sometimes Becky or Anne asked her a question. When they had to leave I went to walk part way with them. Lilly wouldn't come, but that was okay because it had been a good day. Anne thought Lilly was 'sweet,' Becky thought she was 'cute.' None of us said anything about Lilly's Gentile friends.

In school, nobody, my friends included, made mention of the fact that Lilly continued to hang around only with the Gentile girls and had nothing to do with me or other Jewish children. In fact, while my crowd excelled in scholarship, Lilly was putting all her spare energy and time into sports. She soon became the volleyball star of the sixth grade and spent all her free periods in the gym practicing serves against a wall.

Life was almost the same as before Lilly came except when I would run across her in the hall and our eyes would meet for a second before we both looked away, or when I'd see her in the gym or lunchroom. When I didn't see Lilly I was able to forget about her. So though things weren't ideal, they weren't too bad and I figured I could stand living like that until some distant time when we would grow up and go our separate ways.

After six months, I'd gotten used to the situation, and wasn't even conscious of any real problem. A new pattern was established, even to my getting up to push Lilly down in her bed and cover her when she had her night horrors every week or so. I knew she went to church when she got out of school early, and for all I knew on Saturday too, when the rest of us were in *shul.*

One time after school, I was brave enough to follow her to church and then right in. My knees were quaking as I hauled open one of the heavy doors and slid inside. I was sure some officials would accost me immediately, to thunder at the Jew defiling their holy place. I found myself in a dim, high-ceilinged hall. The only light came from stained glass windows above the entrance doors. My heart thumped so hard I could barely catch my breath, and if the hall hadn't been empty, I would have turned and fled.

I rushed toward an open door hoping I'd see Lilly, and burst into an immense space, dark and cold. I couldn't see where the ceiling ended. Rows of pews led to a well of light on a raised platform that seemed several blocks away.

Lilly was a dwindling figure walking up the aisle—I could hear the click of her shoes on the stone floor echoing distantly. My shallow breathing squeezed the air from my body which trembled out of control. An isolated figure here and there sat or knelt in a pew or at a bank of candles at the front. I was awed by the vastness of everything—massive pillars soaring up like tree trunks in a forest, huge windows made of thousands of pieces of colored glass, aisles stretching between hundreds of seats. Golly, I thought, where do the kids stay when they come to church?

I stood against a wall at the back, staring at Lilly who dipped her knee as she entered a pew to kneel and, I guessed, to pray. Soon she stood, walked over to a statue where rows of candles were burning and lit one herself. That's when I left. How could this be my cousin, I wondered? Why did she want to be in such a lonely, scary place?

I began to realize how far apart we were in every way. When I tried to figure how it could've happened, my head began to ache and I had to stop thinking about it.

One day in study hall Catherine Czarnowski, the Polish girl in my home room class, passed me a folded piece of paper, and gave me a meaningful look. We had never really said or had anything to do with each other, so even before I unfolded the paper to see what was in it, I hated the whole thing. I knew it had to be about Lilly because Catherine was with her a lot more than I was. They were always together at lunch, with Lilly talking a blue streak, and they spent a lot of free time in the gym and also after school for all I knew.

I opened the paper with shaking fingers. It was a note in the same neat, schoolgirl hand we were all taught. It read, "Meet me after school at the Crown Street school entrance. Come alone. I want to talk about you know who."

Catherine was sitting a few rows in front of me. When I looked up, her eyes were on me waiting for my answer. I nodded once, and she got up immediately and left the hall. I couldn't guess what Catherine wanted or what would happen. I wondered if there were a lot of them and if they wanted to beat me up and if Lilly would be there to help them.

I didn't want to go and wished I hadn't agreed to meet her, but I was trapped. If I didn't show up, she'd get me somehow at another time.

Just when I thought I had things worked out with Lilly so I could live with them, something else came up. Bitterly I thought of how happy I'd been before and how I hadn't known enough to appreciate it. I'd give just about anything for the days when I was an only child.

The afternoon dragged along until suddenly it was gone. I told Anne I wasn't going home, I had to go to the school library, and when she offered to wait for me I practically yelled at her to leave me alone. For about the tenth time she told me I wasn't the same since Lilly came. I hugged her and said I was sorry and I'd try to be nicer but that she had to go and leave me alone any way.

I was keeping Catherine waiting but I felt as if I had lead in my shoes. I got into my coat, fumbling with the buttons because my fingers wouldn't work right, put on my scarf and mittens, and picked up my books. I'd stalled all I could. I was the last one out of the room, and now I almost ran to the rear doors to get it over with.

She was standing just outside on the top step and she was alone, which was a relief.

Her nose was red with cold and her very pale skin looked blotchy. I thought she was ugly and colorless. Her hair was almost white, so were her eyebrows and lashes. And her eyes were mean when she looked at me, so I avoided them when I could. When she saw me she said, "It's about time. I'm freezing."

"I got here as fast as I could," I mumbled.

"Let's walk," she said.

"Where to?"

"Just around."

We walked down the steps, across the school yard and out the gate.

"I want to talk to you about Lillian," she said.

My mind seized up as I tried to locate a Lillian among the people I knew.

"About who?" I said stupidly.

"Lillian, Lillian, the girl who lives with you."

"Oh," I said, "you mean my cousin Lilly."

"Her name is Lillian and she's not your cousin."

"What?" I said. I couldn't seem to understand what Catherine was talking about. It was like one of those dreams where everybody knows what's going on but you.

"Lillian LeClerc is not your cousin. Don't make believe you're surprised. It's just a mistake she ended up in your house. She doesn't want to be there. Don't you think it's awful to make her stay when she doesn't belong to you and doesn't want to have anything to do with you?"

Of all the blows I had taken connected with Lilly, this was the worst. I gasped until the cold air burnt my throat and lungs.

Finally I said, "Where did you get all those ideas from? Why would we take someone who didn't belong to us?"

Catherine pushed her lower lip out at me. "I didn't make this up, y'know. Lillian told me she was happy where she was and Jews made her leave. She doesn't want to stay with a bunch of Jews. Why don't you let her go where she wants to?"

"Did Lilly ask you to talk to me?"

"She didn't have to. Lillian's too nice to ask for favors and she's too scared to talk for herself. Someone's gotta help her."

I couldn't believe it. All the Gentiles in school thought my family kidnapped Lilly and was keeping her against her will! If the idea weren't so frightening I would have laughed at how silly it was. My mind went babbling along and I remembered the story of 'The Ransom of Red Chief,' where desperados kidnap a kid for the ransom money and end up paying the family to take him back. I would give every single thing I owned if someone would take Lilly away.

"Look, Catherine, Lilly is an orphan. Her mother and father, my aunt and uncle, were killed in an extermination camp. They put her in a Catholic orphanage so she wouldn't be killed by the Nazis, but my aunt made everybody swear Lilly would go back to her family when the war ended. All her papers and records prove she's my cousin. If we were keeping her against her will would we let her out to go to school?"

Catherine's face was set and stubborn. I was fascinated with the way her nostrils flared when she got excited. "All I'm saying is they made a mistake. They mixed up Lillian with someone who *was* your cousin. You've got the wrong one and you gotta let her go."

A doubt entered my mind along with a flicker of hope. "How do you know? Do you have proof?"

"Yeah, Lillian says the pictures they showed her of her mother and father, she never saw them before, and she never knew anything about Jews until they forced her to leave The Home and brought her to England. If she was a Jew wouldn't she remember some of the things Jews do?"

"Then how did she get all the papers that say she's my cousin and why did my Aunt's neighbors say that Lilly is Lilly and not someone else?"

"I told you," Catherine said with elaborate patience, "they mixed things up. You know how it is in a war, everything gets lost and mixed up."

I walked along for some time thinking. What if Catherine was right and Lilly wasn't my cousin at all? Lilly acted like an enemy and if she wasn't Jewish, keeping her might ruin our whole family. Finally I said, "I don't know what you expect me to do. I don't decide about what happens to Lilly. If it were up to me I'd let her go wherever she wants."

This seemed to be what Catherine was waiting for. "Well, you could tell your parents. Tell them God will punish them for keeping the wrong person."

That annoyed me. "Why would my parents want to keep the wrong person, someone who isn't a relative or even Jewish?"

Catherine spoke promptly, without thought, as if she were stating a well-known fact. "Well everyone knows Jews take Christian children away and do bad things to them."

It was like cold water in my face. "Who told you that—your parents? You're disgusting," I blurted. "You have a lot of nerve talking to me like that."

Catherine spoke hastily as though realizing she'd lost ground by showing me her hand. "Well maybe *your* family doesn't . . . I'm not saying your family is deliberately doing that."

"Oh, is that so! It sounds to me that's exactly what you *are* saying even though you don't know any or anything about Jewish people. Maybe your family takes Jewish children to do bad things to. You should mind your own business, y'know."

"That's not true! I love Lillian and I want to help her. I don't want her to suffer."

"Well how does it help to tell her the people she lives with kidnap Christian children? To tell you the truth, I wish I'd never seen or heard of her, or you either."

I took off then, running hard, as if I could put distance between myself and the awful things Catherine had said to me. I was sobbing. The tears running down my face felt as though they were freezing there; my nose began to run. I didn't even know if I had a tissue in my pocket. A block before my house I slowed down to a walk, and juggling my books in one arm, hunted through my pockets. I found an old scrap of tissue and wiped as carefully as I could. Then I walked around the block a few times, waiting for my eyes and nose to stop being red. By the time I thought I could go home, my teeth were chattering, and I wasn't sure whether it was from the cold or from the terrible things Catherine had said.

In the house, I went straight up the stairs to my room, while Mama came out of the kitchen to look after me, calling, "Saraleh, where are you going? Are you all right?"

I always stopped in the kitchen to kiss Mama, get my milk, and talk, but I couldn't face her then, not if my life depended on it.

I called, "I'll be down in a minute Mama, I have to go to the bathroom."

In the bathroom, I washed my face with soap and hot water, then cold water, and as I did, tried to sort out all the peculiar feelings I was having.

For six months I had been drowning in a sea of open antagonism and secret hatred. From Catherine I learned that the lies which had fueled the Holocaust were all stacked up ready for use, like seasoned cord wood. My safe, secure life seemed to be just another fantasy. Maybe after all, I was only a Holocaust survivor, but from New York instead of Auschwitz. More and more I was feeling like a little girl in need of parental guidance. I had to talk to Mama and Papa and maybe Yosuf.

When I came into the kitchen, Lilly was already at the table finishing her milk and cookies. I kissed Mama then slid into my seat without looking at Lilly.

"So Saraleh, how was school today?"

"Okay, Mama."

"Just okay? What's wrong?"

"Nothing Mama, it's just . . . there's nothing new to talk about."

"Well, Lilly was telling me she got a hundred on her math test today."

I stared at Lilly and resentment and anger must have been in my face, because she looked first surprised, then blank.

I said sarcastically, "Well, isn't that nice."

Lilly knew what I meant, because she turned away.

I finished eating as fast as I could and as I was rinsing my glass, said, "C'mon Lilly, I want to show you something."

Mama told us to take off our school clothes, and we went upstairs together, me leading the way. I closed the door to our room so Mama wouldn't hear, and before I could get cold feet, said, "I'll bet you can't remember anything about your mother or father, Lilly, you were so young when they left you at the orphanage."

She looked at me for a moment then said, "I remember plenty of things. Also they came to see me in The Home until after I was seven years."

"So then you know the pictures you have aren't your mother or father but some other people?"

She frowned. "They are my pictures, and they are my mother and father."

"How can you be so sure, things were all mixed up because of the war."

She stared at me.

"I mean," I went on, "if you're not Lilly Janislowicz but some other girl, a Christian girl who doesn't belong here, my mother and father would definitely want to know, so they could send you to the people you really belong to."

She said nothing.

"Don't you have anything to say, Lilly? If you're not my Auntie Esther's girl, no one wants you here. Your best friend, Catherine Czarnowski, thinks we kidnapped you to force you to become a Jew," I saw Lilly suck in her breath, "so why don't you tell us who you really are, so you can go where you belong?"

All of a sudden I saw red; I mean I really saw red. I guess I got so angry the blood rushed right into my eyes.

I marched over to where Lilly was standing near her bed and pushed my face into hers. "You're a rotten, nasty liar, either way. If you're Lilly, then be Lilly and if you're not, then say who you are!"

Lilly looked scared. "I'm Lilly," she whispered.

"Then why do you go with the *goyim*? Why do you tell them terrible stories about us and about the Jews? If you're Lilly, you're a Jew and your parents were Jews. Why do you go to church? Why won't you come to the synagogue? If you're a Christian girl, say who you are and we'll give you back." My voice had been rising and ended with a squeak. I wasn't going to let Lilly off the hook this time. I was going to make her talk if I had to wring it out of her. I kept her backed against the foot of the bed glaring into her face.

Her face was pale and her eyes wide open. She whispered, "Your Papa is my real uncle, but I didn't want to leave Belgium. I wanted to stay in The Home or with my mother's friends. They had no children. They would have adopted me."

I backed off. "So why didn't they let you stay where you were?"

I saw Lilly swallow hard, as though something was stuck in her throat. Her eyelids and nose turned red—she looked as if she'd be crying in a minute. But I cared more about finding out what happened than if she was happy or not.

"They showed me a letter my mother wrote before the Germans took her and my father away. She begged her sisters and brothers to find me if she didn't live and take me back with them."

I was quiet a long time. Finally I said, "So everybody's doing what your mother wanted; what are you so mad about?"

Lilly then made the longest speech I'd ever heard from her. "My mother! My mother!" she said fiercely, throwing her hands up in the air. "What did my mother care? She could have take me to England. But my father could not go into England, so my mother choosed to stay with him instead of to save me." As Lilly got more agitated and spoke faster, her English became more foreign sounding. Her face was red and her eyes filled with tears.

"The Sisters and Fathers becomed my mothers and fathers. They treat me okay, I was happy. The other kids are the same like me, no real mothers or fathers. I don't want to leave. I don't want to be Jew. Jews killed God. If I stay with Jew, I will roast in eternal hellfire, and the synagogue is a place for the devil. I am Lilly but I do not want to be here."

I couldn't sort it out; there was so much I didn't understand. I wasn't angry any more, just really helpless. The problem was too big for me. Lilly was miserable and I was miserable and the people who had started it all, even though they weren't around anymore, were still causing us to be miserable. I went and sat down on the side of my bed and Lilly sat on the end of hers.

"Lilly," I asked, "what do you mean, the Jews killed God? How could anyone kill God? He's not real—I mean like people."

Her eyes grew rounder than usual. "Oh yes. The Jews did kill Jesus Christ, God's only begotten Son. They made the Romans put Him on the cross to crucify Him."

I was really puzzled. "Lilly, I don't know what you're talking about. I didn't kill anybody. I'm not even thirteen years old. My parents and your mother would never do anything like that. And the synagogue is full of lights and beautiful scrolls, and the Ten Commandments that God gave us to follow. We sing and pray. There aren't any devils in the synagogue. You can come and see for yourself, you don't have to believe me."

"No," she shook her head so vigorously her braids swung out from her head, "the Sisters told me. They were good to me."

I began to get exasperated again. "Do you think I killed God?! Do you think your Mama and Papa killed God?! Can you believe that? You're Jewish, when did you kill God, Lilly? When did you make them put God on a cross?"

Now Lilly looked completely baffled. "*Sais pas. C'est vrai, mais . . . sais pas.*" Her shoulders sagged. She looked smaller than usual.

I leaned toward her again. "How could it be true? Lilly, you didn't get it right. You were excited or something and didn't understand what they meant. But now you can find out for yourself. You don't have to listen to anyone."

Mama opened the door and came into the room. "What's the door closed for, girls?" Then seeing us still in our school clothes, "Why aren't you ready for supper? We eat in a few minutes. You know better than to keep Papa waiting, Sarah. Go and wash up, both of you, and I want to see your hair combed, Sarah. It's too late to do yours over, Lilly. Now hurry, girls."

I marched past Mama to the bathroom and out of the corner of my eye saw her shake her head over me. I figured it'd be easier to talk to Yosuf before I tried to talk to Mama and Papa.

Twice a week we had gym, which wasn't one of my favorite subjects. Some of the girls were really good at climbing ropes and dribbling basketballs, but though I managed okay and always ended up with a 'B', I wasn't sorry when the end of the period came and I could get out of my gym suit. For one thing, our gym suits were an ugly green. They buttoned down the front and the bottoms were like bloomers. If an elastic snapped, you had this big wide thing flapping around your leg. Even the girls who liked gym didn't like the gym suits.

Each girl had a locker with a combination lock, and the locker room always smelled sweaty from our sneakers and the suits, though we were supposed to take them home once a week to wash and iron. The locker room was always cold, except in June when it was very hot, and whenever I put on my suit it felt clammy, as if it was damp. I usually went into the gym covered with goosebumps and with blue-looking legs and arms.

Sometimes, instead of having us work out on the horses or parallel bars or ropes, the teacher would set up a game of basketball or volleyball with another class. In fact a couple of times, my class played Lilly's class. Lilly was a real good player. She was one of the shortest girls on her team, but that didn't seem to get in her way. She was very fast and very strong, and could return a ball to almost any spot she wanted. You could see she loved to play and that her team depended on her to make points.

Though Lilly's class was sixth grade and we were seventh, when she was playing, the best we could do was make a draw. Well, the day after Lilly and I had that talk about killing God, our gym teacher set up a volleyball game between Lilly's class and mine. We chose Allie Snider, who was our best player, for captain, and she put me in the center position where I did best.

Lilly was on the other side of the net smiling and laughing and talking with her friends. With them, she acted like a normal girl. It used to make me jealous, but now I didn't even care any more. Most of the time she played the net position because she was able to score so often. This time though, she was in the center position. We volleyed for first serve and my team won. That gave us a little advantage and the first volley went on quite a long time with some good returns back and forth.

I enjoyed volleyball. It was a neat game with real team spirit and I was pretty good at holding up my end.

We scored on that first volley and got to serve again. I delivered the serve to the rear of the court and was back in my place just as the ball got to Lilly. She looked my way as she punched the ball and I saw it come straight at me, fast and hard at the level of my head. I ducked just in time and heard it whiz by my ear. The girl in back of me volleyed the ball toward the net, and the team put it over.

The next point and the one after that went to the other side. Allie said, "C'mon kids, let's give 'em a run for their money. Let's make the next point."

We actually did, tying the score. On our next serve, Lilly got the ball, and this time when she sent it over, I couldn't get out of the way and it slammed right into my chest, knocking the wind out of me and almost bowling me over.

Miss Olson, the gym teacher, said, "Be careful, girls. Don't aim your volleys at each other." So I knew it wasn't my imagination.

I was still trying to catch my breath, wondering whether Lilly was hoping to kill me outright on the volleyball court and get rid of me that way.

The funny thing was that it didn't make me angry to know she was out to get me. If she hated me so much there must be something wrong with me. I guess I wasn't much use to my team after that. My arms and legs felt heavy and I had a hard time getting under the ball much less punching it any distance. The other girls were covering for me; maybe they knew I wasn't feeling so great.

That was the day I found out you have to concentrate as much on sports as you do on history or math if you want to do a good job. I don't know why they call it playing; it's as much work as any other thing and in my opinion, not as interesting. But I learned to have more respect for how hard you have to work to be good at sports.

So there I was, mostly taking up space and trying to stay out of the way of the girls on my own team, when I saw Lilly hit another ball my way. As long as I live, I'll never forget the look on her face, even if I can only describe it as being just plain mean. She put all her strength into that ball, jumping at least a foot in the air to send it back. I didn't have a chance, it came at me so fast, or maybe I was so discouraged I really didn't care.

The ball blocked out everything, and the next thing I saw was a bunch of stars. I don't remember anything after that until waking up flat on the floor with a wet towel on my face. I heard a lot of excited talking going on. My nose felt funny like when you breathe up chlorine water in a pool, and my head hurt.

I tried to sit up, but I felt a hand on my shoulder and Mrs. Olson said, "Lie still, Sarah, You've been hit in the face by a ball. The nurse will be here in a minute."

Then I remembered that ball all right, and my only thought was, well, Lilly, I hope you're satisfied now. Someone took the towel away; the nurse was bending over me. Mrs. Olson was next to her, and all the other kids were gone. The nurse touched my head and face, and it sure hurt around my nose and right eye.

Finally she said, "Well, young lady, you're lucky. It doesn't look as if your nose is broken, and all you'll have is a beautiful shiner. I guess we'll send you home with a note for your parents. It'll help if your mother puts some ice on that eye."

"My head hurts," I said.

"No wonder," Mrs. Olson said, "I was glad to see your head was still where it belongs."

"I'll tell your mother to give you an aspirin," the nurse said. "Let's get you on your feet."

I wanted to get up. It felt strange being flat on the gym floor like that, and it was hard too. But when I sat up I was dizzy and took my time moving after that.

The nurse said, "I'm going to drive this one home; I don't think she should walk very far."

Mrs. Olson said, "C'mon Sarah, I'll help you get dressed."

Boy! I felt like an invalid. What would Mama say seeing me come home in the middle of the day in the nurse's car? I began to get angry. Poor Mama didn't do anything to deserve getting scared and upset over. It wasn't just between Lilly and me anymore. She was beginning to mess up the whole family. The big question was, what could I do about it?

When the nurse put me in her car, she said, "I've called your mother, Sarah; she's expecting us. I told her it's nothing serious, so we don't scare the wits out of her."

We were home in two minutes; it was only four blocks from school. Mama was out on the stoop waiting and looking worried. They hustled me into the house and sat me down. The nurse told Mama what to do and then left.

Mama got ice out of the freezer, wrapped it in a towel, and told me to go into the living room, take off my shoes and lie down on the sofa. I was glad to do it; I was pretty tired by then. Mama put a towel on a pillow under my head and put the pack on my eye. It stung at first but then it felt good.

Mama said, "Mrs. Olson said you got hit by a ball. How did you get hit by a ball right in your face, Saraleh?"

I was glad I didn't have to look at her. "It was just an accident, Mama, we were playing volleyball."

"And who was the one who hit you?"

"Just one of the girls. It's not so bad. I'm not hurt too much. The nurse said I'll have a black eye. What's it look like, Mama? I never had a black eye before."

"Well Sarah, I like you better without it." So I knew then she was feeling better. "But when Papa sees this, I don't know what he'll say."

What Papa said was, "*Gott in Himmel!* And we think they're safe in school! Who ever heard of girls playing volleyball?"

And Mama said, "Who ever heard of children getting hurt playing volleyball. They must play it like football."

Lilly came home late. If Mama and Papa weren't so busy with me, they would have started worrying about her long before. As it was Mama kept looking at the clock and saying, "And where is Lilly? What kind of day is this? One hurt is enough, I don't want to hear any more bad news today."

Just then Lilly came in and started right up the stairs. Papa stopped her by calling, "Lilly, come in here before you go upstairs."

She came in slowly. I was sitting up on the sofa getting a rest from the ice pack. She didn't look at anybody, and Papa said, "Why are you so late, Lilly? We were beginning to worry and if it weren't that Sarah got hurt and we were busy with her, we would have been out looking for you already."

Lilly dug her toe into the carpet looking down all the while. "I stayed at school later for extra work," she mumbled.

What a liar, I thought. She was just scared to come home. Probably thought I squealed on her, like a Nazi. She should know all about that; she acts like one.

Papa said, "Don't do that again without telling Mama where you'll be. Now go up and change for supper. We'll be late enough already, with all this commotion."

Lilly didn't argue about leaving; she got out fast. Then Mama said, "Are you feeling all right, Sarah? You should get out of those school clothes, and if you want to eat in bed, I'll bring you up a tray."

"I'm okay, Mama. I'd rather eat with everybody. My head doesn't hurt anymore."

They let me go then. I figured they wanted to talk without Lilly or me around. I went up the stairs with my head feeling light, as if it wasn't attached to me as tight as usual. I was pretty mixed up about Lilly. I still wasn't used to the idea that she hated me, so that hurt. But I was getting tired of trying to understand her problems. I was thinking about getting her alone somehow and beating her up until she yelled 'Uncle.'

I sure wasn't going to pretend that nothing was wrong. I was going to snub her, no matter what she said or did. When I came into our room, Lilly was in her play clothes, on her bed with her back to me as always, pretending to be asleep. I marched right to my closet without trying to be quiet just as if I was all alone in the room. I took out my play clothes and laid them on the bed. Then I went to my bureau mirror and looked at myself for the first time since the ball hit me. All around my eye was swollen so that I looked lopsided, and it was a real purplish color with parts of it dark blue. The skin was shiny, so now I knew why they called a black eye a shiner. While I was admiring my eye and wondering how long I would have to look like that, I heard Lilly say, "Sarah, does it hurt a lot?"

I just went on about my business as if no one was there but me. I unbuttoned my blouse and unzipped my skirt.

"I didn't want to hurt you so much," she said.

I took off my skirt and blouse and hung them up, never looking at Lilly as if she didn't even exist.

"If you tell your parents that I wanted to hurt you, I will tell them that you are lying."

So that was it! She didn't care about me one bit! She was just scared for her own skin. What did she think Mama and Papa would do to her? Torture and beat her like in the concentration camps!? I wasn't smart enough to keep giving her the silent treatment which probably would have punished her worse then anything else, but that was too much! I was so furious I was about to burst.

I wanted to shout but didn't so Mama and Papa wouldn't hear. I hissed, "You are disgusting! You know that?! You tried to kill me! And if you didn't, it wasn't your fault. And if you had killed me, how do you think Mama and Papa would have felt? But then I'm sure you don't care at all. You don't care about anybody but yourself. I didn't tell Mama and Papa because I didn't want to upset them, not because I care about what happens to you. What you need is a good whipping, but they don't hit children, so I'm telling you, Lilly, from now on stay out of my way because the next time you do something to hurt me, I'm gonna get you alone somewhere and beat you up. Meanwhile, don't you come near me or talk to me about anything!"

I grabbed my sweater and pulled it over my head, forgetting about my sore eye because I was so angry. I saw a few more stars before I got the sweater on.

"Sarah, I was so mad because you called my friends liars. I just wanted to get even," she said.

"Oh," I said sarcastically, "do you know another word for liar that you like better? And do you think you have the right to hurt someone because you're mad at them? I'm mad at you. I think I'll wring your neck, okay?"

"I didn't tell Catherine to talk to you." Lilly's head was down and her lower lip was trembling.

"You must've told her *something* to make her think she should talk to me like that."

Lilly didn't say anything. "Y'know, Lilly," I said, "before you came I was so happy to think you'd be my friend and sister. The only thing you are is my enemy. If you want to go someplace else, it's okay with me. I'll help you leave any time you want. Now I don't want to talk to you any more."

Boy, it felt good to get all that off my chest. I didn't know how long it would be before I had another run-in with Lilly, but I knew I had to talk to Yosuf as soon as possible.

On Friday nights after supper, our mothers were in the kitchen, our fathers and Duvid were in the living room, and Lilly was in the bedroom. Only now I realized how hard it was to talk to Yosuf in private. If we went into the spare room to talk, we would attract more attention than if we stood on the dining room table to recite the blessing.

I waited until we started the chicken course, when everybody was busy talking, passing dishes and dishing out. Quietly I said to him, "Yosuf, I have to talk to you privately about Lilly, and not just for a few minutes, and pretty soon too."

One of the things I always liked about Yosuf is that he never treated me like a baby. Someone else might have argued with me and told me to talk to my parents but Yosuf knew that if I thought I couldn't, there was a good reason. He would understand I couldn't tell them Lilly was ashamed of being Jewish and of living with Jewish people.

Yosuf was the family genius, not just because he was the top of his class in every subject and would graduate from high school at sixteen, but because he understood a lot, knew a lot, and knew how to find things out if you had to know something.

When he didn't say anything right away, I knew he was waiting for a time when he wouldn't be noticed. I was clearing the dining room table and only the two of us were in the room when he said, "What time do you get out of school on Monday?"

"Three o'clock."

"Can you make an excuse to be home later than usual?"

I nodded.

"Okay, I'll meet you at the public library, Monday at three-fifteen."

I nodded again and took a stack of dinner plates into the kitchen. Yosuf went into the living room where the men were.

It was easy. I didn't even have to make up a story. I told Mama I'd be going to the public library after school for about an hour.

There was a bench in the entrance hall where I would meet Yosuf. It was probably more private sitting there talking as if we met by accident than if we were seen with our heads together at a table in a corner.

Anne didn't even ask any more if we were walking home together—I turned her down so many times—so that was no problem. After school I ran all the way to the library. The library clock said three-ten when I got there. I looked in all the rooms but Yosuf hadn't arrived yet, so I went out to the hall bench. Just as I got there, Yosuf came in. We sat down with our books stacked on either side of us.

"What's going on, Saraleh?" Yosuf asked right away.

I had thought about everything I was going to say so I wouldn't waste a minute.

"There's a Polish girl in my class who's friends with Lilly. She talked to me last week. She said that Lilly isn't my cousin but a Christian girl that we got by mistake. That Jews take Christian children, *steal* them and do bad things to them. I spoke to Lilly about it. Lilly said she knew she was Auntie Esther's child, but that she's an orphan because Auntie wouldn't leave Belgium to go to London when she could have saved herself and Lilly."

"That's true enough," Yosuf said, "she wouldn't leave Uncle Leon."

I nodded to show that I knew that too, and went on, "But Lilly is furious with her mother and at the aunts and uncles who took her away from the orphanage. She says she was happy there and wanted to stay. But," I rushed on before Yosuf could say anything, "the most important thing is Lilly hates Jews. She says we killed God, and the devil lives in the synagogue. I tried to talk to her about it but what she said doesn't make any sense to me, except now I know why Lilly is the way she is."

Yosuf looked worried. "Yosuf, do Mama and Papa know all these things? Someone should talk to Lilly. I don't think it'll get any better if we just wait. You know a lot . . . can't you help?"

Yosuf leaned back to think. He was staring straight ahead and I looked anxiously at his nice, familiar profile. He had a lot of curly hair and a high forehead. He wore thick tortoise-shell frame glasses that were always sliding down his nose which was straight and small. He'd push the glasses up with a finger and the next minute they'd be sliding down again. A dark fuzz was beginning to show on his upper lip. Well, he was sixteen; he'd soon be a grownup man.

"Well, Sarah, you're right, I think we have to do something," he said finally. "Let me think about this for a couple of days. I'll do some research and maybe I'll talk to some people. Maybe even the rabbi, not about Lilly but about the problem of the deicide lie."

I looked perplexed.

Yosuf smiled. "All that means is the lie about Jews killing God."

I was surprised. "You mean it has a special name?"

"Sure. It's a big thing with the Gentiles. Saraleh, maybe it's time to talk to your parents about Lilly."

My eyes filled with tears. "Yosuf, I'll have to tell them she hates us and hates Jews. I'm supposed to be her sister and take care of her. They'll be so disappointed. Can't we do something ourselves, first?"

Yosuf looked worried and sighed. He shrugged and finally said, "I'm not even sure we'll be able to change her mind, but we can try."

I heaved a sigh of relief. It was good to move my burden over to share with other shoulders, and even though Yosuf was a skinny beanpole, he looked like a tower of strength to me. "Thank you, Yosuf."

We stood, picked up our books and walked out together. When we got to the corner, we said goodbye and took our separate paths home. I walked with a lighter heart than I'd had in days.

CHAPTER FIVE

MY FAVORITE SWEATER WAS MISSING. FIRST I FIGURED IT WAS IN the wash. Though I hadn't put it in, Mama might have. Then I thought it might have gotten mixed in with Lilly's things; sometimes our things got mixed up. But before I could look for my sweater, I noticed that a book I liked very much was gone. In each of my bureau drawers, I kept a bar of perfumed soap; they were *Chanukah* gifts. One of them was gone. I had to face it. Since I had talked to Lilly about Catherine, more and more of my things were disappearing. She sure keeps me busy, I thought. If it isn't one thing it's another.

I didn't want to accuse her and I wasn't going to go to Mama or Papa, but I didn't want to keep losing my things either. It wasn't that she didn't have her own stuff, her shelves were almost as full as mine by now. I was ashamed to consult Yosuf. This was a small problem compared to the one I left with him. Okay, Sarah, I told myself, you figure this one out yourself. It took a day of hard thinking before I came up with what I thought would work. That very afternoon I made sure to get home before Lilly. I went to her neatest drawer and chose her most nicely ironed petticoat; the one with lace around the neck and armholes. I folded it into a tiny package, put it into a small paper bag, and slid it between my mattress and the spring, in the middle where it wouldn't show

78

when the sheets were changed. Then I took her book of *Dogs of the World*, put it in another paper bag, and stuck it in the back of the closet shelf under the boxes of out-grown clothes Mama collected for the Hadassah bazaar.

Lilly had a collection of stamps from letters she got from Belgium and London. She'd steam them off carefully, spread them out on a dish towel to dry, then store them in a little wicker box. I was sure she kept track of every one of them. Some of them were beautiful; my parents thought it was a great way to learn geography and other things. I picked out five of the most beautiful ones, put them in a little envelope, and stuck it in the pages of my dictionary. That should do it, I figured.

I got results in less time than I expected. That night when I was getting ready for bed, Lilly was putting out her clothes for the next day. I didn't look at her but knew anyway exactly what she was doing. I heard her open the bureau drawer. I heard her scrabbling around in it. I heard her taking things out, opening other drawers, closing them then opening the ones she had before, and so on.

Good! She was searching for something, probably her best petticoat. She blew out a long, exasperated breath.

I looked up innocently. "What's the matter Lilly?"

"I cannot find my good petticoat."

"Did you look everywhere?"

"Yes! I am looking everywhere now," she said as if I were an idiot.

"Maybe it's in the wash."

Vigorous head-shaking. "No, no, I just yesterday pressed it."

"Oh, that's too bad. Do you want me to help you look?"

She gave me a peculiar look. "No, I will find it myself. Maybe it will turn up."

"I certainly hope so," I said fervently as I jumped into bed.

Some nights when Lilly got into bed she took her box of postage stamps and looked at them one after another, spreading them out side-by-side on top of her quilt. I hoped tonight would be one of them. She was in her nightgown all ready for bed. I willed her to get her stamps, and as if she were obliging me, she did. I quickly buried my nose in my book and held my breath. I heard her climb into bed. Then there was a long, long silence.

She got out of bed, not to return the box of stamps. I peeped
over the book. She was standing by her bed looking at the rows of
stamps laid out on the cover. She looked in the box again; I could
see it was empty. She got down on her hands and knees to look
under her bed. I felt a bubble of excitement rising in me and
hoped I wouldn't giggle and give myself away.

Mama came into the room. "Lilly, what are you doing under
the bed?"

"My stamps are missing," came her voice, muffled by the bed.

"They're all on your bed," Mama said.

"Some are missing."

"Are you sure? You have so many, how do you know?"

Lilly stood up and gave Mama a look she usually reserved for
me. "I know my things. I know what I have got. Five of my best
stamps are missing."

"Well, they'll surely show up. You must have taken them out
and forgotten."

Lilly's eyes narrowed and her voice grew hard. "Do not tell me
what I did. I never took them out, but someone else did."

"That'll be enough, Lilly. You will not talk to me like that. Put
your things away and get into bed, it's time to go to sleep."

"My good petticoat is missing too," she burst out. "Someone
is stealing my things."

"Lilly, if you keep on I'll call Papa up here to talk to you."

I don't know why Mama supposed that would work with Lilly.
It worked with me but I loved Papa and couldn't stand to disap-
point him.

"He's not my Papa and you can call him as much as you want.
I want my things back. Until I get them, I am not going to bed."

Mama wasn't going to let Lilly push her around. "I'll give you
five minutes to put your things away and get into bed, young lady.
Then if you want to stay up you can take your quilt and pillow and
go into the spare room, but you can't stay in here and keep Sarah
up." Mama left the room before she could get an argument.

Lilly looked around in despair, and for a moment I felt really
sorry for her. "Don't worry, Lilly, you'll find your things. I'll help
you look tomorrow."

There were tears in her eyes as she gathered her stamps
together lovingly and put them in their box.

When Mama came back Lilly was in bed with the quilt over her head. Mama told us good night and turned off the light. That night Lilly had a real bad night horror, and after I was getting back into my bed, I hoped I hadn't made a mistake about what had happened to *my* things.

Yosuf was taking longer than I thought he would. A whole week had gone by after we met in the library and nothing had changed. Except in school at lunch time, whenever I walked by the table where Lilly, Catherine, and the others sat, as soon as Catherine caught my eye she would put an arm around Lilly as though to protect her from me. I thought it was a pretty corny thing to do, and would give Lilly a little sarcastic smile. It looked to me like Lilly wasn't so comfortable any more when I did. Then I got tired of the game and just walked by without giving them a glance.

Of course Lilly didn't find her petticoat or her stamps, and a couple of days later, missed her book. She came over to me then, one day as I was walking home from school. It was the first time she had walked with me in the street since her first day of school almost eight months ago.

"Hey, Lilly," I said, "what will your friends say when they see you walking with me? Aren't you afraid?"

She ignored what I said. "You have been taking my things," she told me.

I opened my eyes wide. "What are you talking about Lilly? Why would I take your things when I have all my own things? But y'know it's funny, my things are missing too; my good blue sweater—I haven't been able to find it since a week ago Thursday, and my book of wildflowers is missing and one of my bars of sachet soap. Gosh! Do you think we have a thief in the house? Or maybe Mama's taking our stuff and selling it, for Hadassah or something. I mean if Jews steal children, why shouldn't they steal ordinary things?"

Lilly got very red in the face, dropped her books on the ground and punched me on my shoulder. She took me by surprise. Before I could recover, she grabbed a handful of my hair and pulled.

I was wild with fury. The pent up anger, frustration, humiliation, and rejection building in me because of Lilly broke like a surging wave. I flung my books out of my arms and grabbed her wrists in my hands as hard as I could until she let go of my hair.

Holding her so tight she couldn't get loose, I began to shake her back and forth like a rag doll. She kicked out and caught me hard in the shin. I let go of one hand and slapped her in the face with all my might. She was kicking wildly and I backed off to arm's length but still held on to one of her wrists. I twisted her arm behind her and pushed it against her back.

Suddenly we were being wrenched apart. A couple of the bigger girls I didn't know were separating us and one of them said, "Okay, kids, that's enough. Settle your differences without fighting."

The girl holding Lilly said, "I'm not gonna let you go until you calm down. When you promise not to fight you can go."

I wasn't surprised. The older girls always broke up fights between the younger kids, and I was willing enough. My shin was killing me and I could see the beautiful black and blue mark I was going to have. Lilly's wrists had the imprint of my fingers all over them and there was a red mark on her face where I hit her. If my parents saw this they'd have a fit. Lilly looked as if all the fight had gone out of her. I felt as bad as she looked. The girls let us go and left.

My books were scattered all over, loose sheets of paper sticking to the sidewalk. Lilly's stuff was only a little better because she had less than I had. I was still breathing hard and could hear Lilly puffing away. When I finished picking up my things, she was standing near me waiting. I began to walk slowly, limping a little to favor my left leg.

"Well," I said, "do you want to talk about how we find our missing things?"

She nodded.

"Maybe we can work out a deal. I'll trade your things for my things."

She said something so low I couldn't hear. "What?"

She whispered, "I don't have your things any more."

"Really," I said, "and what did you do with them?"

"I gave your sweater to Catherine and the book and soap to two of the other girls."

I could have killed her right then and there. I stopped in my tracks and she stopped too.

"Is that what they taught you in your Catholic orphanage? Is that what you learn from your Gentile girlfriends?"

Lilly had her chin pushed into her neck.

"Anything is okay if you do it to a Jew, right? Jews killed God, so any way you treat them is okay. Your mother and father were Jews and they got killed for that. Well, you're only another lousy Jew, no matter how you pretend you're not."

Lilly had began crying, the tears gushing out of her eyes in a way that surprised me. The snot was running out of her nose and she was sobbing as if she couldn't catch her breath. I didn't care. I was glad.

"Now what am I supposed to do? What do I tell my mother when she wants to know what happened to my new sweater? I say, 'Oh Lilly stole it to give one of her *goy* girl friends, the one who thinks we steal Christian children.' "

Now I was crying. "Y'know what, you jerk! You don't get any of your things back! I'll watch you *plotz* in front of my eyes before you see any one of your things again! And you better keep an eye on everything you own because you'll never know when something else is gonna disappear."

I had to stop talking. I was crying so hard I couldn't catch my breath. We stood, the two of us, facing each other and crying as hard and loud as anyone could.

I wanted to make Lilly suffer. She'd stabbed me in the back, stolen my nicest things to give to kids who detested me. I could see them all laughing with Lilly egging them on. My disappointment was only the smallest part of what I felt. The bitterness of Lilly's hatred was a raw pain inside me and I wanted to hurt her back.

But through the haze of my tears I saw a small girl, coat pulled half off one shoulder, eyes and nose red and swollen, the mark of my fingers on her left cheek. Tears ran from her eyes in rivers and dripped off her chin and jaws, staining the front of her blouse. One sock was down around her ankle, she had a bruise on her shin, and her shoes were scuffed.

My urge to make Lilly miserable suddenly evaporated. She looked so alone—for the first time she looked like an orphan. If I left her now her heart might not break, but I felt as if mine would.

I stopped crying first; my head was starting to throb and ache. Fortunately, I had a wad of tissues in my pocket; we needed every one. I mopped my eyes and cheeks, and blew my nose again and again.

Hiccupping uncontrollably, I went to the gutter and threw the wet tissues down. Then I went over to Lilly, whose eyes were squinched shut like a baby's, and tried to mop up her face. She leaned against me sobbing. I pushed a tissue into her hand and said, "Here, blow your nose; it's running all over."

Blindly she wiped at her nose, saying between sobs, "It is mean that I took your things, Sarah. I will never do it again. You can keep my stamps and petticoat. I don't care."

She started crying all over again with her head against my shoulder. I patted her back the way Mama did me when I felt bad.

Finally she stopped crying too. She looked a terrible mess and I supposed I looked just as bad. It was awfully late and Mama would begin to wonder and worry about us, but we couldn't go home in our condition. We went back to school, and sneaked in through the side door to the girls' room in the basement. We washed our faces in cold water and I put some paper towels soaked in cold water on my leg. Lilly ran cold water over her wrists. I combed my hair; Lilly re-did one of her braids. When we'd fixed whatever we could, we had to go home.

"Does it hurt too much?" Lilly asked, pointing to my shin which was now swollen and had a black and blue mark about an inch in diameter. At least the skin hadn't been broken.

"Only when I touch it," I said.

"I'm sorry," she mumbled.

I shrugged. "We'd better hurry."

It seemed very late when we got home, but the clock in the hall said only half-past three. "Maybe we'll be lucky and my mother won't notice."

I was conscious that I had stopped referring to my mother as Mama to Lilly. In my heart, I understood Lilly was not part of our family. Perhaps that was the day I gave up on the idea she ever would be.

Considering that an earthshaking thing had happened to us that afternoon, and that many of the safe and expected circumstances of my life had changed or been destroyed, externally everything was pretty much the same. Mama was busy putting groceries away from her weekly shopping and barely glanced at us when she asked why we were so late. She didn't even seem to notice that we came in together, something we almost never did except by accident.

She didn't see my shin until a few days later, because I made sure to wear knee-length socks until the bruise began to fade.

It was almost a week after that when she asked me why I never wore my new sweater. I told her the biggest lie of my life. I said I had torn a big hole in the back catching it on a nail, and I was so afraid she'd be angry, I threw it away. Boy! Did that make her mad! She called in Papa and Lilly to tell them how irresponsible and stupid I'd been and said she was sure it could have been mended.

I kept my head down and Lilly's was as low as mine. Papa expressed amazement at my poor judgement and asked what was happening to me. Mama said she would take the cost of it out of my allowance. I didn't even care; I just wanted it to be over.

Later, Lilly came over to me when we were alone in our room and said she'd give me the money back out of her allowance. I just nodded but didn't know what to say. The money was only part of my problem. The worst part was what Mama and Papa thought of me and I couldn't do anything about that. But with Lilly making the offer to pay me back I took the opportunity to talk to her.

"Why did you give my things to those girls?" I asked. She shrugged and looked away.

"If you wanted to give them presents, you could have bought some or given them your own things. Why did you take mine?"

She whispered something.

"What?" I asked.

"You have a lot of things," she said just loud enough for me to hear.

"You have almost as much as I have," I shot back. I was angry because it wasn't fair and because I felt guilty that she was right.

Her face got red and her brows came together in an angry frown. "You have everything. A Mama and Papa and a nice house and you do whatever you want."

I felt my mouth fall open. It was so unfair. I didn't make her lose her parents. "I didn't make you lose your parents," I blurted. "Mama and Papa want you to be their own child just like me, but you don't want to. I want you to be my sister, but you don't want that. You just want to be mean to the people who want to help you. Why?"

"I don't want to be here." She looked around desperately.

"What's wrong with here?" I looked around too, at our room. Mama had worked so hard to make it nice for Lilly.

"I don't like to be with . . . . " her voice trailed off.

"With what, Lilly?" I prompted. "Come on, tell me. What are you afraid of . . . ? I'm not gonna kill you or anything."

"Jews." She was barely audible.

I felt sick. I felt my cheeks go stiff and my eyes burn. "Yuck! You're so stupid. You're a Jew yourself." I pushed my face at her trying to make her look at me. "A Jew, a Jew, Lilly. How can you not be with yourself!? What's the matter with you? The only thing wrong with being a Jew is the way *you* feel. I always felt fine until you came along."

She flashed me an angry look. "I did not have to be a Jew, not after my parents died. Plenty of Christians wanted me."

I sighed and hit my forehead with my hand. "But you're not there now, right? So what's wrong with here? Do Mama and Papa treat you bad? Don't you think they want to love you? So what if we're Jewish? I don't understand you, Lilly."

"You do not know nobody likes Jews?!" she jeered. "You do not know anybody, just Jews and they do not count. Catherine really knows, not you, not your Mama and Papa. Jews, they are not nice people, that is why everybody hates them, and I'm . . . not . . . going . . . to be . . . a Jew," she ended, emphasizing each word.

I didn't know what to say any more. My head hurt from trying to figure it all out and trying to say the right things to her.

"I don't know what to do, Lilly," I said, really discouraged. "It makes me angry when you say things like that about us, and I know they're such lies and that no matter what we do or how much we try, you still hate us and think such terrible things. Can you tell me what to do?"

"Yes," she said, "leave me alone. Tell your parents to send me back to Belgium to the orphanage."

My heart sank like a rock. If I went to my parents with such an idea they would be horrified. Papa would be ashamed for his dead sister's sake, especially after all her suffering. Maybe I was to blame for starting the conversation with Lilly. If I hadn't made her talk to me and tell me all those secrets she might have gotten used to us and to living with Jewish people. Maybe after a while she'd see it wasn't so bad and then later, even get to like it, at least a little.

I couldn't resist another question.

"Where did you find out that Jews aren't nice, Lilly? I never heard that till you came."

She shrugged and turned down the corners of her mouth. "The other kids in the orphanage and Sister Mary Luisa said Jews cheat people. That's why no one helped them when Hitler came. And everyone knows they killed the Son of God, so they are being punished. Catherine says her priest says the same. That's how I know."

"Oh!" I gasped, "those are such lies! We're not like that . . . no one I know is! You live with us, do you think we do those things?"

Lilly dropped her eyes and pouted. "I don't know," she whispered.

"You don't know!" I squeaked. I threw up my hands. "I give up. I just give up! Okay, Lilly. I'll leave you alone, that's all I can do. But if you want to go back to the orphanage *you* go tell my parents. I won't do it."

I went to the bathroom, locked myself in and stared in the mirror. I had red blotches on my cheeks and my eyes looked hot. I felt sick and was sorry I started the whole thing. I turned on the cold water and threw handfuls on my face wishing I were someone else and lived far away from Lilly. I hoped she'd ask my parents to send her to Belgium and they would, so life could become normal again.

Later I put Lilly's things back. I figured she wouldn't be taking my things any more. I was right, and besides that, I found my book on wildflowers back in the bookcase one day, and my bar of soap in the bureau drawer. I don't know how she got my things back, and didn't even want them now because people who thought I was so awful had touched and used them.

I felt low all the time. I'd given up on anything happening with Yosuf because three weeks had gone by and he didn't tell me anything. When I asked him on Friday what was happening, he told me to be patient. It was easy for him to be patient, he didn't have to live with Lilly.

In some ways things were better between us. She didn't look daggers at me any more and sometimes even said a few words first about things we needed to do in the house. As for me, I avoided talking to her whenever I could, and just nodded or shook my head whenever she said anything to me.

I told myself if Yosuf didn't do something soon, I would ask Mama and Papa if I could have my own room again. I'd be happy to go into the spare room to get away from Lilly, although it was smaller and not as light.

I was beginning to worry about everything, even in school. A lot of times I didn't hear my teachers, and missed a lot in my classes. Mrs. Trask kept me after school one day and asked if something was wrong. She said I wasn't paying attention and a few of my test marks were lower than usual. What could I say?

I couldn't tell her what was happening, so I just apologized and said I would try to do better. Almost everything was becoming a drag. I stopped spending time with my friends and doing extra-curricular activity. The only time I felt better was when I was reading a book I liked and could forget everything about my own life. I caught Mama and Papa looking at me in the worried way they used to have for Lilly. It was a very bad time. Altogether it lasted less than two months, but while it was happening I thought it would never end. That was what got me really depressed.

At last one day it happened. Papa told Lilly and me at supper that Yosuf's Hebrew class was having an excursion to the Jewish Museum in Manhattan the coming Sunday. Yosuf was going to take the two of us for a treat, including lunch. My hope was renewed in what he could do for us and I could hardly wait for Sunday.

As expected, Lilly said she didn't want to go and my heart plummeted, but this time Papa said she would have to, Yosuf was being very nice and we weren't going to insult him. Thank God for good manners, I thought, any reason to get Mama and Papa to make Lilly do something that would be good for her for a change.

Later when we were alone, I told her none of her friends would see her, and in Manhattan no one would know who she was. I guess

I reassured her because she smiled after that, and Lilly smiling was something I saw only at a distance when she was with her friends. Maybe also she was glad to have me say something to her again.

Whatever it was, the week turned out to be a good one. I stopped worrying since rescue was on the way, and I enjoyed being able to listen to what went on in school.

We got up early on Sunday morning to get ready. Lilly seemed almost as excited as I was. We both wore stockings and good dresses and Lilly was going to wear her best coat, the one with the fur collar she had come to New York in.

She put it on and it looked peculiar. She had grown quite a bit so the coat was above her knees, the sleeves about an inch too short. Mama showed Papa how Lilly had grown, and looked pleased when she told him they would have to buy a new coat for Lilly.

Since it was a special day, Mama made us pancakes with syrup for breakfast and let us have a drop of coffee in our milk. Then we each got an extra quarter from Papa to buy anything we wanted. Already the day was turning out to be more fun than I'd had in ages. I thought wistfully that things might have been like this most of the time for Lilly and me if she weren't so crazy. I didn't think it was going to be easy to change her, either.

Yosuf came soon after we finished breakfast. He was wearing his good blue suit and nice gray overcoat, and his hair was combed down flat and shiny. He looked nice, but I would have been glad to see him anyway.

We rushed to put on our coats and he examined us up and down and said, "I have the two prettiest cousins in all of Benson-hurst."

I laughed and even Lilly giggled. Mama told us to be good and listen to whatever Yosuf said, and Papa told us to have a good time. On the subway, Yosuf sat between us, but he talked mostly to Lilly. I didn't mind at all because I knew he was starting what I asked him to do. He talked about the Jewish Museum and how it told some of the history of one of the oldest and most important cultures in the world. What Yosuf said was very interesting: I was learning things too. He said that two of the most important religions in the world, Christianity and Islam, were based on the Jewish religion, and that the Jewish people had brought the idea of One God to the world. He said Jews could be proud because of all the people in the world and in history, the Jewish people had contributed the most good and done the least harm.

Every once in a while, he would stop and look right into Lilly's face and ask her if she understood what he was saying; a couple of times he asked her what she thought of it, but she just shook her head or shrugged. Once when she wouldn't look him in the eye, he said he knew he was telling her things that were different from what she had been taught, but he expected her to argue with him, and he would prove to her he was telling the truth. By the time we got off to change to the uptown local, I was so proud of him and so proud to be Jewish that Lilly seemed even crazier to me than before.

We met Yosuf's class in the museum lobby. There were five other boys, the teacher, and us. I could see we were expected because the teacher, Mr. Gurstein, shook my hand, then Lilly's and said, "We are happy you are here, Lilly, we have a lot to show you."

Then we started. We saw beautiful scrolls and Torahs, Torah covers and breast plates, candlesticks, spice holders, wine cups and books, commandment tablets and Passover plates, embroidered yarmulkas—which Lilly said were like the skull caps some of the priests wore—and tablecloths, and more things than I can remember. But the best part was Mr. Gurstein and sometimes Yosuf or the other boys would explain what it meant or what something was used for and how this or that thing had been adapted to be used by Christians.

Mr. Gurstein pointed out there were no pictures allowed in synagogues because human beings were not meant to see God or try to guess what he looked like. Lilly said there were a lot of statues and pictures of God, Jesus Christ, in church. Mr. Gurstein said we Jews listened to God's commandment not to worship any god other than the One God, and worshipping graven images was idolatry. He said statues and paintings were graven images. Just about then Lilly began to get a stubborn look on her face; Mr. Gurstein said we would stop for lunch.

We went to a cafeteria a couple of blocks away, picked a nice corner, pushed two tables together, and put our coats on the chairs before we went on line to choose our food. I took a roll and a vegetable plate and hot chocolate, Lilly took a cheese sandwich and hot chocolate, and Yosuf took tuna fish and milk. I was having a very good time and I wondered if Lilly was enjoying herself at all, or if she was just waiting for the moment when she could escape back to her Christian friends. Whatever she was thinking or feeling, I figured I might as well enjoy what I could, while I could.

When we all started eating, Mr. Gurstein asked Lilly if she knew that Jesus was a Jew and a rabbi? Lilly stopped in mid-bite and looked at him skeptically.

He smiled at her and said, "That's right, Lilly, he really was a Jew, ask any priest. Every priest and nun knows it."

"If Jesus Christ was a Jew, why did the Jews kill him?" Lilly said hotly.

"This is going to be hard for you Lilly, because of what you've been told, but it was the Romans who wanted Jesus to die, and they killed him. There were some Jews who were working for the Romans who went along with it, but most Jews didn't even know about Jesus."

Lilly had put down her sandwich. She looked completely confused. "I don't believe you," she said. "The Jews killed Jesus because they didn't want to believe He was God."

Mr. Gurstein said, "When you get older, Lilly, you can read many books about that time. Jews believe in The One God. Christians call Him 'God the Father.' Jesus believed in the same God the Jews believed in then and believe in today, and never anything else. Jesus did not claim to be God. It was many years after he died that people began writing about him. They never even met him. They made up almost everything they wrote to get people to join them and become Christians."

Lilly's forehead was a bunch of furrows and she was pushing what was left of her sandwich around on her plate.

Mr. Gurstein looked at her with a sad face. He said softly, "I know how hard this is for you, Lilly. I just want you to remember these things, and as you get older learn for yourself. You should know you're part of a wonderful people, who have steadfastly loved God and His teachings to be good, and through almost two thousand years of terrible, terrible prejudice and persecution, still remain faithful to their promise to follow God's commandments. It's something to be very proud of, and some day I hope you have the strength and courage to tell people who try to make you ashamed of what you are that there's something wrong with them, not with you.''

It got very quiet when Mr. Gurstein stopped talking. All of us but Lilly kept on eating, while she poked a piece of her sandwich with her finger. Her head was down, and her mouth was the compressed line I hated so much. She was behind the solid wall I could never break through.

"I want to go home," Lilly said.

Yosuf raised his eyebrows at me and shrugged. Mr. Gurstein made a gesture with both his hands that said, ''Well, we did the best we could.''

Yosuf spoke then. ''When we finish eating, I thought we'd go for a little walk in Central Park because it's such a nice day. We could go to the zoo.''

Lilly didn't say anything, but I was delighted. I didn't want Yosuf to stop trying yet. No matter how inadequate he and his teacher and friends were, they were a million times better than anything I could do. I wanted to lock Lilly up in a nice quiet room and make her listen until she saw that it was all right to be what she was, and that it was wonderful.

Mr. Gurstein and the other boys were going back to the museum, but Yosuf, Lilly, and I went to the park and walked down to the zoo. It was a long walk, but it was a nice day, really warm for April. Yosuf walked between us and pointed to squirrels and birds, naming some of them for us. Soon Lilly stopped sulking and looked as if she were enjoying herself again. Yosuf bought us a bag of peanuts and we shared them with the monkeys. We laughed at the cute way the monkeys took them out of our hands and peeled off the shell before popping the nuts into their mouths. After about an hour of the zoo we sat down with our peanuts, and the squirrels came right up to our feet begging for a handout.

Yosuf said, ''Lilly, I hope you've had a good time today.''

Lilly nodded. ''Mostly, yes.''

''Now I'll tell you,'' he went on, ''that I invited you and Sarah so I could talk to you about how unhappy you are to be living with Auntie Malkah and Uncle Mikhel. It's not a good thing to live like that, Lilly. You can make yourself sick, but you also make the people you live with sad. I know you didn't ask to come here and live with us, but your Mama and Papa didn't ask to be killed either. Everybody here wants you to be happy—all the aunties and uncles and cousins, and especially Auntie Malkah and Uncle Mikhel and Sarah. We're all good people, Lilly, we never hurt anyone. We never killed Jesus or anyone else. Do you know that by now?"

Lilly looked up at Yosuf and nodded. I knew she didn't do it just to please him.

He went on, "Awful things happened to you, Lilly, but now you can start over with people who love you and want to take care of you. Do you understand me, Lilly?"

This time I thought Lilly really had been paying attention because she hadn't been doing any of those things with her forehead and lips.

Then she said, "Yosuf, I know what you are telling me. I understand what you are saying, but it is still true that so many, many people hate the Jews, they kill everybody. A Jew is not safe, because Jews killed Jesus Christ, but even if it is as you say, a lie, they are still hated and still killed like my mother and father. I am scared. When I did what the Sisters and the Priest said, they did not hate me, they loved me. So what is wrong that I want them to love me?"

I felt like crying, it sounded so sad, and I think Yosuf felt the same because when he started to talk his voice was shaking. "Leahleh," he said, "there's not one thing wrong with wanting to be loved." When he talked again, each word came out slow as if he was thinking at the same time.

"But can people who don't like what you're born as really love you? If you're a good person and your beliefs are good, why should anyone make you change if you don't want to? And if you change to what they want, can you ever trust them? A lot of Jews who'd become Christians were killed by Hitler and people like him. The Nazis said, 'once a Jew always a Jew,' even though some of the people had been Christians for a long time. So in the end it didn't make any difference."

It was very quiet when Yosuf finished. I heard the birds chirping in the tree over our heads. A little kid was chasing pigeons, and his mother told him to stop. The sound of cars and buses on Fifth Avenue drifted back to us. It was so peaceful; the things Yosuf had been talking about didn't seem real. They were like a fairy tale, where wicked witches and sorcerers are only imagination, so everything comes out right in the end.

Lilly's head was down and she twisted one of the brass buttons on her coat, first one way then the other.

At last she said, "So if it is known I am a Jew, I will never be safe."

Tears were rolling down her face. Yosuf saw too, put his arm around her, pulled her close, and just sat holding her. It was getting dark and colder when we left to go home.

On the subway Lilly fell asleep with her head leaning against Yosuf's arm. He and I talked about what had happened that day. I said even if Lilly never changed her mind, I had learned a lot about feeling good to be Jewish. I told Yosuf that since Lilly came there were times when I felt bad about being a Jew.

Yosuf said, "I think we have to talk to your parents about Lilly, this is too much for a kid to handle all alone. Saraleh, I don't know how much better she'll get. She's very scared. Older people will have to try to help her."

"Yosuf, if the Nazis had found out about Lilly, would they really have killed her too?"

"I guess so. They killed over a million Jewish children. A lot of them were burnt alive, when the gas chambers were too full."

"How could they do such terrible things? I don't understand, Yosuf." And I started to cry.

He put his arm around my shoulders. "I don't know, Saraleh, I don't know."

CHAPTER SIX

YOSUF MUST HAVE TALKED TO MAMA AND PAPA BECAUSE AT THE beginning of the week they told Lilly and me it was time for us each to have our own room. They told Lilly she could pick a color for her walls or even choose a wallpaper. Lilly perked up a bit then, which was really something because she never said much or looked too happy around us anyway. But she'd been so solemn and quiet after our trip, even a little change was noticeable.

We rushed to get her room fixed up because Passover was just around the corner and we all had to clean the house from top to bottom to get rid of any *chumetz.* Mama had to get all the Passover dishes, pots, pans and silverware out, and pack all the *trefe* dishes and pots away for the ten days of Passover. It was a big job and everybody worked at it, even Papa who brought down boxes full of stuff from the closets and put away the boxes packed with the everyday things. I loved the excitement, and to see all the things I had forgotten in the whole year since last *Pesach.* I loved the house when it was ready; everything sparkled and smelled clean and fresh. I loved the Passover food even though I got tired of *matzohs* by the end of the week. It was hard to take *matzoh* sandwiches for school lunches. If I wasn't careful, by the time lunch time came around, my *matzoh* sandwich would be all cracked or just a lot of crumbs.

Lilly chose pale blue for her room, and Mama dyed her bedspread two shades of blue. It was a lot of work because first she had to bleach out the gold color or she would have ended up with green. When the room was finished it looked really pretty. Papa built some shelves for Lilly's books and other treasures, and her bureau matched because it was dark brown wood. At first my room looked kind of empty, I'd grown so used to having Lilly's bed and bureau in it, but at least now I wouldn't be afraid to disturb her or have to hide something I didn't want her to see.

I came into her room carrying the last armload of clothes from my closet and I said, "That's it, Lilly, I can't find any more of your things in my room." I put them on her bed. "This is a nice color. You must be happy to be on your own."

"I have never had my own room," she said. "In the orphanage we had ten girls to a room."

"Didn't you have your own room when you lived with your parents?"

"I do not remember too much. I remember only sleeping in the same room with them."

"Well," I said, "I guess you'll really enjoy this then."

She shrugged. "And if I do not, I will have to learn to like it."

To reassure her I said, "When you get used to it, you probably won't ever want to share a room again."

She shrugged again and kept on hanging her things away. I got the feeling she wanted me to stay, so leaning against the bed I said, "Of all the holidays, I like *Pesach* the best. All the relatives get together for the *seder*s and the food is yummy and even when you're in school it still feels like a holiday."

"I don't know what *Pesach* is and I don't know what a *seder* is."

"Oh," I said, feeling stupid. They wouldn't have told Lilly about Passover in a Catholic orphanage and even if her parents had done the *seder*, she'd be too young to remember very much.

"Do you want me to tell you about it, Lilly? Or you could borrow some books from Yosuf, he has some neat books full of beautiful pictures, about Passover and other things."

She kept methodically putting her things away, rearranging her bureau drawers, straightening her shoes in the bottom of her closet. "What do you do at *Pesach*?"

I told her about the dishes and *matzoh* and *seder* and the story that was read every year all over the world about how the Jews were led out of slavery by Moses to the desert where they spent forty years before they entered the Promised Land with the Ten Commandments. When I finished, so had Lilly; all her stuff was put away.

"I would also like to read a book about it. Will you ask Yosuf?"

"Sure. He can bring it Friday."

Yosuf brought a few books. One, the one I liked best, was a big, flat book with beautiful pictures. There were Jewish slaves working on the Pharaoh's pyramids, and Moses smiting the Egyptian foreman for beating a slave. And manna raining down from heaven to feed the Jews in the desert, and Moses coming down from Mt. Sinai with the Ten Commandments from God and seeing the Jews worshipping the golden calf. The pictures were in rich colors and each plate was decorated with a border of flowers and fruit with real gold paint. I loved the book and so did Yosuf.

When he handed it to Lilly he said, "You know about Jesus and the last supper, Lilly?"

She nodded. "Yes, I know about the last supper. It is just before Jesus was crucified."

"Yes, well, the last supper is *Pesach*, Passover. Jesus was having his Passover supper with *matzoh*s and all the other things. That's why Passover and Easter often come at the same time."

She looked surprised and began to shake her head.

"Yes. Really, Lilly, I'm not telling you stories. Ask a priest or a nun. They'll tell you it's so. Don't ask your little friends because they won't know any more about it than you do."

It was news to me too. Before Lilly came, no one ever told me the Christian religion was based on ours. I wondered if Lilly ever asked her Gentile friends if they knew that Jesus was a Jew.

Everyone I knew was Jewish. None of them ever mentioned Jesus. The name was like a curse you put, not on others, but on yourself. If you wanted to carry around a bad luck charm, the name Jesus was it. No one asked why this was so. It was a given, like going to school or making your bed.

The connection between Judaism and Christianity never came up. No one forbade talking about it, no one even thought about it. It was understood that such conversation was a breach of the

fundamental principles of protocol and etiquette. With my
friends, if one of us inadvertently mentioned 'that name,' the
others would make the sound of spitting, the formula against evil
spirits.

For the first *seder* all the relatives came. That meant Yosuf's
family of course, but also Uncle Shmuel, Auntie Rachel and their
two grown children, Murray and Deborah, and Deborah came
with her husband Irving and their baby girl, Rosie. We had to put
all the leaves into the dining room table and Mama cooked for
several days before. We always had chicken and the only thing I
didn't like about Mama preparing chicken was the way she would
singe off the pin feathers over the gas flame before she cut it up
and salted it for koshering. The smell made my stomach queasy
and gave me goose bumps.

I always got to make the *charoses*, and my reward was licking
out the bowl. This time Lilly shared the job with me. I showed her
how I peeled and cored the apple, then chopped it very fine with
the chopper in a wooden bowl, then chopped in the walnuts very
fine, and added a little red wine so the whole thing became a
delicious paste. She liked it as much as I did, and the smells in the
kitchen were making our mouths water.

We set the table with the good white linen cloth, then set out
the plates, really close so we could get everybody in around the
table. Papa's big chair we filled with pillows so he could sit
'reclined' as all free men did for Passover. We set out the wine
goblets; the children had special ones. Mine had a silver filigree
base and the glass was a beautiful red, as pretty as the color of the
wine. In front of Papa's place, we put the *matzoh* cover with three
*matzoh*s inside for him to hand out to everybody. In each place on
the napkin, we put *Haggadah*s, the booklets telling the story of the
Exodus from Egypt. At the back of each Haggadah in English and
Hebrew was a statement: 'Compliments of the Manishewitz *matzoh*
Company.' Mama brought out the big *Pesach* platter with the burnt
egg, a chicken bone, bitter herbs which made my eyes tear because
they were slivers of raw horse radish, and the *charoses* I had
prepared with Lilly helping. I went to the kitchen and brought out
the big bowl of salt water and put it down alongside the platter.
The wine bottle was next to Papa's place, and another one was on
the side board with the candles Mama would light when it was

time. When we were finished the table looked beautiful, with only enough room down the center to put the food.

"Very nice, girls," Mama said. "Hurry, go get dressed."

We had new outfits for Passover. Mine was a wool suit in a silvery gray that Mama said matched my eyes, and a silk, long-sleeved blouse with a long tie to make into a bow. The saleslady called the color 'electric pink,' I called it 'yummy.'

Lilly's suit was a clear blue and her blouse was light brown, like her hair. I had shoes with a one inch heel that made me feel truly grown up with my new silk stockings. Lilly's shoes were almost like mine, except hers were brown and mine were black.

It was nice to have my room all to myself again, and it was more fun to see Lilly completely dressed up when she was finished instead of when she was putting on her clothes to get ready.

We were dressed long before any of the relatives came so we sat in the living room very primly on the sofa, our skirts spread out around us to keep them from creasing. Lilly must have caught some of the holiday spirit because her eyes were shining and her cheeks were flushed. For the first time since I knew her she looked pretty to me.

Just then she said, "You are very pretty today, Sarah."

I almost fainted, but before I could, I told her, "So are you, Lilly. Blue is 'your color.' " I had heard Mama say that to Auntie Aviva once and thought it was very chic.

The door bell rang and because Mama was upstairs dressing, I went to the door and let everybody in. They all came together and the room was immediately full of people. Everybody put their coats and hats in the closet and the men put on their *yarmulkas*. Baby Rosie was adorable and very good considering all the noise and fuss going on. Papa came into the room before Mama, and greeted everybody with "*Gut yontif*" and hugs and kisses all around. Then Mama came in and after more hugging and kissing and "*Gut yontifs*," we went into the dining room and sat down. It was time to light the candles. The *seder* would last four hours because Papa didn't cut corners; he read every word, and we sang every song.

By the time the first part of the *seder* was finished and Mama and the Aunties brought in the first course, I was ready to eat the table cloth. The trouble with waiting so long to eat was that I ended up stuffing myself.

I was too old this year to steal the *afikomin* for a ransom present, and I thought it was too bad that Lilly would miss out on knowing how much fun that could be. But at least Duvid was still young enough to crawl under the table and steal the piece of *matzoh* Papa hid and had to buy back in order to continue the *Pesach* service.

Lilly and I sat either side of Yosuf, and regularly he would lean toward her to say something. I knew he was explaining what was happening as we went along.

I never learned what Lilly thought or felt at her first real *seder*, because although she was no longer openly hostile toward me in our house, we never talked about intimate things. She avoided me in school and would rarely walk with me on our way to or from school. Lunchtime, she usually sat with Catherine and the others, though once in a while she would sit by herself at another table until it filled up with kids who came in late and had to sit anywhere. She started doing this during Passover when our lunches were made with *matzoh*s, and I guessed she didn't want her Gentile friends to see and ask what she was eating.

It was during this Passover that Lilly had one of her night horrors and woke the whole family. I don't know if it was because she was alone in her own room, or if it was because of what happened to Yosuf's book, but she screamed so loudly, we all came running. I got to her room first because I was closer, but Mama came next in barefeet and her nightgown. Papa followed tying his robe as he ran. I was already trying to wake her. She was sitting straight up as usual with her eyes wide open. The difference was that she was screaming; the sweat was pouring off her.

Mama said, "What is it, Saraleh? What's happening?"

"It's Lilly's night horror," I said.

"What is that?" Papa asked, then said to Mama, "Malkah, get a towel and a wet cloth, Lilly's fast asleep."

Mama ran to the bathroom and I said, "She does this all the time, but it hasn't been so bad before. I usually just push her down and she goes back to sleep."

Mama came and put the towel around Lilly's shoulders and began to wipe her forehead and face with the cloth.

Papa said, "You mean this has happened before? Why didn't you tell us?"

I shrugged. "I don't know. It was just something Lilly did. I figured it had to do with what happened to her, and she never bothered anybody but me before."

Papa shook his head and looked upset, but didn't say anything else. Lilly stopped screaming; she was just whimpering now and her eyes were closed.

Mama said, "She can't go to sleep like this, she's drenched with sweat. Sarah, get me a nightgown from her drawer."

Papa walked to the door. "We'll call the doctor tomorrow, maybe he'll have something to say about it." He left the room so Mama could change Lilly.

She was quiet now but didn't seem to be awake or asleep. "I wonder if we should wake her up or let her just go back to sleep," Mama mumbled. "*Oy veh*," she said, "*tsuris b'lytin.*"

I knew what that meant all right. I'd heard it often enough during the war and whenever Mama heard any bad news about friends or relatives. It meant—Oh woe, people have such trouble!

I almost fell over the next day after school when Lilly came to my room and said, "Sarah, will you come into my room? I have got to show you something."

I didn't even care what she was going to show me although I was curious. I just felt a thrill thinking she was becoming more friendly. When I got into her room she closed the door, and then I saw she was very pale and her hands were shaking.

She said, "Something terrible has happened and I do not know what to do."

"What is it, Lilly?"

"I did a terrible thing, but I did not know it would happen."

"What did you do, Lilly?" I was ready to believe that Lilly wasn't exaggerating. My own experience with her was enough for me.

"It is Yosuf's beautiful book."

Oh no, I thought, poor Yosuf. "What happened to Yosuf's book, Lilly?"

She was biting her lip and breathing hard and talking low and fast. I had to strain to understand her.

"At lunch I took it to show Catherine and the other girls to ask them about these things it tells about. When I wasn't looking somebody took it and made marks in it."

"What!" I shouted. "How *could* you do that Lilly? Let me see the book."

Of course she was crying already. It seemed to me Lilly would do something terrible and then as soon as anyone learned about it she'd start to cry. She was on her hands and knees in her closet pulling the book out from behind her shoes where she had hidden it. I wondered if she thought it would go away or heal itself. She was blubbering when she handed me the book. The cover looked okay. I sat down and opened the book in my lap. On the picture of the slaves building the pyramids, crosses had been gouged into each of the figures. The picture was ruined, the colors scraped off or the page torn right through. I turned to the next illustration, and the next. Each of them had been defaced the same way. On one of the printed pages pencil marks had been criss-crossed all over the page. I was horrified and felt sick to my stomach.

"Oh Lilly, how could you do this to Yosuf's precious book!"

She got hysterical. "I did not, I did not, I did not, do it. No, no I would not do that to Yosuf's things. I swear it was not me. It was one of the girls, I do not even know which one."

"But why did you take it to them? Why did you let them hold it so they could do this?"

"I thought they could tell me about it, the story in the book."

I was mad and disgusted. "You mean you wanted them to tell you if it was all okay. Don't you know better by now? Now you know what they think of it. Are you satisfied?"

I knew I was being cruel, rubbing salt into Lilly's wounds, but I loved Yosuf with all my heart and I was aching for him. Although most of the time I felt sorry for Lilly, she hadn't given me much reason or chance to love her, and her pain didn't bother me nearly as much.

Lilly was wringing her hands, something I had not seen her do before, so I knew she was really upset.

"Sarah, what should I do, what should I do, what should I do?" she kept saying.

"I don't know Lilly. You've got to tell him sooner or later. When you give him the book he'll see it."

"But can I buy another book so he will not know?"

I wasn't much help and I didn't feel like putting myself out for her either. "I don't know, Lilly. I don't even know where to buy such a book. Besides, where would you get money for something like this? It's very expensive."

"I have some my parents hid for me with their neighbor," she said. "Oh Sarah, do not talk about money now. You must help me get Yosuf a new book."

I didn't even know where to look for a book like that except to ask Papa, and then, of course, Yosuf would know. For a minute I felt desperate like Lilly looked, then I got disgusted. "Look Lilly, you get yourself in these awful fixes, then you make me worry about it. This time *you* figure it out. I don't know what to do."

When I said that she got even paler, and said something in French that I didn't understand. "What?" I said.

"I will kill myself," she said very fast, "I will kill myself, then it will be all over. I will not be worried anymore."

"You know, it's a sin to talk like that," I said. "Anyway, it's crazy to talk that way about a book. No matter how nice it is, it's only a book. No book is as important as a person."

"I do not care. It is so bad what I did to Yosuf. He will hate me."

"No he won't, Yosuf isn't like that."

I was beginning to weaken—the same old things about Lilly the orphan were going around in my head—but then I got an idea.

"What we could do," I said really slow because I was thinking out the idea while I was talking, "is take the book to the librarian at the public library. Maybe she could tell us how to get another one."

Lilly's face lit up and she laced her fingers together in front of her like the pictures of people praying. "Oh Sarah, that is a very good idea. Can you do it right away?"

I wasn't going to let her get away with that. "If we do it, we're both going to do it together. I'm not going by myself."

"But what if they see me?"

"You mean your friends, the ones who did this?" Lilly had the most nerve of anyone I had ever met, and she could get me madder than anything in one minute or less. "I don't have to go with you. You can do it alone." I turned around and began to walk out of her room.

"Yes, I will go alone. I thank you for telling me what I must do."

I didn't stop or turn back, but I was surprised because Lilly sounded like she meant it when she said thank you.

I was so glad I hadn't said I'd do it, I could've cried. She could do it just as well as I could. Anyway, it must've worked out okay because about a week later Lilly gave Yosuf back his book. The cover looked a little shinier to me, but maybe that was because I knew it was a new book. Otherwise it was exactly the same.

It was such a relief to have my own room again, there were times when I could almost forget about Lilly being in the same house. Besides, things did get better. She always ate with us now, though she never said much. I guess we all got used to her sitting there while we talked about things in our usual way. Mama and Papa stopped trying to include her in the conversation, though Papa asked us both about school. The most she said was that it was okay. She never brought any friends home, though Mama said she could if she wanted to.

I knew why she didn't and I wondered if Mama and Papa knew. When I had my own room back, Anne and Rebecca started coming over again, but Lilly always had her door shut tight. After the first couple of months I told them all about what was happening. Before then, I made excuses about Lilly having to get used to things. Rebecca kept saying she didn't know how my parents let Lilly hang around with the *goyim*. I told her to mind her own business. Anne said her mother thought we were brave to take in a kid like Lilly, there were so many stories about how 'disturbed' the survivors were and how hard it was to get them to be like everybody else.

I said I'd really rather not talk about Lilly all the time, you'd think there was nothing else in the world and what did we talk about before we ever heard of Lilly? We stopped after that and the next topic was boys, because after school, that was most important. Anne still liked Yosuf and said she watched him in synagogue while she was supposed to be following the service. Rebecca liked this boy, Solly, who was really her neighbor. That was how she got to know him. He was in the eighth grade. He came to all Rebecca's birthday parties and she went to his. He was okay, but Rebecca was taller than he was and she looked like his big sister when they walked together. I didn't think it was romantic, but I never said so.

There was a boy in my algebra class, Marvin Weinblatt, who kept staring at me. He was two rows over and one seat behind me. Every time I felt this funny feeling on the back of my head, and I turned around just a little, he'd be staring at me. He never even tried to pretend he wasn't looking when I'd catch him, and so I'd turn away first. It made me feel shy and sometimes when I had to answer a question, I'd feel so embarrassed I'd stammer, which I never did other times. I didn't know whether I liked it or didn't. But when Anne and Rebecca and I were all together talking about boys, I'd talk about Marvin Weinblatt, and tell them how I'd catch him staring at me. Then they'd "ooooh" and "aaaah," and wonder how I could start a conversation. But I didn't want to, and I never did.

Anyway, knowing someone like Yosuf made all the other boys look like little kids who acted silly. If I ever had a boyfriend he'd have to be someone like Yosuf, or I'd rather do without one.

Lilly got home from school later than I did, but she was always home an hour before supper. The only time she came home before me was when I went over to Anne's or Rebecca's house from school. But Mama always knew where I was.

I didn't know if Lilly was sneaking off to church or to Catherine's place or to her other Polish girlfriends. I didn't even want to know because whenever I knew something about Lilly it seemed to get me in trouble. That's the way things were all the way into June when we had only one month more of school. In school it looked like everybody forgot that Lilly was my cousin; at least nobody said anything anymore. She and I didn't even look at each other in the halls, and because Lilly was smart and got good grades, the teachers never asked to see my parents.

On open school week, Mama and Papa visited all our teachers, Lilly's and mine, and told us they heard good news about both of us.

CHAPTER SEVEN

MY BIRTHDAY WAS MARCH TWENTY-FOURTH, AND I WAS THIR- teen. Lilly was going to be twelve on June third. Since I was a young lady I had a grown-up party. Mama let me serve tea with the ice cream and cake instead of soda. I invited four more girls besides Anne and Rebecca, and Yosuf and Duvid came because they were my cousins. Duvid made a pest of himself blowing bubbles in his tea, which was disgusting, but he's only eight so that explains it.

Anne was practically fainting over being in the same room with Yosuf; she could hardly lift her cup without slopping it over.

Lilly was shut up in her room and I thought that was too bad, the table looked so nice and the cake was beautiful. Mama had it made at the bakery, with chocolate icing, rosebuds and fancy lettering that said, 'Happy Birthday, Sarah.' Yosuf went upstairs and I don't know what he said to Lilly, but when Mama brought out the cake with fourteen lit candles—thirteen and one to grow on—Lilly came into the room with Yosuf. Everybody sang Happy Birthday, and I made a wish and blew out the candles. Then I cut the cake and handed out pieces on real plates, not paper ones. Lilly sat down next to Yosuf and had some too.

After a while everybody forgot Lilly was there, especially when I began to open my presents. The best one was a beautiful new sweater from Mama and Papa, nicer even then the one Lilly had given to Catherine. After the presents we played games, but not kid ones like pin the tail on the donkey. We played musical chairs while Yosuf controlled the music on the radio, turning down the dial suddenly to make it stop.

Lilly stayed near him all the time watching us play, and once I saw her forget herself and laugh when Beryl and Miriam ended up in the same chair. It was a really good party. When everybody left, we kissed and said what a good time we'd had.

Yosuf and Duvid stayed for supper, but only Mama and Papa had much appetite. We had leftover cake for dessert.

Before Lilly, or B. L., as I came to think of it years later, I remember life as being simple: predictable and peaceful. I can't remember any real unhappiness. Lilly brought intensity with her. Intense fear, anger, confusion, self-doubt, inferiority complexes, hate. She represented all the negatives in my life. She was a contrast to all the wonderful times: the holidays, the birthday parties, the outings with Yosuf, being with my friends, doing well in school. All the things that went on in an easy, natural rhythm. But Lilly was there in the corners of my mind the way a toothache throbs on even though aspirin has numbed the pain.

Yosuf was like a magician with Lilly. Sometimes I think if she could have lived with him and Uncle Chaim and Auntie Aviva things might have turned out all right. I suppose Lilly loved him the way all little girls seemed to, and no wonder. He made us feel pretty and smart and good. He did it spontaneously, without effort; it wasn't put on for an occasion.

I asked him about my thirteenth birthday party and how he'd gotten Lilly to come out of her room. He shrugged and said he didn't really remember doing anything special; just said something about how nice it would be for all of us if she came down.

A couple of weeks before Lilly's birthday, one night at supper, Mama asked Lilly if she would like a birthday party. She swallowed what she was chewing and said without really looking at Mama, "No, thank you."

I saw Mama look at Papa who said, "We cannot let an important occasion like a birthday go by without something special, Lilly. If you don't want a party, maybe you would like to do something else, like go to a movie or eat at a restaurant. Before you say anything, you think about it, and let us know later or tomorrow, okay?''

Lilly nodded and went on eating. At least Mama didn't have to worry about Lilly's appetite any more. She ate as much as I did, and helped with the dishes, and cleaned her room. It made things easier, but she was never part of the family. It always seemed as though she was living with us because she had nowhere else to go.

Later when Lilly went up to her room, Mama and Papa asked me if I had any ideas about how to celebrate Lilly's birthday. I really didn't and I also didn't care if she had a celebration or not, but I wouldn't say that of course.

What I said was what popped into my mind. "I don't know; anything as long as Yosuf is there."

Mama and Papa looked at each other, then Papa said, "Thank you, Saraleh, that helps."

A couple of days later, Yosuf came over after supper, just as Lilly and I were finishing the dishes. Lilly heard him in the dining room and began to hurry to get finished. Papa called us into the living room and after we said, "Hi, Yosuf," Papa said, "Lilly, Yosuf offered to take you and Sarah to see a show in Manhattan for your birthday. Would you like that?"

Lilly just looked at Papa. Yosuf said, "Lilly it's a marionette show; do you know what that is?"

Lilly shook her head. Yosuf said, "It's a play that's all done with dolls. People move the dolls but you can't see the people, so it looks as if the dolls are really moving and talking."

Lilly's face was beginning to light up, but that probably would have happened anyway just from looking at Yosuf. "It's fun, Lilly. The play is a fairy tale called Rumplestiltskin. If you never read it, Sarah can show it to you. Would you like to go?"

Lilly smiled shyly and nodded and I almost could hear Mama and Papa sigh with relief.

"Good. I'll pick you girls up on Sunday at eleven o'clock sharp. Wear your nicest dresses. The play starts at one o'clock in a fancy theater on Fifty-seventh Street. We'll take a little walk on Fifth Avenue to get there. When the play's over, we'll go to the Automat for milk and cake."

I was beginning to get excited about Lilly's birthday after all. I would have a great time just doing all those interesting things and being with Yosuf.

Sunday was a beautiful day, sunny and warm but not too hot. I wore my favorite summer dress, lemon yellow, princess style with white lace around the neck and sleeves, and I had sandals that made my feet look grownup. Lilly's dress had puffed sleeves and a wide ribbon for a belt. It had tiny rosebuds all over a light pink background. When we were all dressed up, Papa inspected us and said we looked like a garden of flowers. Yosuf came soon after, right on the dot of eleven, and we started off.

When we were on the subway he showed us a little folder that was all about the play we were going to see and the people who made and worked the marionettes. The pictures were in beautiful colors. I could hardly wait to get there, and even Lilly seemed excited, the way she was when she was with Catherine.

We walked on Fifth Avenue, stopping to look in the windows of the stores, where all the clothes and the dummies wearing them looked beautiful and expensive. There weren't any prices on things the way there were in the stores in our neighborhood.

The theater was in a small building that had statues of fat, naked little children carved around the windows and doors, and other figures and faces up near the roof. The inside was smaller than our neighborhood movie, and the seats were red velvet. We were in the center of the second row, and the stage was tiny. In the middle of the stage, there was an even littler stage in a box with a red velvet curtain.

The lights went out slowly and the curtains of the little stage parted. There were these beautiful dolls, moving and talking, and before long they didn't look small or like dolls any more; they looked normal. I forgot everything, even that it was Lilly's birthday. It was the most wonderful thing I had ever seen. When it was over, and the lights went back on, everybody looked like giants and everything looked as though it was made for giants. Yosuf told us that was called an illusion. I said it was such a funny feeling because it was easier to get used to illusion than to the way things really are. Yosuf said sometimes people liked illusions better than the real thing.

We went to the Automat and Yosuf gave each of us three nickels to put into the slots and get out milk and a piece of cake. When we finished, we walked to the subway and went home. The celebration wasn't over yet and Yosuf and I knew that Mama and Papa and the uncles and aunties would be at our house with a surprise birthday cake, and presents. I chose a present for Lilly, not because I felt like it but because I was expected to. I got her a hair brush and comb set at Woolworth for seventy-nine cents, and wrapped it in gift paper.

When we walked into the house, everybody said, "Happy birthday, Lilly!" and went to hug and kiss her, except Duvid who shook her hand. Mama came in then with a cake with pink frosting and thirteen lit candles (one to grow on), and Lilly made a wish and blew them out. Mama cut the cake for her while she opened her presents and thanked each person, including me. I thought it was a very nice birthday party, better then Lilly deserved. I wondered if the wish she made on her cake was that she would soon not have to live with us anymore.

Every year we went away for August when it got really hot in the city. We went to a place in the Catskill Mountains. It was on a beautiful lake and there was a big main house with little cabins around it. The cabin we rented every year had a kitchen, a toilet with a shower, and two small bedrooms. It had a front porch that faced the lake. Papa took us up in a big rented car so we could bring along all the things we needed for the month, but it was too far for him to come up every night after work, so he would come up early Friday afternoon before *Shabbat* and go back Sunday night. The train station was about a mile away, and the people who owned the place would go to pick Papa up and take him back.

I never missed anybody when we were in the country, there was so much to do. The owners had cows and chickens, and Mama bought eggs and butter and milk from them. They had a lot of cats and sometimes kittens and an old dog who just lay around sleeping in the sun. When I wasn't watching or playing with the animals, I'd be swimming in the lake or rowing in one of the three boats they had. A lot of times there were kids my age, and some of them who lived in the Bronx or Long Island became my pen pals.

Even though I had to wait a whole week to see Papa, the month always went so fast it seemed as though we just got there. I used to play a game to slow down the time. If I was on the lake rowing, I would put the oars in the boat and hang my head over the side. The sun made the water sparkle and I'd look down into the water to see the grassy stuff waving back and forth and sometimes see a fish swim by, and I'd think, I'll stay here like this without moving, and as long as I don't move, nothing else will. Everything will stop, I'll be here forever. And I'd smell the water which was so sweet, it was the nicest thing I could smell. I'd stay a long, long time, but of course I had to move no matter how much I wanted not to, and before I knew it, another day was gone.

Because Lilly was going to be with us this year, I wasn't exactly as thrilled about being in the country for a month, without my friends or Papa or my own room. Going back to sharing with Lilly, even for a month, was making me queasy, and the idea of her mooning around sulking or acting as if she couldn't stand being in the same world with me spoiled everything before we even got there.

When I thought about it, the idea of staying at home with Papa and seeing Anne and Rebecca every day, going to the public swimming pool or to Coney Island, suddenly looked like a lot more fun than being in the country with Lilly and Mama. I was desperate enough to say one night that since I was a young lady of thirteen maybe I should stay at home and take care of Papa during the week and come up weekends with him. Papa smiled and shook his head. Mama said, "Ridiculous!" and Lilly gave me a quick look that told me she knew very well why I didn't want to go to the country.

Anyway, I had all of July to enjoy before I had to go away for a month with Lilly. I didn't know there'd be other problems in July. With no school, Lilly couldn't see her friends any more unless Mama and Papa knew about it.

The first day of July I could hardly wait to get out of the house. It was beautiful and sunny, and Anne and Rebecca and I planned to go to Prospect Park, visit the zoo, and just walk around. Our mothers made us a picnic lunch.

But there was the problem of Lilly. After breakfast she went up to her room and shut the door. Mama went after her, knocked on the door, went in. I couldn't hear anything because of the closed door. Later when Mama came out she didn't look too happy. When I collected my lunch and kissed her goodbye, she said, "Have a good time," the way she always did. But she looked like she was thinking of something else.

We had a wonderful time in the park. We lay on the grass after we ate, talking and looking at the sky and the clouds. The first day of summer vacation was always the best because it was neat being out of school on an ordinary day thinking of all the days we had left that would be just as good.

But when I got home the place was doom and gloom. Lilly was still in her room and Mama told me she hadn't come out all day. I wanted to say that if Lilly wanted to miss out on all the fun, that was her business, but I couldn't say that because Mama was so worried. Lilly came down for supper and for the first time we all talked about her problem. Mama told Papa that Lilly had spent the whole day in her room and wouldn't even go into the backyard.

Papa said, "Lilly, you can't spend all of July locked up in your room, you'll get sick." Lilly just shrugged.

He said, "Why didn't you go with Sarah to the park?"

Very low she said, "I did not want to."

Mama said, "And why didn't you at least go outside and get some fresh air in the backyard?"

She said, "I am all right. I do not need so much fresh air."

Papa said, "That's not only for you to decide, Lilly. You cannot spend every day in the house."

Lilly sat looking at her plate and shoving her food around the way she had when she first came.

Mama said, "See, she has no appetite because she didn't get any exercise."

I was dying to say something about Lilly's friends and how she didn't want to be seen with me and my friends because we were Jewish, but I was ashamed to say it.

Then Papa said to me, "Sarah, do you know anything about this? Why is Lilly behaving this way?"

Boy, I was in a pickle, and Lilly threw me this scared look. I knew she didn't want me to say why she wouldn't go out, so I started to shove my food around on my plate.

When Papa spoke again I could tell he was angry. "The two of you are going to have to make up your minds to tell us what is going on here. If there's something either or both of you have done, you have to solve it between you, or tell us so we can help you solve it. And until you do, you will both behave the way Mama tells you. You, Lilly, will go out on nice days. If you won't go out with Sarah, you will go out with your own friends who Mama knows, or you will go with Mama, or you will go into the yard. But you will not sit up in your room. Finished!"

I trembled. When Papa said, "Finished!" that was it. And I knew it because he said it only when there was no other way. Maybe two or three times a year.

Even though Lilly didn't care about Papa the way I did, I could see she was impressed because she still looked scared. I wondered how she was going to get out of this one.

We ate supper without talking much, even though Mama and Papa tried to act as though nothing out of the ordinary was happening. After Lilly and I did the dishes we were both glad to go to our rooms, though it was still light out and at any other time I wouldn't have minded taking a walk with Mama and Papa. Of course, the minute they said they were going out and the door closed downstairs, Lilly was in my room.

"Can I talk to you?" she said.

Whatever was coming wasn't going to be fun for me. I knew her already. "What do you want, Lilly?"

"What should I do, Sarah? I will die if I have to go outside and they see me."

I felt really mean. "If you gotta die, I guess you gotta die, Lilly."

The tears began to spurt out of her eyes.

"Oh, no," I said, really exasperated. "What do you want from me? Your *friends* (I made it sound sarcastic) know you live with Jews. They gotta expect to see you with them sometimes, especially in the summer when you're home all the time."

"I told them I was going away for the whole summer, that is why I cannot go outside. They will see me."

I rolled my eyes up to the ceiling the way Auntie Aviva does when she's exasperated. "You got yourself in a fix again and you want me to figure it out. I can't figure it out. You'll be gone all August, but unless you tell my mother and father the truth or make up some lie to get them to send you away somewhere for July, you're gonna have to tell your friends the truth, that you're gonna be here for July.''

She just kept right on crying. I said, ''You're so ashamed to do anything that will insult your friends. Don't you care *anything* about the people you live with or Yosuf or any of your other relatives? Don't you care about how we feel, even a little?''

She was really wound up now, sobbing and wringing her hands. ''You are used to being a Jew. No one told you it is bad.''

''No one but you, Lilly.'' She ignored me as if I hadn't said anything.

''But for me it is too hard. I am not used to it. Everybody will stare at me. They will know. I care, yes I care, but God doesn't, and people who are important do not. What difference if *I* care? I cared about my mother and father. So what did it matter?''

She sure knew how to make me feel bad. Every time I made up my mind to ignore her she'd get me involved anyway. Just remembering what happened to her mother and father did it. No matter how good her life would be, she'd never get them back again.

''Listen, Lilly, why don't you just tell your friends we changed our minds and you have to stay here against your will. You're only a kid. They know you can't do anything on your own. It's even against the law.''

''They think Mama and Papa know they're my friends and that I spend all my time with them.''

Whenever I thought it was as hard as it could be, Lilly came up with something worse.

''Now how did they get that idea? Who do you suppose told them that?'' I made a long pause to let it sink in. ''Well, either you tell them you lied or you tell Mama and Papa you're ashamed of being a Jew and ashamed to be seen with any of us because we're Jews. Either one will solve your problem.''

Lilly let out a wail, so that instead of looking forward to the summer, I wished it was all over and we could go back to school when I wouldn't be so messed up with Lilly and her problems.

The next day I woke up late and felt great, until I remembered Lilly. I wished I could fall back asleep again, but then I heard Mama in Lilly's room. It turned out that Lilly had a fever and they called the doctor. That's the way it went for a whole month. The doctor thought it was allergies and did some skin tests, and gave her an injection once a week. But Lilly stayed in the house practically all of July, and Anne and Rebecca and I had to spend some time with her in the house keeping her company, which I could have done without, but at least Anne and Rebecca got to know her a bit after all. It was a relief to leave Bensonhurst to go to the country. I know Mama was thrilled to get out of the city. As for Lilly, her allergies disappeared like magic, and Mama wondered if she was allergic to something in our house.

It was scrumptuous being in the country on the Moskowitz farm. I felt like running and jumping and rushing around to see everything right away, but we had to help carry things into the cabin. After that Mama let us go out to play. I could hardly wait till my bathing suit was unpacked. Meanwhile I could go to the barn.

Now Lilly was sticking to me like glue. I didn't exactly mind but I wasn't used to it either. So I just went on about my business and let her tag along. First I visited Jafit the cow. I loved her. She was a small Jersey cow and looked to me like pictures I've seen of deer. Her name in Hebrew meant beautiful. She remembered me from last year because when we came into her stall, she raised her head from the straw she was chewing and mooed at me and pushed my fingers with her nose. I kept stroking her face and after a while Lilly stuck out her hand and touched Jafit's head. When Jafit turned her head fast, Lilly jumped about a mile in the air. It was so funny I laughed, and after a while Lilly laughed too.

Then I climbed into the loft to see if there were any kittens this year. I knew all the places where Golda the cat went to make a nest. We were in luck. On the third try I found a nest with three kittens. I told Lilly we mustn't touch them. They were still too young, and if Golda smelled us on her kittens she'd move them to another spot. So we just crouched down and watched them. One was all yellow like Golda, one was tiger stripe, mostly gray and white, and the third was all gray. Their eyes were still closed and they kept making little sounds. I told Lilly Golda was getting old because her litters were getting smaller. Last year she had five kittens, and the year before, seven.

We climbed down, and at the bottom of the ladder Pahsie met us, wagging his tail pretty fast for an old dog like him. Pahsie was short for Pahskunyak, which meant 'pest' in Yiddish. Then I took the long path around the barn and through the woods to get to the lake. By the time we got there the sun was down low and made a wide streak of yellow-gold on the water. I ran out on the dock and lay down on my stomach so I could put my hand in the water. It felt warm and smooth. I could've jumped in right then with all my clothes on. Then I went to inspect the boats. They were pulled up on the shore and were painted different colors this year. I was about to push one off and take a little row around when I heard Mama.

"Saraleh, Lilly, come in. Time to wash for supper."

The first day was mostly gone already! It felt as though we'd just gotten there.

I didn't rush to go into the cabin. Instead I kept turning around to look at the lake, and finally Mama came out on the porch. "Sarah, don't make me call you again. You have a whole month to be out. You'll set a bad example for Lilly."

We went right in after that. Even though I wanted to be outside I ate a lot because I was starved. Lilly ate quite a bit too. Mama seemed satisfied for a change. She said, "Maybe we'll put some weight on these girls this month."

When we finished the dishes and put everything away, Mama showed us where she put our things and told us to make sure to put on suntan lotion before we went out for the first couple of days.

"I don't want to come here next weekend and find two lobsters instead of girls," Papa said.

Then Mama let us go out, and even though the sun was down it was still light on the lake, so we pushed a boat into the water and I rowed it around for a while until Papa called us to come in. The mosquitoes were beginning to come out anyway. I told Lilly that I'd teach her how to row tomorrow.

After I got undressed and washed I could hardly wait to get to bed I was so sleepy. I didn't even care that Lilly was in the same room.

I was always the first one up when we were in the country. If I could've stayed awake all the time I'd never have gone to bed at all. I got up very quietly and opened the bureau drawer a couple of inches because it squeaked, just enough to pull out my bathing suit. It was a new one this year; a one-piecer with thin straps, and all red. It made my figure show. What were just bumps last year were too big to be called bumps this year. They weren't too big, but big enough for me. I pulled on the suit and put on my blouse from yesterday, then put on my sneakers and, holding my breath, tiptoed out through the kitchen and opened the screen door a crack because it squeaked too. As soon as I was out I ran down to the water. I felt like yelling I was so happy, but I didn't dare make any noise. I got a boat into the water and rowed out to the middle of the lake, then drifted along looking for all the things I remembered from last year. Soon it got warm and I took off my blouse and before I knew it, Mama was calling me to come in for breakfast.

I must've looked pretty red because Mama said, "Talk to her, Mikhel."

"Saraleh, you must listen to your mother, especially when I'm not here all week. She told you to put on sun tan lotion. Your nose and back are all red. You won't enjoy anything if you make yourself sick. And you're responsible for Lilly. If she sees you disobeying, why should she listen?"

I didn't tell Papa what I thought about the last thing he said, I just kept on gobbling my sunny-side-up egg, dipping my bread into the yellow.

"Do you have to be up at the crack of dawn?" Mama said. "Some vacation if you get less rest than you do at home."

"Okay, Malkah, let the child get up if she wants. She can spend time indoors in the winter. Just as long as she doesn't disobey you."

"I'm sorry, Papa, I'll be good. Can I go swimming after I do the dishes?"

"You wait an hour after you finish eating. You know that."

Sure I knew but I figured I'd try anyway. I didn't see what my stomach had to do with moving my arms and legs in the water.

After we washed the dishes I told Lilly to put on her bathing suit. Hers was a two-piecer, with a flower design. I didn't see why she needed the top piece, she was mostly flat as a board, but of course she wore both pieces.

When we got out on the lake I showed her how to row, both oars together, then one at a time, and how to steer and turn and not dig the oars too deep in the water. Then I let her try. She learned really fast and was strong, something I knew for a fact already. I let her row and hung my head over the boat to watch the water going by. Then I put my hand in the water and felt it push against me. All of a sudden something nudged my hand. It must've been a fish! This was fun. I never had anyone row me around before. Lilly liked it too, so we did that for a long time. Then we switched and I rowed her.

Before we even had a chance to swim, Papa was calling us to come in for lunch. This was terrible. I hadn't even played my game to slow down time.

We got into the water in the afternoon. Lilly did a dog paddle and got around all right, but I showed her the side stroke, and the crawl, and the dead man's float. And by the time Mama called us to come out to get ready for supper she was pretty good at all the strokes.

The next day we met a few of the kids from the other cabins. My old friends from the other years weren't back this time, but there were twin girls, ten years old, who looked just alike. We couldn't tell them apart and they wore the same clothes, which didn't make it any easier. Then there was a boy, about Yosuf's age, but he said we were just kids and we should "get lost"; he had pimples all over his face anyway.

Before I knew it, it was time for Papa to go to the train. We begged, and Mama let us go to the station with him. We went in the truck, and Lilly and I sat in the back which was open, hanging on to the sides while the hair blew all over my face. Lilly's hair was in braids but the loose bits around her face and ears blew straight out and up.

At the station we jumped down to kiss Papa goodbye, then got in the cab with Mr. Moskowitz to drive right back. We waved to Papa as long as we could see him. And now the whole first weekend was gone already.

That month was the high point of my life with Lilly. We were suspended together in a perfect world for children. Our reason for being in this small paradise was to play all day long, with time out for minor chores like doing the dishes, which made play all the more valuable and treasured. We were away from everything that threatened; Lilly from her Christian friends and a world that made being Jewish a shortcoming. The Moskowitz farm was a Jewish world of ninety acres, including the lake, and because of this Lilly was able to relax, could stop looking over her shoulder to see if she were being observed consorting with Jews. She was free to enjoy my company, which allowed me to enjoy hers. We shared everything and did everything together. It was a time of my early fantasies come true. We began to share thoughts as well as time and place.

After my mother, Lilly was the first to know when I started menstruating. I had been prepared and knew what to expect, but it still came as a shock. I spent three uncomfortable days, the sanitary napkin between my legs feeling as big as a house, and I resented every moment I had to stay out of the lake. I was very sorry for myself I remember, but presented the event to Lilly as an exciting rite of passage which confirmed that I was truly a young lady. Given enough time, she too would reach this exalted state.

There came a day when I felt confident enough to ask Lilly what she remembered about her parents. We were sitting on the dock with our feet in the water. It was a hot day; we'd been swimming and the sun was drying our suits.

I said, "The first thing I remember when I was a baby is Mama holding up a rattle and me reaching out and grabbing it. Mama says that's amazing. I was only five months old. What's the first thing you remember, Lilly?"

She lifted her foot out of the water, watched the droplets run off, then put it back again. "The first thing . . . I was sitting on my Papa's lap playing with the buttons on his vest or his shirt, I do not remember which, only the buttons. But maybe it was my Mama singing to me in my bed, one or the other."

I thought how sad it was that Lilly's parents weren't there to tell her.

"When I was little," she went on, "my Mama made long curls in my hair. In the orphanage they made the braids."

"Did all the kids in the orphanage have braids?"

"Yes. We helped each other. The big girls did the little ones. Then each other."

"Did you mind not having curls?"

"Not much. We were all the same. Sometimes we had our hair loose. On Christmas, we got dressed up. It was nice. The tree was beautiful. We sang songs and one Christmas, I don't remember which one, we got an orange for every two girls. It was good."

I saw Lilly swallow the spit collecting in her mouth over the memory of half-an-orange. I moved my feet in the water and focused my eyes on the trees and underbrush across the lake. They looked black in the bright sunshine. "Do you remember the kind of place you lived in before the orphanage?"

She was quiet for so long that I turned to look at her. She was sitting very still, looking down into the water. Her lips were parted the way they are when you're asleep. "Lilly?" I said.

"I remember a tall, narrow house. We lived near the top. I remember looking out the window into the street and at the neighbor's house across the street. But then my Papa nailed boards all across the windows and we couldn't look out any more. It was dark inside all the time."

"Why did he do that?"

She shrugged. "He was afraid," she whispered.

I couldn't understand. "How did that help?"

She gestured with her hand, palm up. "*J'n'sais pas.*"

I was surprised. She hardly ever spoke French at home any more.

"It was the bad time," she went on slowly. "Every night, Mama took me across the street in my nightgown to sleep at the neighbor's. When I was older, maybe ten, the neighbors told me it was because if the Nazis came to take my parents away they would not get me, too."

Suddenly I felt chilled to the bone. I took my feet out of the water, put them up on the dock, and hugged my knees trying to stop my shivering.

Lilly looked at me. "You have goosebumps, Saraleh," she said. "It is not cold."

My teeth were chattering. I reached for the blouse I had dropped on the dock and put it on. "That must've been awful for you," I said through clenched teeth, trying to keep them from rattling.

Lilly turned back to the lake. "Yes. Sometimes at night I would cry for my Mama and Madame LeClerc would hold me in her lap and rock until I fell asleep. I was mad at my Mama when she came to get me in the morning. I cried and hit her, but she just hugged me and took me home."

I felt a lump beginning to grow in my throat, but still I wanted to hear everything. "Then what happened?" I whispered.

"I remember one night my Mama didn't take me to the neighbor, but when it was very late and dark, she dressed me in all my clothes, one on top of the other, and my Papa put some things in a sheet and tied it up. Then we left the house. My Papa carried the sheet on his back and my Mama carried me and told me to be very quiet. The next I remember is we walked and walked. Sometimes they carried me. I was tired, I wanted to go home. Once when I was crying, my Mama gave me a banana. It was very delicious. We walked a long time and one night we slept in some hay, outside. I itched all over. Then there was water and boats. We stopped and waited a long time. I played with some rocks and sticks and watched the bugs running in and out of holes in the ground. Then I got tired and hungry and cried. Later, we started walking again until we were back in our own house. Then my father put boards on all the windows."

I was confused by Lilly's story. "What happened? Where did you go when you walked so much?"

"Years after, the neighbors told me that my parents tried to escape to England on a boat. That was the reason we walked so far."

"Couldn't they get a boat? Why did they come back?"

"The neighbors did not tell me. Maybe they did not know."

"What did your Mama and Papa do then?"

"Soon after we got back to Brussels, my parents took me to La Hulpe—to the orphanage."

I felt the lump in my throat again. "How old were you, Lilly? Were you scared? Were you lonely?"

"I was five years old. Yes, I was scared. There were so many children and only the Sisters. I wanted my mother. I cried all the time. Everything was so big. My Mama and Papa came a couple of times to visit me. It was terrible when they left. I remember sitting on the floor and screaming and screaming until my throat hurt. Someone picked me up and gave me something sweet to drink.

Then my parents did not come any more. Madame Le Clerc came
. . . sometimes M'sieu, too."

I could hardly get the question out. "Was that when . . . did
you know if . . . were your parents dead?"

"I didn't know right away. Madame said my mother and father
were okay. She showed me cards with pictures and writing on the
back, and read me what my parents wrote. But by the time I was
seven, I *knew* they were dead. No one told me. Anyway, by then I
liked the orphanage. I was used to everything. They were nice to
me."

"Your poor Mama and Papa!"

"No!" Lilly's voice rang out across the lake. "My father was a
coward! He made my mother go to die with him instead of letting
her take me away to England. They didn't care! I hate them!"

She jumped to her feet, ran up the dock and into the woods.

I was stunned by Lilly's story and the depth and intensity of
her anger. How could she be angry with her mother and father, I
wondered? They didn't want to die. They didn't want to give her
away. But I began to understand how complicated the problem
was —how hard it was going to be to make up to Lilly for all she
had lost—how enormous the task of making her feel secure. Then
I realized there was no way to make up to her for what she'd lost.
And I couldn't think of any way to make her feel safe. In fact Lilly's
fears were affecting me. I began to dread the day we would have
to go back to the city.

Being with Lilly during that marvelous month left no room for
making time slow down; if I could have watched us in action we
would have looked like a Keystone Cops movie, rushing through
each day with too much to do to ever catch up. I felt we had turned
a corner, we were now going to become the family I had dreamed
about almost a year ago. This wasn't some childish misapprehen-
sion on my part—my mother and father indicated by their good
humor, relief in the expectation that the worst was over. Lilly was
finally adjusting and now only the normal everyday crises of raising
children was in the offing.

The Moskowitz farm was our personal Shangri-la. Once our
stuff was loaded into the rented car, and we piled in ourselves to
start the five-hour drive back to Brooklyn, Lilly crept back into her
shell, retreating visibly behind blank eyes and the compacting of

her body that I noticed the first day we saw her in the ship terminal. She said nothing unless one of us spoke to her, replied only in monosyllables to direct questions, and I don't think she looked out of the window once.

I felt my heart sink with dread and sorrow. I was becoming fond of Lilly and hated to lose her. This was much worse than never having made contact at all. I couldn't figure out what to do with my mixed up emotions and ended with a non-specific yearning, an aching hunger for things to be different, for life to be a golden summer day in a quiet country place, safe for animals and children and all helpless creatures.

Luckily there was plenty to do getting ready for school and the High Holidays, which left little time for regrets and moping. Not only did the house need to be cleaned from top-to-bottom, and Lilly and I were old enough to be included in almost all the work, but we had to get ready for school, which meant looking over, cleaning, and repairing our clothes. Then decisions had to be made about what new clothing was needed, and what school supplies could be bought before the first day of school.

Mama took us downtown for shopping, and until we were on the subway, I got the feeling Lilly would have been happier wearing a bag over her head. She was so worried about being seen with us, though the chances of meeting any of her friends in our neighborhood were small. But once we got home from the country, finding out what was going on in Lilly's head became just as difficult as before the little window opened between us during the month we were at the Moskowitz farm.

Not that things were exactly the same. In the house, Lilly didn't brood or sulk the way she had before we went away. There were times when she acted almost friendly. But in school I saw no change in her behavior. She was sucked back into the Gentile group with Catherine at the center, just the way a vacuum cleaner sucks up dust.

CHAPTER EIGHT

I WAS SO HAPPY TO SEE ANNE AND REBECCA AGAIN! WE SPENT AN entire day exchanging news about the things we'd done during August. Yosuf had grown almost two inches in just one month and it must've all been in his neck. When he saw us, he kidded Lilly and me about the Cardozo Spanish blood showing up in our suntan.

My eighth grade homeroom teacher was new in our school. Mrs. Weiss was young and pretty and nice. School was going to be a breeze.

I told Mama and Papa now that I was thirteen, I intended to fast the entire day on *Yom Kippur*. I tried the year I was twelve the ways girls are supposed to, but lasted only till lunch time. This year I *knew* I would be able to fast the whole day.

Lilly and I were going to wear our Passover suits for *Rosh Hashanah* and *Yom Kippur*. Luckily we hadn't grown that much in six months, and Mama had bought them a little big for us to grow into. School was open on *Rosh Hashanah* and *Yom Kipppur* since they weren't legal holidays. But the building was almost empty because there were only a couple of kids in each class who weren't Jewish. In some classes, all the kids were Jewish. Most of the teachers were too, so all the Gentile kids who had to go to school were put into one classroom with a couple of the non-Jewish teachers.

Lilly wanted to go to school, which shocked the whole family to the roots. Papa said, "Now, if you want to stay in the house, Lilly, you may. But you will not go to school; not on the High Holy Holidays. Not while you are in my house. Finished!"

You could see Lilly didn't like it, but she stayed home and didn't say anything after that.

I began my fast at sundown with Mama and Papa, and went to *shul* with them in the morning. It felt funny to leave the house without brushing my teeth and with no breakfast. Lilly ate, of course; Mama made her a good breakfast, and when she was done and did her dishes, she went to her room and closed the door.

When lunch time rolled around and Mama and I left *shul* to go home, my stomach felt like it was stuck to my backbone. At least that's what the kids say when they get very hungry. Mama and I went home after the morning service, but Papa stayed on. He and Yosuf and Uncle Chaim and Uncle Shmuel would be in *shul* all day until the blowing of the *shofar,* which was the end of *Yom Kippur* when everybody could go home and eat.

Mama started lunch for Lilly as soon as we got home, and I couldn't understand how she could do it. The smell of food made me dizzy; all I could think about was when I'd be able to eat and all the things I would eat when I could. Lilly came down and sat at the kitchen table eating her tuna fish sandwich on rye bread, and while I watched her my mouth watered so much I almost choked on my spit.

Mama looked at me and said, "Saraleh, would you like something to eat? Nobody wants you to get sick."

That stiffened my spine. I shook my head and went out of the kitchen and poked around the living room until I had an idea. I went back to the kitchen and said, "Mama, I'm going over to see Anne for a while."

She nodded and I left. I figured if I distracted myself I'd forget about my stomach. No such luck. Anne was having lunch. She told me to sit down and her mother offered me a sandwich. I tried to be nonchalant when I said I was fasting this year. Anne looked at me and as soon as she swallowed what she had in her mouth said, "Maybe I'll fast next year."

"We're supposed to start when we're twelve."

Anne shrugged. "Even if I start later, I'll have plenty of years left to atone."

"That's not the point." I said, "The point is doing a *mitzvah* when we're supposed to, not when we want to."

Anne took a big bite of her sandwich and said, "I'd rather eat."

A few minutes later I left.

By three o'clock, I decided to give up because I knew what it was to be dying. I was ashamed to be so weak and even considered sneaking some food, but not only would I not be atoning for sins if I did, I'd be adding one by lying to Mama and Papa.

So I went into the living room where Mama was reading and said, "Mama, I'm starving. Can I have something to eat?"

Mama looked up and smiled. "You've been very brave, Sarah. You've fasted almost the whole day. God doesn't want children to suffer."

Mama sat with me while I ate a sandwich, trying not to gobble so I wouldn't make myself sick.

When I was able to I said, "I didn't know it was so hard to fast. The only thing I thought about was how much I wanted to eat."

Mama nodded. "Hunger is a terrible thing, but when you're older it gets easier to fast for one day. I always think that when I fast for *Yom Kippur*, I'm not only observing God's commandment, but also getting to understand just a little bit how painful it is to be hungry, and remembering how many people don't have enough to eat."

I thought about that for a while. I wondered what I would do if, as hungry as I was, I hadn't been able to eat because there was no food. It was too horrible to think about and I pushed it out of my mind.

Once the holidays were over, we settled down into our usual routines. The leaves turned wonderful colors and came drifting down to carpet the sidewalks and streets. I loved to crunch through them and jump into the places where they piled up against the trees, before the street cleaners came to sweep them away. It got colder and Mama looked over our winter things. Lilly's coat with the fur collar went into the box for the Hadassah bazaar and she got a new navy blue one with a double row of buttons and a hood. My last year's coat would still do. Too bad. I would have liked a new coat too.

I was able to forget about Lilly again, more or less. She went her way, I went mine. Most of the time, I even forgot to look for her in the lunchroom to see if she was sitting at the Polish table or alone at another table.

One day after school when I was waiting with Rebecca for Anne to come out so we could walk home together, Catherine came walking across the yard and right up to me.

She ignored Rebecca and said to me, "I want to talk to you alone. Send your friend away."

I was so surprised, I didn't know what to say for a minute, but soon I answered, "I don't want to talk to you, and anyway if you have anything to say to me you can say it in front of my friend."

"Oh, no I can't. It's private, between you and me and the lamp post."

I didn't know what to do. I really detested Catherine and she scared me. But I knew she wanted to talk about Lilly and I was curious too.

Anne came up just then and said, "What's going on?"

Catherine said, "I want to talk to Sarah in private, so why don't you and your friend leave us alone?"

Anne looked at me and Rebecca. She said to me, "Saraleh, do you want us to go away? We could go over to the tree and wait for you there if you want to talk to her privately."

I felt really relieved. The tree was a big oak about twenty feet away from where we were standing. Anne and Rebecca would be able to see us but not hear us. It was a good compromise because it made it more our decision than Catherine's, and I wouldn't be with her all alone.

I said to Catherine, "I'll talk to you right here with my friends by the tree and that's it."

She gave me a dirty look, then shrugged and said, "Okay."

Anne and Rebecca walked away, not too fast, and when they got to the tree I turned to Catherine. "Well, what do you want?"

She had the nerve to say to me, "Do you care anything about Lillian?"

"If you're talking about my cousin, Lilly, I want to know what business of yours is it?"

"It's my business because she talks to me about it and because I'm her best friend."

I knew it was true and it made a bitter taste in my mouth.

"Y'know what she says all the time now?" Catherine went on, "She says she's gonna run away where no one will ever find her."

"So maybe she wants to run away from you too, Catherine."

Catherine stuck out her lower lip. "Oh no she doesn't, smart aleck! She just wants to get away from you," she moved her face so close to mine, I felt my eyes begin to cross, "and she says if she can't run away, she'll take poison and kill herself! So if she kills herself it'll be your fault!"

I felt my heart lurch. Catherine was beginning to scare me, so even though I didn't trust her as far as I could throw her, I figured I might learn something about what Lilly was saying to that bunch. "Is that so! Don't make me guess . . . what does Lilly say she wants?"

"She wants to go back to Belgium and live with the neighbors who looked after her when she was in the Home. Or she wants to go back to the Sisters and become a nun. And if she can't go back any more, she wants to live with a proper family, not yours."

Her nerve took my breath away. I could feel myself beginning to shake. "And what have *you* been telling her, *dearie*, about how awful Jews are and how she'll be punished for living with us? D'you think that has anything to do with what Lilly says she wants?"

"I don't tell her anything that she doesn't know already."

"But you help, don't you, and if she's not sure about how awful we are, you make her sure, right?"

Catherine just kept giving me a dirty look. Suddenly I was really curious and I wanted to understand. "Catherine, why do you hate me so much? I never did anything to you. You don't even know my mother and father, how can you hate them?"

She stood for a minute looking as if she wasn't going to say anything, but I kept waiting. Finally she said, "All Jews are the same, I don't have to know any of them."

I kept pushing as if I wanted to hurt myself. "What is it we're the same about, besides having the same religion?"

She hesitated but for such a short time, I could have been mistaken. "Jews killed Jesus Christ and they cheat people too. In business and things. They're rich and they make everybody else poor."

My heart was pounding and I was shaking again. I was sure it showed and I didn't want her to think I was scared. "So that's what you're telling poor Lilly. It'll be your fault if she kills herself. You should be ashamed of yourself trying to scare a little kid who's family's been murdered for nothing. I don't know what kind of god *you've* got that teaches you to hate people who are different from you. I'd be ashamed to believe in a god like that! Shame on you, Catherine!"

I turned around and walked over to where Anne and Rebecca were waiting, and I must've looked really peculiar because they seemed anxious and got on either side of me. Rebecca took my books and Anne took my arm and we all walked home together.

On Friday night I went straight to Yosuf. I just took him in a corner and told him about Catherine. He went to talk to Papa. Later, after everybody finished eating and Lilly and I started to clear the table, Mama told us to go with Yosuf, he wanted to talk with us. Only when I was older did I realize how worried and helpless everyone must have felt to resort to leaving this problem in the hands of children even for an hour.

Years later I learned that immigrant families often used their children as interpreters and representatives to officialdom, when the adults had not mastered English. The children matured early and did a creditable job. Perhaps some subconscious residue of this tradition had influenced my family.

Lilly went willingly enough with Yosuf. I took the chair from my room for myself, Yosuf sat in Lilly's chair, and Lilly sat on her bed.

Yosuf didn't waste a minute. "Lilly, Auntie and Uncle and Sarah are worried about you. This girl Catherine spoke to Sarah and said things that scared her."

Lilly got a little pale and she asked me, "What did Catherine say to you, Sarah, when did she talk to you?"

I told her.

"I did not tell her to talk to you," Lilly said.

Yosuf said, "But she thinks she's helping you by doing it. And if she keeps saying the same things to you that she said to Sarah, how can you learn to live with us?"

"She is lying. I did not say those things about running away and taking poison."

"Why did she tell that to Sarah?"

"She wants me to be with Christian people. She is always bothering me to leave here."

"Will she stop bothering you if you tell her to?"

"No! She will never leave me alone!" Lilly said passionately.

"Do you want to go back to Belgium to become a nun, or live in the orphanage or with the LeClerc's?"

"I did want to, when I came here."

"And do you now?"

There was a long silence while Lilly looked first at Yosuf, then down at the button on her blouse that she was twisting first one way then the other. We could hardly hear her when she said, "I think I will be too scared to go back to Belgium now."

Another long pause. "Is there anything you would really like to do, Lilly?" Yosuf asked.

She shook her head. "I do not mind to live here but I cannot be safe if I do. I am afraid of Catherine and the priest and the Sisters."

"Someone could talk to them, Lilly, and make them leave you alone."

"No! No! They would kill me if they knew I told anyone!"

She was so agitated, Yosuf put his arm around her and patted her back soothingly. "Okay, okay, calm down. We won't do anything you don't want and we won't let anyone hurt you either."

"You cannot stop them if they want to. And, Yosuf, what if they are right and God really sent Jesus to be the Messiah? And God is really punishing the Jews for not accepting His Son? If God killed my mother and father because they are Jews, then if I am a Jew He will punish me too, and you and Sarah and Mama and Papa, and everybody . . . . "

She began crying. Yosuf looked at me with such misery in his face that I felt like crying too. He stood up and took a tissue from the box on Lilly's bureau, went to her and with an arm around her shoulders, wiped her face until the tissue was soggy. Then he went back for the whole box.

When Lilly stopped crying Yosuf kissed her cheek. "Listen," he said, "this is a terrible problem for a small girl. It's too hard to understand—even grownups don't understand why the Catastrophe happened, how God could let it happen. But I believe that God would never send such a terrible thing full of hate and destruction to punish His children to make them love Him."

"But God made people and people made the Catastrophe," I said. "Why didn't he stop them?"

"Sarah, my Hebrew teacher says people are like little children who have to learn how to do the right thing. God has to let us make all our horrible mistakes without interfering every minute or we will never grow up," Yosuf answered.

"But, Yosuf," I protested, "if God can do anything, why didn't He make us perfect, like Him?"

Yosuf sighed. "I guess we're one of His experiments, Saraleh. An inventor makes a lot of models before he gets his invention to work right. Maybe that's what God is doing with human beings."

"Then I do not want to be a human being," Lilly said fiercely. "It is too hard. I am too mixed up. I do not know what I am supposed to believe. It is not fair that I should have to know who is right."

"You're only a little girl, you don't have to worry about things like that now, Lilly. When you're grown up you can decide."

"But they say I must decide now or terrible things will happen to me."

"What if you tell them that for now you decide to be Jewish?"

Lilly turned beet red, then pale. She jumped to her feet and began a frantic hand-wringing, and foot-hopping, whimpering all the while. I found it terrifying, and Yosuf must have been frightened too, because he sent me downstairs to get Papa and Mama. I ran to tell them. I was glad to sit in the living room with Auntie and Uncle and Duvid, being happy I was me and not Lilly.

It was so quiet, even Duvid was just playing with his pocket toy, trying to get the little b-b's into the clown's eyes. Watching him, my eyes got very heavy, and the next thing I knew I was waking up and Yosuf, Mama and Papa came into the room. I knew it was very late without even seeing a clock.

Auntie Aviva said, "Nu, what's happening with Lilly?" They looked the way you do when somebody is in the hospital.

Papa said, "Lilly has been spending her time with some girls in school, *goyim, antisemitkehs*, and she's been seeing a priest after school."

There was an audible shocked intake of breath from Auntie Aviva and Uncle Chaim.

"*Oy veh*," said Auntie Aviva.

Uncle Chaim said, "For how long is this going on?"

"Since she started school."

Auntie Aviva put her hand on her cheek, and rocked back and forth. "*Oy veh, oy veh!*"

Papa said, "There's no use bemoaning this. Lilly is very frightened and all mixed up. We must help her if we can."

Uncle Chaim said,"*If* we can? Of course we will help her but what should we do?"

"I'll see the rabbi tomorrow after services and we'll talk about it. Until then we'll try not to worry. He may have some ideas. We will see."

Papa sounded very strange, as though he didn't really know what he was saying. He kept rubbing his chin with his hand. I was getting more scared now myself. I was thinking I should have gone right to Mama and Papa when all this started, on the very first day of school.

Yosuf was looking at me, and he said, "Sarah, don't blame yourself for what's happening to Lilly."

Papa heard and his eyes were very sad when he looked at me. "Saraleh, Yosuf is right. This is a very hard problem even for grownups. You did the best you could."

Mama came over to where I was sitting on the sofa, and sat down next to me. She hugged me, smoothed back my hair, and kissed my forehead. "You should go to bed now, Saraleh," she said very softly. "It's very late. And you shouldn't worry anymore. We will worry for you. Okay?"

I nodded and kissed her and got up. I kissed Auntie, Uncle, Yosuf, and Papa, said "goodnight" and went upstairs. Lilly's door was open but it was dark and quiet in her room. For a minute I wondered if she was asleep or not, then I went to my room and got undressed. I was so tired I just fell into bed without washing or brushing my teeth.

That night I had the first of my nightmares, the one that comes when I'm deeply disturbed. I am wandering through a dense forest, everything is black and gray and white, like a black-and-white movie. I walk toward a glow in the sky and when I break out of the woods, I smell an odor that reminds me of Mama singeing the pin feathers off a chicken. My stomach turns, just as it did when I was a little girl, but I keep walking toward the glow in the sky even though the odor gets so strong I can hardly stand it. I come to an open space, like a compound. There are shadowy figures moving about, but I can't distinguish any details and though I'm filled with a sense of dread, I keep moving toward the glow which seems to be coming from behind a long low building. As I approach the building I'm suddenly aware of a deep, wide, long trench in front of me. I know I can't cross or go around it. I look down and I'm horrified—the trench is filled with murky water and in it float bits and pieces of human beings—arms, legs, fingers, ears. I want to shriek and run away but I'm rooted, speechless, to the spot. Then I look up toward the building on the other side of the trench, and see Lilly at a window. She's pressed against the glass, looking directly at me. Her mouth is open in a scream, her fingers claw the pane. I know she is asking me to rescue her. I reach my arms out to her, and a figure grabs her from behind and pulls her away. The last I see, fading into the dark interior, is Lilly's open screaming mouth and her arms stretched out toward me. That's where it ends. Invariably I wake up screaming.

That first night, Mama had her arms around me while the vision of Lilly being pulled away was still vivid. The lights went on, Mama dried the sweat off me with a towel and changed my nightgown. Papa sat near me holding my hand. I told them the dream and Mama's eyes filled with tears.

Papa shook his head. "How will we ever heal these wounds," he said.

Mama sat near me holding my hand until I fell asleep. I didn't dream anymore that night.

It was an unusual Sabbath at our house the next morning. All of us were subdued and Mama and Papa looked exhausted, as though they hadn't slept much the night before. The sense of peace and well-being characteristic of the atmosphere in our house on Saturdays was missing, and Lilly and I sat in the kitchen over our breakfast with our heads bent to our plates. The oppressive dream was still with me, and I had the eerie feeling Lilly knew as much about that dream as I did.

Mama said she was going to stay home with Lilly; I could go to *shul* with Papa. I didn't feel like going to *shul*, but I felt even less like staying at home where it was so dreary. I didn't say anything, just got ready to go.

Outside I felt better being in the fresh, cold air. Puddles of water in the gutters and on the sidewalk had frozen over and when I stepped on them, the ice cracked like glass. I liked the sound, but this morning I didn't pay any attention to it. I walked alongside Papa. He didn't hold my hand any more when we were out walking, and he had his head bent looking at the sidewalk in front of him, his hands clasped behind his back. Usually when we walked to *shul*, we talked and looked around, pointing out things to each other, but I knew Papa was thinking about Lilly, and I didn't feel much like talking either.

Then Papa said, "From now on Saraleh, whatever happens between you and Lilly that bothers you, you must tell me and Mama. No more trying to fix it yourself, or being ashamed to tell us. You understand what I'm saying?"

I nodded. "Yes, Papa. I'm sorry I didn't tell you before."

Then he said, "You and I and Mama did not make Lilly's troubles. She came with them, never forget that. We will try to help her get over them." He rested his hand on my shoulder. "You are a good girl, Saraleh. You are being a good sister to Lilly. We are proud of you."

Papa's compliments were so rare I felt giddy hearing them. But still there was a hard heavy spot in my chest when I thought of the talk with Lilly and my dream the night before. The next moment, we reached the synagogue.

We were always early on *Shabbat* morning. Papa greeted some of the other men, 'the regulars,' who like him were always there to form a *minyan*. When he stopped to talk to the rabbi, I left him and went to the balcony.

I fell asleep twice. Each time Rebecca nudged me awake, and for a minute I didn't know where I was. Anne asked me what was wrong with me and I told her I thought I was catching a cold. It was a relief when the *kiddush* was over and I could go home. I went home alone because Papa stayed to talk to the rabbi.

When I got home, Mama offered me lunch. I said I wasn't hungry, but I was tired and wanted to go to bed. Mama felt my forehead and Lilly looked at me. Mama told me okay and I went upstairs, pulled down the window shades, got undressed and went to bed. I fell asleep right away and didn't wake up until the next morning. I wasn't hungry and I didn't have any dreams.

All that week there were conferences going on in the house with the aunties and uncles and Lilly included in some of them. The rabbi came once and spoke to Lilly in the dining room while I was sent to my room to do my homework. When Lilly was introduced to the rabbi, she looked more scared than usual. Less and less she had the blank look that scared *me* when I saw it. Instead she looked as though she would run away if she could and had someplace to run to.

They kept her out of school the entire week. It was my job to bring her homework assignments from school so she wouldn't fall behind. She wasn't sick, but her teacher knew all about Lilly not being in school because she had everything ready for me each time I came in.

In school I caught Catherine looking at me a few times and knew she was dying to find out what happened to Lilly. This was the first time Lilly'd been out of school except for the Jewish holidays. I was so glad I could ignore Catherine because Lilly wasn't around for me to worry about or feel obligated over. I felt she was safe, not as safe as when we were in the country, but safer than when she was in school.

At the end of the week Mama and Papa sat me down for a talk. Lilly was in her room; we were alone for the first time in days.

Papa started. "Sarah, the rabbi took all of Lilly's papers and went to see the priest she's been going to. He did this to prove Lilly's parents were Jews who were killed in the camps and that they wanted Lilly to stay with the faith and be raised by Auntie Esther's relatives. The rabbi asked the priest to stop the children and people who are telling Lilly being Jewish is bad because they are making terrible emotional problems for her."

Papa spoke slowly and distinctly as if for his own sake as well as mine. "The priest said since Lilly spent her formative years in a Catholic institution, except for the accident of birth, she is a Catholic. He said Lilly may be a Jew only in a legal sense. The only consideration he would make is because we are Lilly's legal guardians and she must live with us, it is detrimental for her to be told we are not good people, so he might instruct the children in that way. But when she is able to make her own decisions the whole thing will have to be re-examined, and if she wants conversion to Catholicism, he will be there to help her."

While Papa spoke he looked more and more sad, and sometimes his lips got tight as if he was angry. I noticed some white hairs mixed in with the black in front near his forehead, and while he was talking he'd rub his chin with his hand. It made a sandpapery sound. Mama, who always looked young to me, all of a sudden looked much older. She had lines around her eyes and furrows on her forehead.

I had plenty of ideas why they must be feeling bad. I knew I would miss Lilly if she left. For all the times I wished I could give her away or have her disappear, I thought of her as our family, and we were such a small family. Now some strangers were trying to take one of us away. It was not a good feeling. To lose her to the goyim would be to lose her completely. My only experience with Gentiles was of hostility, which meant if Lilly became one of them she also would become my enemy and I would never be able to have a friendship with her.

Mama began to talk. "We're thinking of sending Lilly to a small private school for girls for a few months, until things calm down here. It's upstate. This Jewish couple run it and all the girls are Jewish. Maybe Lilly will learn something about her own people if she has the chance to be with them. The rabbi says it's a nice place."

"Does Lilly know?" I asked.

"We spoke to her about it."

"And what did she say?"

"Lilly doesn't say much," Papa answered. "Yosuf will talk to her and try to find out, and we thought you could too."

I nodded, but I didn't think I'd find out much more than they had. Yosuf might, though.

That night after supper, Yosuf came over and Mama and Papa left him and Lilly and me alone in the living room with tea and cake. If it weren't such a serious occasion, I would have been able to enjoy the idea of being grownup, entertaining company in a grownup way. As it was, I was nervous. Lilly looked much more like a little kid now than she had when we first brought her home. She didn't have that stiff, blank look like a big doll with nothing inside. I didn't know whether this different look was good or bad. But I hoped it was good.

Yosuf said, "Have you been bored at home all week, Lilly?"

She shook her head. "No. I do my homework and Mama is teaching me to use the sewing machine. I am making myself a blouse. When I finish it, I will make a dress."

Yosuf smiled. "That's great, Lilly. Have you been thinking about what happens next? Whether you go back to school here or away for a while to a school in the country?"

"I have thought. But I don't know how to think about it."

Yosuf waited. That was what was so good about talking to him. He gave you time to think about things and if he asked you a question he let you answer it. He didn't make up an answer for you.

"If I go away, I will be alone again. I do not know the people where they will send me. What if I do not like it? What if they do not like me? They say they will bring me back if I do not like it, but how do I know they will? What if they never come for me again?"

Yosuf nodded but didn't say anything.

After a while, Lilly said, "If I stay here and go back to school, Catherine and the others will want me to be around with them and go to church with them, but Mama and Papa say that is making problems for everybody at home. They say Father Vaughn will talk to the girls and explain why I am living here, and it will be better, so maybe that will be all right. But if I hang around the Jewish kids, Catherine will get mad at me, and if I hang around the Polish kids, Mama and Papa will be sad. Can I go to school and not be with any of the kids?" She looked very serious and tilting her head, said, "You see this is not an easy problem, Yosuf. I do not know how to think about it to make a good decision."

We all sat silent for what seemed like an hour to me. Then Lilly told us things I had never heard before.

"When I was in the Home in La Hulpe, things were not so bad. I was not too lonely. We had enough to eat and the Sisters were mostly nice to us. When I was seven, one time after Madame LeClerc visited me, the Sisters said they thought I should be confirmed. That was when I knew my parents were not alive any more. I wore a white dress and veil. They gave me a rosary. It was very pretty and I did not have so many pretty things, just a card with a picture of Mother Mary and another one with St. Francis and the animals. Sister Mary Luisa taught us French. She always talked to me after we finished our lesson for the day. She said no one must ever, ever, know that my parents were Jews because if the Germans found out, they would come and take me away. That was why it was good I was confirmed and did my rosary and knew my catechisms.

"She said Christians had the only real religion and maybe, even though it was terrible what the Boche were doing, the Jews were being punished for not embracing Jesus, the Son of God, as Christ. The Sisters talked to all of us about coming into the order when we grew up. Some of them had been orphans too and now they were part of the family of Christ and very happy. Happier even than some of the people who had regular families. A lot of us orphans said we would go into the order when we grew up. The habits the Sisters wore were pretty; they were gray with white pleated coifs, and all white for summer."

I was so fascinated listening to Lilly, my mouth dropped open, particularly at the part about the nuns and how Lilly thought what they wore was pretty. I asked her, "Where did you sleep? Did you have to work?"

Lilly blinked as though just realizing I was part of her audience. "I slept in a long room, with plenty of windows, ten girls in every room. Everyone had a cot and a cardboard box to hold our things. In summer we tended the vegetable garden and picked apples and pears when they were ready. We did different things. Sometimes washed the floors, sometimes did laundry and ironing, like we do here, only bigger and more. It was not hard. I did not mind. Five hours a day we were taught school subjects by the Sisters and the priests. They came to teach math and science and to do mass and confession, but they didn't live in the Home."

Lilly paused and stared around the room. When she started talking again her face was pinched together and she didn't look at Yosuf or me.

"One time the Boche came into the Home, soldiers with guns. We were lined up in our best school uniforms, in front of this big, fat man with a very red face. He was wearing a funny uniform with a million things pinned on his front. He clicked his heels and stuck his hand in the air and screamed at the Mother Superior who stood very straight in front of us, looking at him. I was glad to be in the back row. I was scared every minute he would see me and take me away because my parents were Jews. After he left I felt very sick and I vomited my breakfast and the Sisters put me to bed instead of making me go to classes." Her voice got very low and I leaned forward not to miss anything she said.

"The Boche were in Belgium for such a long time we thought they would never leave, and two of my friends and me decided we would join the order and always have a safe home where the Boche would not come. When I was ten, Belgium was liberated and M'sieu et M'dame LeClerc came to see me. After, Mother Superior called me into her office and told me my parents were dead in the camps and the LeClercs wanted to adopt me because they never had children of their own. I liked them and now I had another place to go. Mother Superior said I should think about becoming a nun and some of the sisters said I owed it to other poor orphans to make a good home for them just as I had been given."

Lilly glanced at me, then away. Her voice got louder; she began to talk very rapidly. "Before I could decide, Mother Superior called me into her office again. There was a man I didn't know and a Red Cross lady. She said the man was my uncle, from England, and he would take me there to grow up with all my relatives. He spoke English very fast, I did not understand him. I was afraid and anyway, I had two places to stay already. So I did not want to go with him. I did my rosary every day and prayed all the time that God let me stay either at The Home or with M'sieu et M'dame, but He did not answer my prayers, and no matter how Mother Superior said it was God's will, I was angry. Jesus Christ was no better than the Jewish God. So one day, Uncle Avram came with the Red Cross lady and M'dame LeClerc and a little valise and some new clothes, and I said goodbye to all my friends in the Home, and we were all crying.''

Listening to Lilly's story I felt like crying myself and I wondered how she could stay so calm most of the time. It was almost as if she'd read it all in a book—not as though it had happened to her.

"We went to the LeClerc's house in Brussels. They gave me some things they said were my mother's and father's and a photo album and some letters from my mother. In the morning I and Uncle left for England. We went in an army airplane because Uncle Avram was in the army. I was very scared every minute. The soldiers gave me candy and talked to me in English but the plane was too noisy and I didn't understand them anyway. I wished I could be dead with my parents. In London, Uncle Avram took me on the subway to Auntie Fanny's house. A lot of the houses were broken from the bombings. Auntie Fanny and Uncle Moshe had five children and there were only four rooms. I had a cot in the living room. The other children were okay, but I missed my friends in The Home. Then one of the children found my rosary and cards and told Auntie Fanny. She yelled at me and took my things and broke and tore them up and threw them away. I hated her. What right did she have to spoil my things? I cried for a long time and I wouldn't eat. Their food tasted funny anyway.

"Then one day Auntie Fanny told me I would be going to America to live with Uncle Mikhel. Oh, I was so scared. America was so far away. I would never be able to get back to Belgium and find my friends again! I didn't pray anymore because I knew it doesn't work. I just said to myself if I couldn't stand it when I got to America, I would find somehow to kill myself and be over with the whole thing. And then I came to New York and Auntie and Uncle and Saraleh met me at the boat and you know all the rest.''

I had never known anyone with such a terrible story. I thought back to the day we met Lilly at the boat, and of how everything had been wrong. But I couldn't imagine how we could have made any of it right. While Lilly was talking I kept wondering, should she have been left with the people who had become her new family? But then I remembered Auntie Esther, and wondered if I could have left Lilly where she was if it had been up to me.

Yosuf must've been as upset as I was because he wasn't saying anything either. Lilly just sat with her head down as if she was still

thinking of what she had told us. Could we ask Lilly to go away
and be with strangers all over again? But could we leave her in
school where the Gentile girls could tell her every day that it was
a sin and shameful to be a Jew? And could we ever help Lilly get
rid of her fear of being hurt or killed because she was a Jew? How
could she be a Jew if she was going to be so frightened all the time?

What we eventually did was, Mama, Papa, Yosuf, Lilly and I
discussed the possibilities. We sat in the dining room around the
table. It was a family board meeting.

Papa said, "Lilly, Mama and I must decide what is the right
thing to do, but we hope you'll agree with us on what we think is
best. You must tell us how you feel about everything. And we will
do what we can to include things you want. Do you understand
what I am saying?"

Lilly nodded. She looked anxious, but not sullen or removed
from us.

Papa went on. "Yosuf tells us you aren't sure that you would
want to go back to Belgium even if we could arrange that for you.
Is that so?"

She looked uncomfortable. She began twisting a button on her
blouse like she always did when the questions were difficult. Her
voice was almost a whisper, but we were all so still we could hear
her clearly.

"I am afraid it is so different now. My friend Marguerite wrote
me there is a new Mother Superior in the Home. M'sieu Le Clerc
is sick with asthma. Maybe I will have no place to stay if I go back."

Mama said, "Lilly, we don't want you to go back. You're our
flesh and blood, we want to keep you with us."

I saw the glint of tears in Lilly's eyes. Oh, no, I thought. If she
starts to cry, we'll never get anything settled.

Yosuf, who was sitting next to her, put his hand gently on her
head. "Leahleh, I think you can learn how to be brave about being
Jewish. *Il faut avoir de la courage.* You can learn how just the way
you learn math and languages."

She looked up at Yosuf. "But what if God will punish me for
not accepting Jesus Christ?"

Yosuf dropped his hand. We all looked at each other.

Papa said, "Lilly, you have plenty of time to make a final
decision on that. We think that when you learn about religions

and their history, you will see it is not God who made that rule, people did."

Her forehead puckered and I knew she had a lot of arguments for Papa, but when she began pressing her lips together, I knew she intended to keep them to herself.

"I'll bet Lilly is thinking the Jewish rules are also made by people, not God," I said.

Lilly's forehead smoothed out. I felt like a mind-reader.

"Well, Lilly," Mama said, "you are only a young girl—a minor, and you must obey the people you live with. God will forgive you for doing what you have to because you live with us. When you grow up you can make decisions for yourself and then God will hold you responsible."

I thought Mama was very smart to say that. It made sense to me, and Lilly looked more cheerful too.

Papa said, "We want you to grow up to be a wonderful, happy person. I think you must be able to accept what you are, what your Mama and Papa were, not only because *I* think it is good to be a Jew, but because if you fear what you are, or think it is bad to be what you are, you will be afraid and ashamed for the rest of your life. There is antisemitism all over, Lilly. The only way you can escape it is to grow strong and face it and deal with it openly." He paused for a moment, looking at Lilly thoughtfully. "And, I am selfish. I want you to stay what you are for the sake of your Mama, for my dead sister's memory. I can't see her resting in peace if we don't do this."

There was more talk along these lines but everything important had already been said. What we decided was purely practical. Mama would take Lilly to the upstate school and stay with her for a week. If Lilly felt she could stay there, Mama would come back alone. If Lilly had strong doubts, they would come back together. A week later they left.

Mama prepared as though she were going to be away for a year, stocking the house with everything from packaged food to laundry powder. She cooked whole meals and labelled and refrigerated them, one for every day of the week. She instructed me in house and Papa-care, although I knew and already did much of it. Auntie Aviva was a backup for some dire emergency, unknown but nonetheless anticipated. Papa was by no means helpless, and I was knowledgeable and capable. But aside from our annual month in the country which was planned and part of the family rhythm, this was the first time in their married life that Mama would be leaving Papa 'on his own.'

For me it was pure adventure. I was to be in charge of our home and Papa's comfort and well-being—in effect, the lady of the house. So on the Sunday they left, when Papa and I accompanied Mama and Lilly to Grand Central Station and saw them off, waving as the train pulled out, I felt mature, and part of the world of sophisticated people.

It was another matter when we got back home to a quiet and empty house. Papa went to do some work in his little study while I rattled around through the rooms, checking on things already done. Supper enough for a family of six was ready and on the range, my homework had been completed for two days, I couldn't find a book I wanted to read, and it was too early for any of my radio programs.

I looked at the phone. Children, at least in our family, did not telephone their friends at all, much less use the instrument for lengthy conversations. But now I was in another catagory which also included the telephone. Nervously, I picked up the receiver and dialed Anne's number. I could actually see part of her house from where I was standing. Anne's mother answered and immediately I was in trouble. A child would use the telephone only because of a calamity.

When I heard Mrs. Goldberg's voice, I panicked and almost hung up, but didn't dare.

"Hello, hello," she kept saying. "Who is this?"

"It's me, Mrs. Goldberg, is Anne there?" My voice felt weak and I must have sounded as though catastrophe had struck.

"Saraleh? Saraleh, is it you? What's wrong? Is somebody sick?"

This was terrible. I had to correct all the wrong impressions or the whole neighborhood would be on our front steps with doctors and ambulances, fire and police departments.

I raised my voice to what I hoped was a healthy, cheerful volume. "No, no, Mrs. Goldberg, everything's fine, I just . . . Mama took Lilly upstate to the school and everything is fine. Papa's in his study, and I just wanted to talk to Anne on the phone."

"You wanted to talk to Anne on *the phone!?* So it's got to be something is wrong. What's the matter you couldn't walk over? Saraleh, you can tell me, what is it?"

I gave up. "Mrs. Goldberg, I'll be over in two minutes, is that all right?"

"What do you mean, is it all right? Since when isn't it all right for you to come over?"

I said goodbye and hung up in a hurry, then told Papa I was going over to Anne's. The next time I telephoned Anne was three years later to invite her to my sweet sixteen birthday party, and then the call was by arrangement between our families.

As the week went by I missed Mama and Lilly badly. Papa and I took to eating in the kitchen because it was cozier than the dining room. During the week I urged my friends to come home with me after school or found reasons to go to their houses. I was always home when Papa came from work, but only in enough time so that we would have supper at the usual hour. I missed my after-school sessions with Mama over milk and cookies. We went to Auntie Aviva for Friday night supper where I basked in the family atmosphere. I could hardly wait for Sunday when we would meet Mama at Grand Central Station and maybe Lilly, if things hadn't worked out.

Saturday night, after the end of *Shabbat,* I washed and waxed the already clean kitchen floor and scrubbed the bathroom and vacuumed the house. Papa told me I would wear everything out cleaning so much, but I wanted Mama to come home to a perfect house.

When I saw Mama step out of the train, I didn't feel one bit sophisticated. I just ran to her as fast as I could and flung myself into her arms, practically knocking her over. She was laughing and hugging me while I kept my face buried in the collar of her coat. I was so happy to see her I wasn't even embarrassed to be acting like a baby. Papa got to us and reached over to kiss Mama and take her valise, and then I realized Lilly wasn't with her.

On the subway going home Mama sat between Papa and me and told us what had happened. There were twenty girls in the house, a big old farm building on seventeen acres, mostly in fruit trees with a little stream running through the property. The youngest student was nine, the oldest fifteen. The people who ran the school were certified teachers who had taught for years in the public schools and on college levels. They'd started the school in the 'thirties for the sake of their own three children who were by now living on their own. The school had attracted teachers interested in innovative education, and the curriculum included such subjects as Hebrew studies, Jewish history and practices, dance, and tree grafting and pruning.

The atmosphere was relaxed and non-competitive, a very protected environment that Lilly seemed to fit into from the first day. By removing Lilly from the negative influence of her friends, my parents hoped to create a foundation for her to build resources gone dormant or undeveloped. They would keep Lilly there for a year then bring her home.

The family budget was being strained to its limit by the school fee and would probably cost us, among other things, our month at the Moskowitz farm. I squelched the small rebellion in me. I would not allow any part of me to spoil Mama's homecoming or the knowledge that this step was an attempt to return to Lilly part of what she had lost.

During the year Lilly was away, it was as though everything was in suspension—nothing worth mentioning happened, nothing of note occurred, everything was waiting for her return.

Oh yes, life proceeded at an orderly pace. I made the honor roll. I became editor of the school newsletter. Catherine faded into the background. Anne, Rebecca, and I went to our first ballet alone at the City Center in Manhattan. For my fourteenth birthday, instead of the usual ice cream and cake at home, we had a restaurant meal with a cake carried out of the kitchen by the waitress while all the restaurant patrons applauded. Stories of various embarrassing incidents connected with menstruation became, along with boys, a big topic between me and my friends.

With Yosuf's help, I found some of the Holocaust literature that was beginning to come on to the market. Reading about it made me punch drunk as if I'd taken a beating, but I read whatever I could find.

I wrote several chatty letters to Lilly with news about school and home, but never got one from her. I wasn't disappointed. I never expected a reply, and my letters were constructed so they didn't require one. I would write, "I hope this letter finds you in good health," not, "How are you, and how is everything?"

Lilly was coming home for Passover. For at least a week before her expected arrival, I was filled with apprehension. I spent long, secret moments in my room in front of the mirror trying to see myself as Lilly would. I'd use my little hand mirror to get a view of my profile. I'd stop at the door of my room and look through her eyes at my bed, now moved against a wall, at the poster of the Coppelia Ballet near the bookcase, at the serious looking books replacing the doll collection on a shelf.

Sometimes I'd be satisfied. She would find me mature, admirable, more like Yosuf. Most of the time however, I'd be overcome by the old doubts. I was just a spoiled kid, not worth anything but the contempt she was certain to feel.

Fortunately there was plenty to do to get ready for *Pesach*, so between that and school I didn't have much time for brooding. But the night before Lilly was to arrive, I experienced the nightmare for the second time. Mama woke me from my screams, dried and changed me like a baby and sat by my side holding my hand until I fell asleep.

At breakfast Papa told me I should talk about what was bothering me, because if I didn't I might make myself sick. I was awfully embarrassed, as though they had caught me examining myself in the mirror.

"It's nothing, Papa, I'll be all right."

He persisted. "Are you afraid Lilly will be the same as when she left?" I shrugged. "Because if you are, then you must be prepared that she might be, Saraleh, and to be very clear in yourself that nothing is your fault."

I kept my head down, eyes on my plate, wishing he would stop. "Okay, Papa, I'll try."

He left me alone then, and I hurried to finish and get away from the table and the painful subject.

CHAPTER NINE

PAPA WENT TO MEET LILLY AT THE TRAIN. I HELPED MAMA IN THE kitchen, shelling green peas, scraping and cubing carrots, preparing apples for baking, and leaving a big, perfect one for the *charoses.* I shelled walnuts and put them in a small bowl, saving the preparation for Lilly's arrival. Maybe she would want to help make it. Mercifully, Mama kept me occupied, and Papa and Lilly were at the door before I could work up an anxiety attack.

I caught my breath when I saw her. She was almost my height and no longer pudgy. Her hair was shoulder length, thick and wavy. No more braids. She returned Mama's kiss and looked at me and smiled.

I said, "You're all grown up, Lilly."

And she said, "And you're a regular young lady, Saraleh."

I hesitated, not knowing what to do next. She came over to me, took my hand, and kissed my cheek. I don't know what came over me and I could have killed myself, but I couldn't stop the tears which welled up so suddenly they took me completely by surprise. So there I was crying on Lilly's shoulder and she was patting my back, while I kept gulping, "I'm sorry. I'm sorry."

Mama took Lilly's coat and ordered me to the bathroom to wash my face and comb my hair. When I came back to the kitchen, Lilly was in an apron peeling the apple for the *charoses.* We couldn't really talk, because the next two hours were devoted to getting the table and ourselves ready for the *seder*.

At the *seder*, Lilly knew the service and some of the songs and when Yosuf complimented her, Lilly said she'd been preparing herself for it. When we got down to eating, the relatives began asking questions about the school and Lilly described the place and the teachers and the other students. It was clear she liked it and was as happy there as she'd been anywhere.

Later I heard Auntie Aviva remark to Uncle Chaim in Yiddish, that she ought to be, it was costing enough. And Uncle Chaim said back to her in English, it was none of her business since it wasn't her money. I was glad Lilly hadn't heard any of that. She was on the other side of the room looking at Duvid's latest pocket toy. Altogether though, it was a fine first *seder* night, actually the best we ever had. We were happy to be together and you could begin to believe nothing bad would happen again.

When everybody left and things had been cleared away, Papa said he and Mama knew Lilly and I wanted to catch up, so after we got ready for bed, we could stay up awhile, but not too late. I could hardly believe my ears, it was such a special treat. We kissed them goodnight and went up fast.

At the top of the stairs, Lilly said, "When you're ready, Saraleh, come to my room. I have things to show you."

I was so happy I could've burst. I zipped out of my clothes and into my nightgown, bathrobe and slippers in seconds, then forced myself to hang everything neatly on hangers.

Lilly's door was open. She was already in her night clothes and rummaging through her small traveling case. "Come on in and close the door, Saraleh."

I sat down in the chair, and the next minute she said, "Here it is!" With a flourish she handed me a small package.

I looked at it stupidly. "What is it?"

"It's for you," she said. "Open it."

I was clumsy tearing off the paper, but finally exposed a handkerchief with a lace border and the letter 'S' embroidered in one corner. There was also a red and while candy-stripe pencil with a big pink removable eraser on the end and the word 'Onandaga 2B' impressed at the top in gilt letters.

I was touched and embarrassed; I hadn't gotten anything for Lilly. I invented hastily, "I have a going away gift for you, but I can't give it to you until you leave."

Lilly smiled. "That's okay, Saraleh."

I knew she saw right through me. "Thank you very much, Lilly. I love the handkerchief, and the pencil is just what I needed."

"Thank you for writing to me. I read your letters at dinner a couple of times. Everybody said you write very well."

I felt the blush rising up from my collarbone and washing over my forehead. At the same moment I realized Lilly's slightly accented speech was free of the foreign construction that had always made it seem so quaint and exotic. "Lilly," I blurted, "you have changed so much, I can hardly believe it."

"Maybe more outside than inside," she said.

It was an opening I didn't let slip by. "What do you mean?"

"Oh, it's one thing to hide safely in the mountains, and another to be back in the city with all the old things around."

Before I could ask another question she said, "Look, I have some pictures of the school and some of the kids and teachers."

She handed me an envelope and we went through the photos with Lilly naming the people and pointing out the high-lights of the property. She was in several group pictures, and there were a few of her alone, standing in an orchard or in front of a building. She looked sturdy and self-confident. I gave her back the pictures and she put them into the envelope carefully and back in her case.

"Are you happy?" I asked.

"Happy?" she repeated. "I'm not sure what that is." She spoke slowly. "Mostly, I'm not so frightened any more."

I had learned from watching Yosuf to be patient with long silences.

"Much more, I see the things that are funny and make me laugh. It feels good. Lately I am remembering what I dream. I don't know the whole dream yet. I remember only parts. They are frightening, but my Hebrew teacher says it's good to remember." She laughed briefly, not a humorous sound. "I hope she is right. The part I remember is I am running, running, down a long, narrow hall. I am running because someone is behind me trying to catch me. I get to a window and try to get out, but the window is locked. Through the glass I see only shadowy shapes moving back and forth. There is something horrible out there too, but I keep trying to open the window. Then whoever is behind me grabs me and pulls me back. That's when I wake up."

As Lilly spoke the hackles rose on me; my hair felt as though it were standing straight up all over my body. Were Lilly and I locked in the same dream? Which was the dream? This? Last year? My nightmare from which I woke drenched and screaming? Her night horrors? If we were sharing a nightmare, would what happened to her, eventually happen to me?

She was standing over me with her hand on my shoulder saying, "Sarah, are you all right?" I nodded. "Because you got so pale. Are you feeling sick?"

I shook my head. "I'm okay now. I guess I ate too much like always at a *seder*."

I couldn't tell my nightmare to her. I was terrified that both of us would suffer some injury if I did. Instead I asked, "Are you in touch with Catherine or the others in that crowd?"

"No, I didn't even tell her where I was going. There wouldn't be any point to going away if I did."

"Does the priest know where you are?"

"Father Vaughn? No."

"What did you tell them when you left?"

"I told them my guardians thought I was too young to choose my religion."

"Did they say anything?"

Lilly shrugged. "They said it wouldn't be too many years before I could choose. Meanwhile they would stand by me."

"Do you know what you'll do?"

A quick emphatic shake of the head. "Not one bit. The truth is, I find it hard to believe in *any* God after what happened to me. One of the girls at the school is a survivor of the camps. She is almost sixteen. When she was eleven, she worked eighteen hours a day in a munitions factory in Poland and got one slice of bread and a bowl of water with some mouldy cabbage in it a day. She was raped and beaten. She was lucky: her mother, father and younger sister all went to the gas chamber. Can she believe in God? God is for people who have homes and families and plenty to eat, not for Hannah and me."

"But you're learning about the Jewish religion there, aren't you?"

She nodded. "And history. At least no one tells me I will suffer eternal damnation if I don't believe in God. They just tell me to be good while I am alive and not worry about what happens after I'm dead."

"What will you do when you come home, Lilly?"

"I won't think about it until I have to," she said firmly. "That is the way to stay alive. One day at a time."

And so during the Passover week we lived one day at a time. Lilly stayed four days, through the three *seder* nights. Tuesday morning while I was in school, Mama took her to the train station. I gave her a going away gift—a small photo album with mounts for her new collection of pictures.

By the beginning of May I knew we wouldn't be able to go to the Moskowitz farm in August. I consoled myself with the thought of spending the summer with Anne and Rebecca, and having plenty of time to talk about the upcoming term when we would be entering high school. Lilly would be coming home in September and returning to public school. My parents thought Lilly might be advanced a grade to the high school level, but that would depend on a series of examinations to determine how much of the private school curriculum overlapped with the required public school courses.

I was not going to worry about Lilly's return until I had to, and anyway, our attention and energy were being drawn more and more to news of Europe and Palestine. Our Jewish community followed the progress of the fight for a Jewish national state in Palestine closely. Kids came door-to-door with collection boxes, called in Yiddish, *pushkas*. Thousands of dollars in small change were collected for the emerging nation, in *pushkas*. Mama and Papa joined a synagogue-sponsored Zionist group and I often went with them to meetings.

Usually there was a speaker followed by questions and discussion, and always a collection in aid of the fighters or to help the survivors of the Holocaust. One speaker, a tiny, wispy man perhaps five feet tall with a great shock of black hair and brilliant, large eyes behind heavy glasses, spoke with such passion I was haunted by his words for weeks after.

His quiet voice penetrated to every corner of the *shul.* "Have we no right to one tiny spot of earth? Must we forever beg the toleration of another nation to rest somewhere? Must we humbly pack our tents and fade away when nations tire of us? Must we die quietly when we get in the way? Are we to be universal pariahs forever?"

Each question stirred my blood. I wanted to stand up and shout, "No!"

"God gave us Israel," he went on. "His covenant was made with us four thousand years ago. He is waiting for us to return to the promised land. We must save the broken, mutilated remnant of our people in Europe who at this moment languish in camps, waiting, hoping for rescue. The democracies do not want them. And they do not want to return to the places where they suffered unspeakable horrors. In Poland, half of the few hundred Jews who managed to hide and survive the Nazis were murdered by their Polish neighbors after liberation!"

My hands were clenched in my lap. I wanted to go raging through the world redressing the grievous wrongs that still went on—which would never stop until we Jews had our own homeland.

"Can any Jew in his heart remain on the sidelines?" he demanded. "The money we raise is purchasing guns for our soldiers and ancient, rusty freighters for our people stranded in Europe. These boats are loaded—no, overloaded, to the point of suicide, with our brothers and sisters who are being smuggled out of the DP camps and into Palestine, in the dead of night, past British and Arab patrols. After all they have suffered, they must now suffer this terrible danger and added indignity. During the war the British intercepted several of these rotting hulks bound for Palestine and forced them out to sea, and if they sank, and if the refugees starved or died of exposure, that was not their concern. Now they impound the ships and send our people to Cyprus to another kind of prison." Suddenly his voice thundered out, ricochetting around the walls of the synagogue. "*WELL— IT—IS—OUR—CONCERN!* We will not give up! No, never! We will support our people and we will support our soldiers, and we will have a homeland in Palestine as God promised!"

The collection was excellent. I contributed all my allowance and money I had earned baby sitting for my cousin Dorothy. I wished it were a million dollars.

And then summer was gone and Lilly was coming home to stay. She'd be back for the Labor Day weekend.

I had the usual anxiety attacks whenever I thought of Lilly being with us again, and I wondered if she was becoming uneasy also. In junior high school she would meet many of the girls in her old Polish clique. If she moved up to the high school level, there would be Catherine, the most influential of them. I knew they all had a stake and investment in her and were not going to let go, something she knew better than I.

For me high school would be an extension of familiar things. I would move along with most of my present classmates; the high school building was a few blocks away from the one I was leaving. The building and teaching staff would be new. I looked forward to the change.

My reunion with Lilly was good, though she was pretty jumpy, lapsing into silences and chewing her lip. We were the same height now and it looked as though I was going to be the shorter one. Auntie Esther had been as tall as Papa, which was unusual for ladies in those days. Lilly was taking after her mother and it meant clothes buying; she'd outgrown just about everything. Papa said it was the country air. Mama said it was being free of worry. I said, who cared what it was.

The last few days before school, we hung around together, and though Lilly didn't go outside much, she didn't slink around either as though she were trying to fade into the woodwork or wished she were invisible. It was a lot better than it had been and I hoped it would last. I asked her one day whether she thought she'd like to be advanced to high school, and if she had decided yet on a general, academic, or commercial course.

"Yes, I want get to high school as quickly as possible," she said, "and I want a general course so I can major in agriculture. I will buy a farm, far away from any city and I will live there alone. No one will be allowed on my property without my permission."

She said it so glibly, I thought she was joking. "You're kidding!" I said.

"Why should I be kidding? What's so strange about what I want?"

I shrugged. "I don't know. I mean the country is wonderful, but I never heard of a girl running a farm all alone."

"Then I shall be the first one."

"Won't you be lonely?"

"I don't think so. I'll have plenty of animals to keep me company and busy."

"You'll have to go to a city sometime, to buy clothes and machinery to run the farm."

"I will mail order everything."

"Oh, Lilly, do you really want to escape from people so much? What about Mama and Papa and Yosuf, Anne and Rebecca and all the other wonderful people there are?"

"And you think they make up for the others? The Nazi murderers or the British who forced the poor people in the boats out to sea to drown or to return to the camps? The good people never make up for the bad. Never. Never. I can't understand why there are people at all. If the world had only animals and no people, it would be such a lovely place."

I couldn't remember ever feeling more shocked by Lilly, although each revelation of her despair or cynicism or bitterness shocked me anew, and always on a widening level of understanding.

"But, Lilly, you wouldn't be here either if the world had only animals."

"And so what? That would not be terrible. Not to me or to anyone else."

"That's not true, Lilly. You're important to me. I think about you all the time; even when you weren't here, I did. And no matter how angry I got, I always wanted to love you. I would miss you a lot if you didn't let me visit you on your farm."

She was looking at me intently as I said all this, and I was concentrating so hard on expressing myself clearly that I was startled when her eyes suddenly swam with tears.

"Oh, Lilly," I said, "I know how sad your life has been, but you're only thirteen and that leaves lots of time for you to be happy. All of us want you to, Mama, Papa, Yosuf, the aunties and uncles, even your Polish friends want you to be happy."

"I don't believe it!" she burst out. "The Polish girls will like me if I do what they say, and if I become a Christian, won't you and Mama and Papa and Yosuf and all the relatives hate me?"

"Oh, no! I wouldn't hate you, but if you were a Christian, wouldn't you have to hate *us* because we're Jews? Would you talk to us and come visit us? Or would you call us Christ-killers? Even if your mother made a mistake not taking you back to England when she could, it's not her fault that she died and you became an orphan. You always mix that up. How can you keep it all straight if you blame the people who didn't do anything wrong?"

"It doesn't matter," she said. "In the end it's all the same thing. The Jews have been hated for a million years and will always be hated. The only way is not to be a Jew."

I was horrified. After a year at a special school to help Lilly get over her fear, she seemed to be in exactly the same spot as before she left. "Are you going to do what you did before you left, pretend you don't know me or the other Jewish kids?"

"I don't know what I will do," she said impatiently. "I want to be left alone in school. I don't want to speak to the Gentile or the Jewish children. I want to do my work and get out of school as quickly as I can so I can find my farm."

Again the dilemma faced me. Did I keep this to myself or did I tell Mama and Papa? They had spent so much money and expended so much concern on Lilly, yet there didn't seem to be any basic change for the better. She was nicer, more friendly, but that might have happened anyway. It was true she had been with us for barely two years and away one year of that time, but it seemed like forever to me. There was nothing in my mind or heart that could remember the time before Lilly. I couldn't even conjure up an approximation of what I or things in general had been like before she came.

The first week in high school was a tumult of movement and settling in. A few last minute changes of classes, lots of book collecting and supply purchasing, and what seemed like a ton of homework. Each teacher tried to outdo all the others in length of assignment. I hoped they were only testing the mettle of the innocent freshmen, after which normalcy would take over.

I saw Lilly only at home, briefly, during meals. I locked myself away for hours every evening determined I would not fall behind in my homework during the very first week. The second week of the term, Lilly was moved up to the high school and placed in another freshman class. It was policy in those days to keep close relatives separated, twins for example would find themselves in different classes. It worked out well. There was enough competition and rivalry operating without bringing it home to families.

Catherine was in my class and I imagined how delighted she would be to get her hooks into Lilly again. It would be harder— there were many more students, three different courses of study, different lunch and study periods. It was possible their paths would cross rarely, and if I was lucky, not at all. I had no classes in common with Lilly. My lunch period was at eleven, hers at one.

Once a week we were in a study period together. Catherine had the same one too. The high school was so crowded, the auditorium was used for a study hall. During the second week Catherine learned Lilly was back. I watched like a spectator at a drama as our class settled down in the balcony of the auditorium, rustling papers and books. We were permitted some limited whispering, but no moving around. We were not prohibited from moving our eyes and heads around however, and a lot of scanning and spotting was always part of study period. High signs like, 'Meet me later—in the lunch room, gym, library, outside,' were used regularly.

I saw Lilly come in with her class and take a seat on the other side of the balcony a couple of rows down from me. Our eyes met in silent acknowledgement. I swiveled my head to see Catherine who was one row behind me and two seats to my left. Her head was down as she sorted through her books; she hadn't seen Lilly yet but she was bound to. I watched as she raised her eyes and began to scan the hall. I knew exactly the moment she spotted Lilly. She grew attentive, almost rigid, and a look of surprised delight suffused her face. Her mouth opened, she raised her hand. I was sure she was going to forget herself completely and shout and wave. Then slowly her mouth closed and her hand fell, but her eyes were riveted in Lilly's direction. I turned and looked across to Lilly. She was sitting with her head directed at the book in her lap. I prayed she would never look up during the study period, as if that could prevent the inevitable. I turned back to see Catherine, who was in the same attentive position. I knew she wouldn't take her eyes off Lilly. I looked back at Lilly. Same position.

The girl next to me hissed, "Sit still. I can't concentrate."

Well neither could I. It was almost a relief when Lilly did look up and saw Catherine. Her expression was a mixture of apprehension and pleasure, a little smile was paired with anxiously raised eyebrows. A few seconds later I saw her nod and knew a meeting place and time had been arranged. Then Lilly glanced over to me with a look of, what? Resignation? Amusement? Anticipation? I couldn't say, but there was a slight shrug and I figured maybe Lilly had a better handle on things after all.

I wasted the entire study period, which meant I would have an extra hour of homework to do that evening, but there was no way I could get myself to think of plane geometry or irregular French verbs. I had a hard enough time concentrating on my last two classes, I was so intent on thinking of how I would ask Lilly about what happened with Catherine. I would meddle as much as she'd let me, and wherever I failed, I would get Mama, Papa or Yosuf to intercede. I had learned my lesson. Nothing would go sliding by anymore where Lilly was concerned. This was a battle for a human being and if the *goyim* were putting in a lot of effort, so would we.

I rushed home after school, turning down Rebecca's invitation to join her and Anne at her house to do some homework together, then fumed and fretted because Lilly didn't get home until a half-hour before supper. Mama scolded and rushed her off to change and comb her hair while I was stuck with setting the table. At supper, Papa asked the usual questions about school, especially how Lilly was fitting in, and whether she thought she'd be able to keep up and did she need any help, because if we couldn't give her enough, Yosuf had offered to spend time on Sundays. I was pretty impatient and Mama told me to stop fidgeting, I was driving her crazy.

As soon as we were alone doing the dishes, I said to Lilly, "How did your meeting with Catherine go?"

Lilly laughed. "You are very funny, Sarah. I saw you in study hall trying to protect me from the monster, Catherine. We met at the library, then walked around. I told her about the school where I had been, and she told me about herself and the other girls and Father Vaughn and how they all missed me. She wanted to know if everybody was treating me okay. She said she bet I could come live at her house if I didn't like it where I was, and she would ask her parents, if I wanted to."

I felt rage rise in me. Lilly said, "Take it easy, Saraleh. I told her I was okay, she didn't have to worry about me, I could take care of myself."

That didn't help much. Lilly was still placating Catherine.

She went on. "I told her I am not going to get involved with religion now, I am going to concentrate on getting finished with school so I can become independent. I told her I wasn't going to spend time with her or go to church or see Father Vaughn, it's too hard while I'm living with Jewish guardians."

"What did she say to that?"

"She didn't like it but what could she do? Sarah, I meant what I said. I am not going to think about religion until I finish high school, then I'll see how I feel about a lot of things. And I'm not going to bother with the other kids in school. If I want friends, I have you and Yosuf. Anything else is too complicated and hard. I am not smart enough to handle it."

I was beginning to suspect that the kind of injuries Lilly had suffered never really heal, but would keep breaking open regularly like boils or an infected incision.

It wasn't an ideal situation, but it seemed better than the first year. I had given up on the sister idea long before. Being Lilly's friend rather than her enemy was a big plus. Things were looking up.

Lilly was a determined girl. I suppose you learn to be, when you're responsible for your own survival. Whenever I saw her in school, she was alone, not part of any group or clique. She was polite and pleasant and very distant. She immediately became an 'A' student, a favorite with all her teachers. Teachers love students who make them look like whizzes without any extra effort on their part. In our freshman year, we both made ARISTA, the academic honor society, though I went to meetings and Lilly never did. We remained ARISTA throughout high school, had an amiable relationship at home, and nothing to do with each other in school. Lilly showed no interest in acquiring boyfriends or any girlfriends that I knew of. She never seemed lonely or depressed, in fact she seemed happiest when she was alone with her books on animals or her stamp collection.

Some Sundays we'd spend with Yosuf, and they were high points for all of us. Lilly would expand like a flower opening, laughing and joking, like any young girl, and Yosuf would stuff us with information, news, ideas, and stories. We gobbled it all down, nourishing ourselves on his perceptive wit.

Yosuf was too smart to let the subject of religion slide just because it looked as if things were going smoothly with Lilly. Regularly he would test the water with a feeler or a provocative statement. Usually Lilly didn't take the bait, but one Sunday afternoon a few weeks after my sixteenth birthday, there was an exchange between us that left me uneasy all over again. We were sitting in the backyard enjoying the April sunshine of an unseasonably warm day. Yosuf was talking about the Jewish definition of messiah and how the Greeks, in their translation, misinterpreted both the Hebrew word and its Judaic meaning.

"A messiah meant a chief or king, the one who was to lead the Hebrew people to freedom and the defeat of their enemies, something like Ben Gurion in Israel today. It had nothing to do with being God. As for messiah, the annointed one we Jews wait for, when he appears, we'll have peace—an end to wars, hunger, and injustice. Jews can't accept Jesus as a messiah, if only because of the state the world is in. But if the peaceable kingdom ever becomes a reality, a messiah is not God. There's good evidence Jesus never thought of himself as anything but a Jewish teacher, a rabbi. Distortions of his teachings *and* monotheism came from the Greeks who didn't understand what Jesus was preaching."

Lilly always listened to Yosuf with great respect, but she never hesitated to argue with him, and he encouraged her to. Now she said, "Just for the sake of the argument, Yosuf, what if the Gentiles *are* right? What if God really sent Jesus to be the messiah? What if by not fulfilling the prophecy of peace on earth, He is only testing our faith the way He tested Job's, and what if the Inquisition, and the pogroms and the Holocaust are all God's punishment for the Jews not accepting Jesus as His Son, and God on earth?"

Yosuf said, "Christians insist God is love, and Jesus as Christ brings love. There's nothing loving in what the Nazis and the fascists did to the Jews. There's no love in the hatred that produced the Crusades, the Inquisition and the pogroms. How can people do so much evil and claim it is God's message to the world?"

"But what if the people who died in the Inquisition and the Holocaust were the devil's representatives, and the only way they could have been stopped was in the fire, in the Holocaust? Pictures of hell show people suffering for their sins the way the Jews suffered in the Holocaust. So maybe the Jews are demons."

Yosuf's response came quickly. "I prefer the Jewish technique for taking care of demonic behavior. Live decently according to the commandments, uphold justice and let God take care of those who don't believe in Him. I believe he is more capable of doing that than any human agency on earth. Civilized countries have due process, not torture and mass murder. No, it's more convincing that the Nazis, the inquisitors, the sadists and perverts, destroying defenseless people, are doing the devil's work. They fit the description of demons better than their victims. Remember, the Nazis' goal was 'racial purity' not so-called 'love of God'."

Lilly shook her head. "But what if people won't listen, no matter how hard God tries to get them to accept the truth? If they still refuse, doesn't He have to tell them in stronger and stronger ways until they listen? The Jews have been told for two thousand years and they still won't listen . . . what is God to do?"

When Yosuf had had enough he got very quiet and soft-spoken. His words always seemed more meaningful and important that way. Now he said, "A message of hate, insanity and corruption, an abomination of everything good and holy, is a travesty of God's commandments meant to guide us all. To claim the Holocaust is God's work is to make friends with the devil and establish hell on earth. God would never surrender His human creations to the powers of darkness."

"But Yosuf, why would God let His children be tortured in a Holocaust? Isn't He stronger than the devil?"

"Lilly, we're too small to understand everything in God's plan. We can't see very far, while He sees everything. After thousands of years the Jews have their own country again, exactly where God wanted us to be. We were forced to make this gargantuan effort to regain our homeland. We could never have won against such odds if we weren't desperate. The Holocaust gave us no choice."

"Yosuf, that is a very high price to pay. It's not worth it."

"Well, as you yourself said, Lilly, if people won't listen to what God tells them, He has to shout louder and louder. Humans are very wasteful. We do most things the hard way. Because we are immature and inexperienced everything we learn is costly."

"Yosuf, just as you couldn't believe in a God who would use the Holocaust as punishment for not believing in Jesus Christ, I can't believe in a God who would let it happen because otherwise we wouldn't have the State of Israel."

Yosuf smiled admiringly. "Leahleh, are you sure you want to be a farmer? You would make a wonderful lawyer. Think about it before you make your final decision."

Lilly grabbed a fistful of Yosuf's curls and shook them playfully while he screwed up his face in pretended pain. "You are a tease, Yosuf Cardozo, but you're not getting away with it. You know you didn't answer my questions."

"Next time without fail," he said.

Yosuf left shortly after, and because the balmy late afternoon was so pleasant I stayed where I was. Lilly usually went to her room when Yosuf left, but as she sat on, my surprise then turned to discomfort, and I felt compelled to break the silence.

"As smart as Yosuf is," I said, "he can't have all the answers. Nobody can know God's ultimate plan."

Lilly was leaning back in the rickety wooden lawn chair, half-closed eyes squinting against the long rays of the setting sun broken by the roof of the house.

She glanced toward me and said almost lazily, "No, all we know is the plan people make and God is part of their plan."

"What?" I asked. "I don't understand what you mean."

"It's simple. People plan all their terrible things, then they say God wants them to do it, or they're doing it in God's name. They invent a higher power to excuse themselves."

I felt stumped and wished Yosuf were here or that I hadn't started the conversation. "You're right," I agreed, "people use God to justify the things they do. But they do good things in His Name, too."

"I suppose so," she yawned. "When they're comfortable and they don't have to work too hard to do good."

"Lilly! That's so cynical! Do you really believe that?"

She turned toward me, her eyes wide open now and hard. "How could I not believe it? I saw it all myself. I see it happening everyday. People behave decently only when they have plenty to eat and they're safe. Give a little push and they eat each other up. And there are plenty of people who enjoy hurting others. They do it for fun. They don't even have to be pushed."

I could feel desperation welling up from my chest to lodge in my throat. I grasped at the most potent argument I could think of. "And Yosuf? Do you think Yosuf's like that? Would he eat you up if he weren't comfortable?"

"Yosuf is wonderful. If I love anybody, I love Yosuf. But what he would do if he were starving, if he were being tortured, if he was threatened with whatever is his own worse nightmare . . . I don't know. You don't know either, Sarah, and neither does Yosuf. None of us knows until we're faced with it."

"But you do know there were people who endangered themselves and sacrificed their lives to help Jews when they didn't have to. Don't they count? They're people too."

She laughed and the sound was dismal. "They count. And I can count. They can be counted on one hand. They are the weird ones, the saints. We have a few now-and-then, and so what? Things stay the same, basically. We tiptoe around each other. We all hope we won't be the ones to suffer, and if what we are doing is making someone else suffer, we ignore it or say we can't do anything about it. Thank God for God's will! We *need* God for our excuses."

It was getting worse and worse. "How can you live like that!" I blurted, "If the world is a jungle and people worse than animals . . . . "

"Animals are far above people," she interrupted. "If we were like animals the world would be a wonderful place . . . . "

"Okay," I amended, "if people really are monsters, if you see them like that, how can you stand it?"

There was a sudden silence and as it stretched out I began to wonder if I had asked the wrong question. The sun had gone down behind the roof and I felt chilled in my thin blouse.

Lilly sighed deeply. It sounded as if it came up from her toes. "How can I go on? I ask that question, too." Her voice had dropped to almost a whisper. She was really talking to herself. "At least once a day, I ask myself why I go on. And there are many days when I do not have a good answer. There is really no reason. It is all so senseless . . . . "

I was frightened. It had been a long time since I had heard Lilly talk in these terms and never so pointedly. "Ah, Lilly," I begged, "look around you. The earth is a beautiful place. So many people love you and *care* about you. There's so much to enjoy. Please, please, enjoy what there is. Stop turning to look back. Don't let the past poison everything. Take a chance. Open up and live to enjoy yourself."

"You make it sound so easy, Saraleh, but I think it would be easier to, to cut off my right arm. No, I don't know how to do what you say, but don't worry, I have a way. I can manage."

"What way? Manage what?"

She stared at something over my shoulder. I looked around and saw the back porch behind me now in deep shadow, nothing else. I turned back and caught a look on her face I couldn't identify, but now I could no longer see her clearly.

"When things get too bad, I have a way. I have the key." Her voice was low but strong.

"The key? The key to what, Lilly?"

Another sigh. She was only a vague outline in the dusk. "Never mind, Sarah, It doesn't matter. It's late, I'm going in."

Just then Mama turned on the kitchen light and it spilled through the window, making a path on the ground. I got up too and followed Lilly into the house. I told myself Lilly was searching, trying to make sense of things like the Holocaust, when they were impossible to render sensible because they were based on insane premises.

Aside from those leisurely Sunday visits, we were all so busy. The State of Israel survived in the face of all contrary expectations, and established itself against apparently insurmountable odds. To me it was confirmation of Yosuf's premise that this was part of God's larger plan to re-establish Israel for the Jewish people. In my senior year of high school, when I was seventeen, I joined the Zionist Youth Organization. It was time to throw my efforts into Zionist work.

Lilly was sixteen, engrossed in school, planning to go ahead with agricultural studies. I would go to college, but was uncertain of what I wanted for a lifetime career. During this last high school year I hoped to be struck by a blinding light which would illuminate the right path for me.

CHAPTER TEN

THE BLOW THAT ACTUALLY STRUCK WAS SO PROFOUNDLY DEVAS-
tating that the entire family and I were in a state of immobilizing
shock for two days. Passover had come and gone, it was the Easter
week, and the whole school system was closed down. One afternoon while Papa was at work and Mama and I were out shopping,
Lilly packed a bag with a minimum of clothes and all her treasures
and personal papers and moved into Catherine's house.

I was hanging up my jacket when Mama found the note in an
envelope on the hall table. As she read it, she turned white and
her knees buckled. I grabbed her and got her into a chair. I
couldn't imagine what had happened; she had been fine the
moment before. I thought she was suffering a heart attack and
tried to remember what to do in such a case.

"Mama, Mama," I yelled as if she were deaf, "what is it? Are
you having an attack? Should I call Doctor Shapiro?"

She was gasping and shaking her head. I got more and more
frightened. "Oh God," I whimpered. "Tell me what to do,
Mama."

"Glass of water," she gasped.

I ran to the kitchen, shaking so hard I couldn't fill a glass. I
ran back with a little water at the bottom of the glass. Mama was
sitting with her head in her hand, but her color was coming back.

I knelt by her side and held the glass for her. "Here, Mama, a little water."

She wet her lips and leaned back with a huge sigh of sorrow and defeat.

"Mama, tell me what happened so I can help."

She indicated the scrap of paper on the floor near her feet and leaned back and closed her eyes while the tears began to course down her face. Still crouching, I picked up the paper and read the contents three times before the full import penetrated.

There was no salutation. It began: "I hope you believe me that this is very hard for me to write. I have finally decided to convert to Catholicism and so I might as well do it now as later. It is not right for me to stay in your house once I have made up my mind, so Catherine has invited me to stay with her family and I am going there today. I don't ask you to understand but please don't hate me too much. I know you can make me come back because I am a minor but please, *please*, don't force me to. I have struggled and struggled for years with this problem. I cannot see any other way to solve it. Please don't try to see me. I know I am hurting you and don't want to hurt you any more. I thank you very sincerely and deeply for all you have done for me. I wish you the best of luck. Sincerely, Lilly Janislowicz."

By now I was sitting on the floor next to Mama's chair, my legs stretched straight out in front of me, my head leaning against her thigh. I felt quite numb and leaden.

I was only vaguely conscious of Mama sobbing softly above me; my mind was empty. Just one word kept echoing from somewhere, *how . . . how . . . how . . .* and finally the thought formed. *How could you do it, Lilly?* It became a litany, running through my head until it was a senseless rhyme which I clung to. It was a talisman. If I held on to it nothing bad would happen. I don't know how long we sat there, but Mama was the first to move.

I felt her hand on my head, heavily, as though she needed to assure herself I was solid. "Saraleh, Saraleh," she was hoarse and barely audible, "come, get up."

I didn't want to sit where I was, but I wanted less to get up. I had to straighten something out, but what it was kept eluding me, and anyway I had to keep repeating the words in my head to fend off some kind of non-specific disaster. Mama was talking again, interfering with what I had to do. I wished she'd shut up and leave me alone. She slapped me resoundingly on each cheek, leaving me gasping the way I used to when I'd dive into the lake after a good hard rain.

I heard her then. "Saraleh, get up off the floor. I will not let you get sick over this!"

I stumbled to my feet and laid my head on her shoulder. She wrapped her arms around me and held me to her, hard. I wept until I soaked right through her dress. When I stopped, she took me to the bathroom, bathed and dried my face, and led me to the kitchen where she brewed some strong tea for both of us. We sat across from each other at the kitchen table sipping tea. My eyes kept straying to the wet spot on her shoulder, thinking how uncomfortable it must be.

"Mama, don't you want to change your dress?"

She smiled and shook her head. "Don't worry about the dress, Sarah. I'll change soon. As soon as I'm sure you're feeling better."

"I'm okay," I said. "It's just that the whole thing is so strange, I can't figure it out."

"It's a shock, but we'll live through it, the way we live through a lot of things."

"I can't understand why she did it," I went on, "and the harder I try the less sense it makes. Mama, why did she do it, do you know?"

Mama shook her head. "I know what she said, what she told us, but how can I understand? She may not really understand either. Some things we have to learn to accept, because they are the way they are and we can't change them."

"Aren't we going to do *anything*? Are we just going to let her go, just like that?"

"I don't know, Sarah. I'm beginning to think we've done all we can. When Papa comes home, we'll talk about it and probably later with the whole family. We are legally responsible for her. I think we'll have to see a lawyer about our liability if anything happens to her or because of her . . . . Saraleh, I don't want you to make yourself sick over this."

"You scared me too, Mama. I thought you were having a heart attack."

Mama's eyes grew bright with tears and she said angrily, "Lilly has taken enough from us. She's a casualty of Hitler's war; that's enough. If we have to, we'll let her go—push her out of our hearts and forget about her."

The tea was good. I was beginning to grow drowsy and then was overcome by a wave of fatigue so that I could hardly hold my head up. Mama coaxed me to my feet, and took me upstairs. She helped me off with my shoes and dress and tucked me into bed in my slip and underwear. When I woke up the room was dark. My alarm clock read twenty-to-eight, and I couldn't tell if it was the same night or if I had slept through an entire day. I was rested and hungry but lacerated inside. The ache in my heart radiated up to my throat and through my chest to my stomach.

I got up, dressed and went downstairs to the sound of voices coming from the living room. Papa, Uncle Chaim, Uncle Shmuel, and Yosuf were there.

They greeted me calmly and Papa said, "Go into the kitchen, Sarah, and get some supper. Mama and your aunts are there."

The kitchen light seemed too bright. I sat down blinking, and Mama put a prepared platter in front of me. It was warm from the oven, and while I concentrated on filling my stomach, the women talked. I tuned in and out. It wasn't important, they kept saying the same things over and over again in different ways. When would we stop talking about Lilly, I wondered? My whole life was filled with her so I didn't have a life of my own anymore. It wasn't fair. She took up so much space and time and thought and energy. I wanted to wipe out every trace of her. I wanted not to have any memory at all.

I was eating faster and faster; Mama broke into my thoughts. "Sarah, there's plenty of time. Don't eat so fast, you'll make yourself sick."

"I'm full. I don't want any more." I pushed away the plate.

Mama took it to the sink and we went into the living room to join the men. Tea was poured. Cake was passed around. No thinking could be done without the sustenance of tea and cake.

Uncle Chaim said, "There's no question, you must consult a lawyer. If for no other reason, you are trustees of Lilly's reparations money."

"Yes, yes," Papa said, "maybe we will, but that's later on. We are still responsible, no matter what Lilly wants us to do. We must see this family she's living with. Who are they? Is she safe with them? That priest who wants to convert her, he knows he's dealing with a minor. To Lilly it's a simple matter of taking a suitcase out of the house and leaving a note. If only it were so easy!"

Auntie Chaya said, "Who knows? Maybe she should have been left in the orphanage?"

Uncle Shmuel said, "Oh, it's easy to say 'should' now. Who could know the kind of problems there would be? What are we—God—that we can see the future?"

Uncle Chaim said, "What is the point of talking 'should have'? What's done is done. The question is, what to do now?"

Yosuf asked, "Will the family Lilly is staying with talk to any of us? Is it a good idea for us to go see them? Maybe a lawyer should contact them. Taking Lilly without speaking to her guardians is irresponsible."

Mama said, "I'm worried about her. Will they take good care of her? Who are these people? They're only strangers. Are they going to love her and be interested the way we are?"

"Of course not," Auntie Aviva said. "If they hate Jews, how can they love Lilly? She's Jewish."

"But the daughter, what's her name . . . ?" Uncle Shmuel asked, looking at me.

"Catherine."

"Yeah, Catherine, she's the one who influenced Lilly . . . . "

"But she's only a child," Auntie Chaya interrupted. "Who knows if the parents want Lilly just because the daughter invites. We have to talk to them *and* Lilly."

"Lilly doesn't want to talk to us," I said.

"So Lilly doesn't want. Since when is a child left to make such big decisions," Auntie Aviva said.

"Lilly is sixteen. How can we make her talk to us if she doesn't want to?"

Papa said, "Aviva is right. I am not going to leave it the way it is because Lilly wants us to. She is a child. My sister's child, and now my child. I am responsible. I cannot turn my back no matter what."

"At least we should make sure she's safe," Mama said. "I couldn't rest easy if I didn't know she'll be all right."

Uncle Chaim said, "Maybe Yosuf could talk to her. She likes him."

"Yosuf talked to her till he was blue in the face, Uncle Chaim," I said. "She still ran away."

The grownups all turned to look at Yosuf. He gave his characteristic shrug. "I think Sarah is right, but I'm willing to keep trying."

The discussion went on for another several hours, past eleven o'clock at night. Every opinion was expressed time and again and examined from every conceivable angle. A sticky point was not allowed to slip by, but was worried painstakingly until its rough edges got smoothed down or it was discarded as inoperable or inapplicable. We knew all possibilities had been exhausted not by how many hours had passed, but by the silence that finally fell in the room.

We didn't come up with any brilliant solutions, but it was decided to have the rabbi see Father Vaughn again and get an update on his position now that Lilly had taken things into her own hands. The family lawyer, who was my cousin Murray's friend, would contact Catherine's family and ask them to come into his office for a meeting. Yosuf was going to try to talk to Lilly, and depending on what the lawyer said, Papa would talk to Catherine's parents.

In a few days I got back on an even keel. I was once more an only child, alone in the house. It was a little harder than the first separation because this time Lilly had been in the room next to mine since she'd returned from boarding school almost three years before, but I would get over it. When I caught myself thinking of what I would say to or share with Lilly, I would remind myself that I would probably never see or talk to her again. It wasn't so bad. If I could make myself think of her as being dead, it would be even better.

I took on a lot of extra activities. I became secretary-treasurer of my Zionist club, did some projects in my English, History, and French classes for extra credit, including translating French poetry into English, and spent hours with my class advisor going over college brochures and career opportunities. She warned me that I was very late getting my applications for colleges filed and even my high scholastic ratings wouldn't hold doors open for me indefinitely. But I couldn't decide and the incident with Lilly didn't help me focus.

I turned to Yosuf for the nth time. Even forbearing Yosuf was losing patience with me. He suggested an unheard of thing for those days—that I not go directly into college but take a year to find my feet. It sounded good if only because I could drift along for a while.

My advisor objected. She thought momentum was all important in education. Once on the treadmill, you didn't step off until you wanted it stopped for good. Mama and Papa had their hands full with Lilly and were glad to leave me to my own devices.

I started to teach myself shorthand in the evenings and joined the high school typing club where I could use the big office Remingtons with the blacked-out keys. I rather liked being a novice, typing ffffff, rrrrrr, jjjjjj, uuuuuu, while everybody else rattled away at forty and fifty words a minute. Anne and Rebecca were willing teachers and they both offered me the use of their portable typewriters to practice on.

One week after the first high command meeting about Lilly, there was a second gathering. This time my older cousins Dorothy, Irving, and Murray were present. It might have been Passover if the children had been there and the faces a little more cheerful.

Papa reported. "The rabbi saw the priest, Vaughn, who said Lilly was very mature for her age and knew her own mind, so he is instructing her for conversion. Lilly will go through the conversion ceremony in June and become a full-fledged Catholic or whatever they are called when they're converted. Vaughn wants Lilly's money turned over to the church or the people she's living with to administer for her. The rabbi told him it wasn't up to him, but he would advise Lilly's guardians to maintain control of her resources until she reached her majority. The rabbi didn't give any details but I got the idea there was some unpleasantness after that. So the priest is a dead-end, he won't help us."

There were plenty of murmurs and remarks verifying that no one expected anything from a priest.

Yosuf reported next. "I called the Czarnowski's house and asked to talk to Lilly. I guess it was Catherine who answered the phone. She wanted to know who I was and when I told her she said Lilly didn't want to talk to me and to leave her alone. I went to the high school after that, got Lilly's schedule from the office, and caught her in the gym after one of her classes. She wouldn't talk to me. Wouldn't even look at me. She asked me to leave her alone and to tell the family to leave her alone."

Then Murray spoke. "Jonathan (the lawyer) saw the Czarnowski's in his office. They're a couple in their late forties. They have five of their own children and claim they took Lilly in because they felt sorry for the girl being in a bad home. He asked what made them think Lilly's home was bad. They hemmed and hawed for a while and finally admitted all they knew was she was living with Jews and didn't want to. They got this information from their oldest daughter, Catherine, Lilly's friend. They said it was a burden for them to be keeping Lilly without some compensation and they thought they'd be paid for boarding her. Jonathan told them he was advising his clients, Lilly's aunt and uncle, to maintain complete control over her finances until she reached her majority. The Czarnowskis asked if he thought it was fair for them to assume the burden for a girl who wasn't even their own. He said his opinion on fairness was irrelevant, but he did wonder if they wouldn't be liable for some legal action, harboring a minor without the permission of her legal guardians. They didn't look too happy about that, but they didn't seem very happy to begin with. Their priest told them not to talk with Uncle Mikhel unless Lilly's money was turned over to them or the church, to administer for her."

Listening to all this I got a dramatic image of a net tightening around Lilly. What if she were forced to come back to us because she didn't have the money to live where she wanted? Would it be better? I didn't want her in my life again. I didn't think I could stand the seesawing, followed by the shocks to my system of confrontations and goodbye-letters.

I heard myself speaking. "I've been very sorry for Lilly for too many years. I don't want her to be where she isn't happy. Why don't we give her enough money to live where she wants to? She can't live without money. So what if we're responsible for her? We can't be responsible if she won't let us be."

There was silence after my pronouncement until Mama said, "Maybe Sarah's right. My mother always said, you can lead a horse to water but you can't make him drink. Let's keep Lilly's money in trust for her, but we could give her an allowance to live on."

Auntie Aviva said, "How can we let a child make these decisions? She doesn't know what she's doing. She should be made to come home."

I was beginning to think Auntie Aviva wasn't too bright. Unless we chained her, how were we going to make Lilly come home? And even if we made her, how could we keep her if she was determined to run away?

Everybody ignored Auntie. Papa said, "I think we should give up. I say the best thing is to give Lilly an allowance. When she's twenty-one she can have all her money."

The rest of the evening was devoted to small talk, thank God! I told Yosuf what was happening with my college plans and that I was all but decided to put them on hold for a year. I had advanced in my typing to y's, z's, q's and p's and showed him how strong my pinkies were getting.

I had taken to staying late in the high school library after my classes. It was quiet and peaceful and I was able to concentrate. Since Lilly left home I found myself restless in the house, jumping up from the desk in my room dozens of times to go to the bathroom, or for a drink of water, or to look out the window. A couple of times I found myself at the door of Lilly's room staring at her things, which were just as she'd left them. It was better if I didn't get home too soon before dinner. Mama understood and encouraged me to stay out of the house.

One evening I was in the library researching philosophical ideas in America, when someone slipped into the seat next to me. The person leaned toward me and I was about to look up angrily when I heard Lilly's voice whisper, "Sarah, can I talk to you?"

My heart plummeted and did a quick jig all around my ribs. It was a great way to speed up my circulation. I realized I honestly didn't want to see her. Knowing Lilly was too painful and I had talked myself into the idea that it was a phase of my life I had finished. I turned toward her slowly.

She looked the same, slightly thinner, slightly worried. I don't know what I expected.

"What do you want?" I whispered back.

"Can we go outside?" she asked. "We can't talk in here."

I don't think I've ever done anything more unwillingly as I piled my books together, placed a marker in the book I was using, and finally took my handbag and jacket, leaving everything else for my return. She waited patiently until I stood up, then followed me out of the library. The hallways were practically empty, just a few kids like Lilly and me hanging around talking.

I stopped and faced her once we'd gotten away from the doorway. "Well?" I moved back so I didn't have to look up at her. She was a couple of inches taller than I.

"Can we go outside and walk around?"

"I don't think so," I said. "I have a lot of work to do and want to get back to it as soon as I can."

Lilly said, "You told me once, you wouldn't hate me if I became a Christian."

"I don't hate you." Then I amended, "Maybe I do hate you. It's easy not to hate someone in theory. It's harder when you're faced with a real case. But I don't think my problem is that I hate you."

"Well, why won't you come out and talk to me?"

"Because it's not convenient for me now. Does everything have to be at your convenience, Lilly? The note you left that almost gave my mother a heart attack and sent me into a state of shock said you didn't want us to try to reach you or talk to you. Yosuf begged you to talk to him and you told him to leave you alone. But when you want to change your mind, that's okay? How long are you going to play the poor little orphan with everybody kowtowing to you? So tell me what you want and I'll get back to my work."

"The people I'm living with need money for my board."

"Well, you'll be getting an allowance to live on soon. You can give it to them."

"I did get my first check already."

"So what's the problem?"

"They want to be trustees for my reparations money."

I stared at her with contempt for selling herself to buy acceptance from the Gentiles. How could I feel sorry for her any more?

"Do you really want them to get their hands on all your money, Lilly? Can you trust them? Do they care about you, or only what they can get out of you? My parents are giving you more than enough of your money to live on. Should they turn over everything you have for the future to strangers? From what I've heard they aren't very nice. Your money can help buy your farm; are you willing to let that go too?"

"I know I can't make Mama and Papa give me my money . . . ."

I interrupted. "Do me the courtesy of not referring to my mother and father that way."

She flushed and went on. "I know I can't make them, and I do appreciate their not forcing me to come back, but can't you talk to them, Sarah, about the money?"

"Do you like those people that much? Are you that happy living with them?"

"That's all beside the point. It has nothing to do with Catherine or her family."

"I don't get it. Maybe if I can understand, I can help you."

"Can you understand that I want to be like everyone else?" She said it wearily as if she had gone over it innumerable times in her mind and came up each time with the same answer. "In order to do it I need my money."

"Okay," I said, "I heard you. I'll tell my mother and father about what you said."

I started back toward the library door.

She put her hand on my arm. "Wait, will you help me?"

I turned around to her again. "Help you? You're asking me to help you ruin your life . . . please don't ask me to do that." Then I went into the library.

It was the end of my studying. I looked at the same paragraph in the book for an hour, reading and re-reading it, seeing Lilly's face and hearing her voice asking me to help impoverish her. I reviewed the conversation dozens of times.

At last the library lights blinked the signal for closing. I returned the books to the stacks, gathered my things together and left, feeling sorry for myself and vaguely angry, as I walked slowly home. My encounter with Lilly had been a form of punishment.

I told Mama and Papa what had happened and they increased Lilly's allowance by forty dollars a month, which was a lot of money in those days. I put Lilly out of my mind. I never even unconsciously looked for her in the hallways at school. The days got longer and warmer. I filled my days and evenings with work and slept dreamlessly until the week before graduation.

It was an ordinary day. I did nothing unusual; in fact, it was more pleasant than most days because my advisor told me she'd arranged to have me employed in the school library over the summer if I wanted the job. I was mildly excited. I wasn't even out of school and I already had work.

But that night I had my nightmare. As I walked into it, part of me was aware I was dreaming, but even knowing the outcome I went through each step. When Lilly appeared at the window, clawing at the glass, I reached out to her as always and the figure behind her, instead of pulling her out of sight, wrapped long bony fingers around her throat. I saw her eyes bulge, her mouth open wide.

I was choking on my screams when Mama woke me. She rocked me in her arms like a baby.

All the next day I felt exhausted and didn't go to *shul.* In the afternoon I sat in the yard with a book in my lap not reading, just letting the sun warm the top of my head, when I heard the phone ring. A couple of minutes later, Mama came out and said, "Sarah, it's someone who wants to talk to you. I don't know who it is, she won't tell me her name."

A phone call was unusual enough, but who would call and refuse to give a name? Maybe it has to do with the library job, I guessed.

I picked up the receiver. "Hello, this is Sarah."

There was no reply although the line was open. "Hello, this is Sarah. Is anyone there?"

"Sarah?"

"Yes."

"This is . . . Catherine."

Oh, NO! I thought, what now? "What do you want?"

"Sarah . . . ?"

"For heaven sake," I cried, "what is it you want? Haven't you done enough harm?"

Her voice was low but she sounded hysterical. I couldn't understand what she was saying. "If you don't tell me what you want I'm hanging up."

"Lilly's dead," came through clearly.

I could swear she'd said, "Lilly's dead."

"What!!!?" I knew she was trying to drive me crazy.

Her voice came over the line clearly now and expressionless.

"Lilly's dead. We found her a few hours ago. She put her head in the gas oven. It must have been early this morning, we've been out all day."

The voice was fading away. The telephone was heavy in my hand, I couldn't hold it anymore, and, peculiarly, the room tilted and swayed around me.

I opened my eyes and sighed. I was lying on the sofa, looking up at the living room ceiling. Something was awful. Something was horribly wrong.

"Mama," I shrieked, "Mama, I had my dream again!"

"I'm here, Saraleh," she said. I sat up.

She was sitting on the footstool next to me, holding the wet cloth she'd been bathing my face with. I hardly recognized her, she looked so old.

"It's true?" I whispered. She nodded.

"Mama," I bawled. "Mama, Mama, oh Mama!"

I don't really remember much about the next few days. Later, I found out we had been called to take the body. The church wouldn't bury Lilly because she had committed suicide. She was buried the next day according to Jewish law in my parents' cemetery in the section set aside for those who took their own lives, even though she had been converted to Catholicism the week before. Conversion, I learned, is not recognized in traditional Jewish law. Once a Jew, always a Jew.

All Lilly's belongings had been collected and put into the suitcase she'd taken when she left our house. It was returned to us with the body.

I didn't attend my graduation and I didn't take the library job. In fact that summer I didn't do much of anything but sit around staring intently at nothing. When Anne and Rebecca came around I didn't know what to say to them. I could hardly hear what they said to me. My parents asked me if I wanted to go to the country and I could tell them honestly I didn't care. We went but stayed only two weeks. It didn't matter whether I sat on the porch of the cabin or the porch at home.

It was Yosuf who brought me around. He came over the day after we got back from Moskowitz's and sat down next to me on the porch.

"That's enough now, Saraleh," he said.

I smiled. "Hello, Yosuf."

He took my hand and squeezed hard. I looked at him.

"Listen to me, Sarah." He was talking as though I were deaf. "That is enough now, Sarah. Lilly is dead. She's been dead for almost two months, and you are going to start doing everything again. You are going to walk, and talk, and listen, and hear everything and everyone. You are going to come to the table and eat like a person and you will start coming to *shul* again and seeing your friends again. Do you understand?"

"But Yosuf," I said, "I don't want to."

"That doesn't matter. We all do things we don't want to. There is no argument here. This is not up for negotiation."

He was literally shouting in my face with his nose inches from mine. "You will do what I tell you because you must, Sarah, and you will start now, this minute!"

He yanked at my hand and pulled me to my feet and into the house. He introduced me to my mother and father, who looked suddenly small and old and gray. We sat down at the table and Mama served lunch. It was a very nice lunch, a tuna fish salad plate, and I was very hungry. I ate a lot, but I was the only one. My mother kept wiping her eyes with a handkerchief; my father kept rubbing his chin with the palm of his hand the way he always did when he was very tired. Yosuf sat looking at me with his eyes very bright behind his glasses.

I went to the librarian the next day and asked if she still needed help. She said she could use me part-time, if I'd start right away. I called home and told Mama about my job and stayed the rest of the day. I was very tired when I came home, ate an enormous supper, and went right to bed and must have slept without turning over once.

A few days later, Mama told me Catherine had been begging to see me. Mama admitted she hadn't wanted to tell me but was afraid Catherine would get to me without any warning and do more harm than if I arranged to see her myself.

"You don't have to," Mama said. "If you think it will upset you, it's better if you don't."

I shook my head. "I'm not afraid of her, Mama. What can she do or say that's any worse than what's happened? Maybe Lilly left a message for me, who knows?"

Mama looked so worried, I decided to see Catherine right away for the sake of Mama's peace of mind. I called her and we arranged to meet outside the library when I finished work the next day. She was waiting for me when I came out. My resentment was so intense I just glanced at her, but I couldn't help noticing that her normally colorless skin was so pale she looked transparent. We walked to the playground and sat on a bench where an old man sat sleeping on one end.

Since Lilly's death, I had become very patient. I could sit quietly for hours at a time, waiting for something to happen or for nothing at all. I sat next to Catherine, saying nothing.

"Sarah?"

I cocked my head in her direction.

"One of the reasons Lillian left your house was because of a boy."

I turned to her in surprise. She nodded, affirming what she'd said.

"He's in our parish. Lilly met him in church before she went away to that school. Jamie was sixteen then. I told him to leave her alone, but he said he was gonna do her a favor and save her soul. She had a crush on him but I figured it'd be okay once she converted."

I couldn't bear to look at her and turned away.

"When Lillian decided she couldn't stay with you any more because she was gonna convert, I didn't know what to do. My family didn't really want her. I had to beg them to let her stay with us just for a little while. It got worse after they went to see your lawyer. They said Lillian wasn't anything but trouble. Then after she converted, Jamie told her he didn't want to see her any more."

I was caught up in the story. "Why not?" I asked before I could stop myself.

"Lillian wouldn't tell me, so I got ahold of Jamie and asked him. He said he did his good deed for the day—she wouldn't go to hell now, but he wasn't gonna go around with a Jew."

Catherine's voice dropped and began to shake. "He said that anyway she was a creep. I told him he was disgusting to treat her like that and all he did was shrug, like it didn't matter to him at all. I think he tried to take advantage of her and when she wouldn't he dropped her."

"Poor Lilly," I murmured.

Catherine paused for a long moment and I turned to look at her. Her profile was etched against a background of children's swings and sliding ponds. She was looking down at her lap where her hands were busy twisting a handkerchief into a knot. I had never seen her so close or so clearly. She looked very young and vulnerable. Her fine-grained skin showed purplish smudges under the eyes, like bruises. I was surprised to see that her nose was small and neat and that her eyes were hazel, almost brown, and liquid with tears. In my mind they had always been a hard, icy, blue.

When she began talking again her voice was steady. "Things got worse and worse after that. Lillian stopped talking and she hardly ate anything. My father kept making remarks in front of her about 'being in the presence of death warmed over.' I spoke to Father Vaughn about getting her into the novitiate, but he said she was a minor and he couldn't do it without her legal guardians' permission. I really think she wanted to go back to you, but she was ashamed to ask. I thought that once she was a Catholic her problems would be solved. I found out it's much harder than that. She started talking about how the best thing would be if she were dead and I just told her to stop talking crazy, I never thought she'd ... she'd really ... do anything, y'know? She admired you, y'know? When she first came she talked about you a lot, but then she stopped talking about anything, y'know? I feel terrible about it. I didn't think anything like this would happen."

I glanced at Catherine. Tears were sliding down her cheeks although she was talking in a perfectly normal voice.

"Neither did I," I said. "It must've been awful, when you ... when you found her . . . . " My voice thickened and I could only whisper, "Did *you* find her, Catherine?"

She nodded. "My mother and I . . . . Y'see, we went out early to take care of shopping and other things for the kids. On nice Saturdays, like it was that day, we usually all go out in the morning.

The kids went to the beach." There was a long pause. "I felt something was funny right away when we came up the walk, because all the windows were closed. It was such a warm day. But when we opened the door and smelled the gas . . . . " She stopped and struggled for composure. Her eyelids were red and the tears were spilling over. She scrubbed her cheeks with the rope of a handkerchief as if she were attacking an enemy.

"I ran to the kitchen without thinking. My mother was screaming not to go, and opening the windows as fast as she could. When I saw Lilly, I thought she was looking for something in the oven. She was on her knees and her head was sidewise, inside, with the door open." Catherine broke down and sobbed, not trying any more to stem the tide of tears.

My own eyes were flooded and Catherine and the surroundings became an underwater scene, but I couldn't stop myself—I had to know. "What happened then, Catherine?"

She plunged on, letting her voice quaver and crack as it would. "My mother ran in and turned off the gas, opened the back door and the windows, and tried to pull me away from Lilly. Y'see, she was getting . . . she was stiff, y'know, and I was trying to pull her out."

My heart broke right then. "Oh Catherine, Catherine, how awful . . . how awful!"

We were both crying openly now, uncaring about where we were or what we looked like.

"When I got her out," Catherine wept, "her face was so gray . . . then I knew she was dead. I felt so bad—so—*bad*." Her voice rose a hysterical notch. "It was my fault she did it. I thought I was so smart, that I could take care of her and make her life right . . . I *told* her I could."

"Oh Catherine, it was too much for any one person. You didn't know . . . . "

"I was wrong about you too. I was wrong to tell Lilly the things I did about you. I know that now, but I wish I knew it sooner . . . before she . . . . " Catherine's voice trailed off.

We sat for a long time in silence. The tears dried on my cheeks, leaving my face feeling stiff and swollen. I was in a state of mild wonderment over Catherine's revelations about herself. She was a human being like me, full of pain and grief and regret. I had always seen her as *the* enemy; now I was beginning to understand why Lilly had been drawn to her. We three might have been sisters if it weren't for the artificial barriers built by the same perversions that had created the Holocaust.

Catherine was calm when she spoke again. "I even thought of telling you, y'know? But Lilly told me if I did she'd never have anything to do with me again . . . . Anyway, now that she's gone, I wanted to get this off my chest, because I haven't been sleeping too well since it happened. I wanted to tell somebody that I'm sorry, y'know, so thanks for letting me talk to you."

I saw a tear drop off the end of Catherine's chin. She wiped her face with the back of a hand.

An incredible idea began dawning as I looked at Catherine's profile. My impulse to share it was irresistible. "Catherine, you and Lilly and I, we're all of us Holocaust victims," I blurted.

She turned toward me, her forehead puckered in a perplexed little pleat between her eyebrows. "What?"

"Yes, don't you see?" I was excited by the idea, it seemed to explain so much. "Lilly's parents were consumed by it, Lilly went through it, and you and I were touched by the fire. And you know what? None of us who lived through it will ever be the same."

Once it was out it didn't sound as important as when it was in my mind, but Catherine nodded her head as if she understood. I stood up. "Thanks for telling me about this, Catherine. I wish you luck."

I walked away without looking back, thinking of Lilly with a sort of soft melancholy made up of missed opportunities, failed communication, being in the wrong place at the wrong time, fate, predestination, the dream I had the night before Lilly died. If only I were smart enough I could fit the pieces together like a puzzle. With a clear and whole picture in front of me everything would make sense. But now it kept slipping away like a forgotten name at the tip of my tongue.

When I got home, I told Mama and Papa about what Catherine had said and how she had cried. I told them I wanted to look over Lilly's things after supper. When we finished eating, Mama sent me away from the table, saying there were just a few dishes, she would do them. I went up to Lilly's room, closed the door behind me and leaned back, drawing deep breaths until my heart stopped pounding.

The room was very neat; the bed with its ruffled spread was smooth and unwrinkled. I went to the closet. A few things hung on the hangers, a couple of blouses, a skirt and jacket. Mama must have given away the other things. I wondered why she left what she did.

I looked at the shelf over the bookcase. There were a few porcelain figurines—a cat, a horse, an owl, a glass vase with a fake rose. The bookcase held Lilly's books of animals and pamphlets from the Department of Agriculture on dairy farming and commercial fruit-growing.

I walked to the bureau. The top drawer stuck a little. A stocking had gotten caught in the corner. I freed it and turned to the several photo albums stacked neatly on top of one another on the right hand side of the drawer. I lifted them out and sat in the chair with them in my lap.

I sat for a long time, cuddling the albums, stroking the smooth leather cover of the top one. It was the one Lilly had said belonged to her parents. It was very old, the leather soft as flesh, the corners frayed. The album under that was new, the one I had given her three years before. The third one was newer still. I had never seen it. I started with the last one first.

There were pictures of Lilly with Catherine and other children I didn't know. I guessed they were Catherine's brothers and sisters. There were pictures of adults I didn't know. When Catherine appeared in a picture with them, I supposed they were her mother and father. I looked at them closely, curious to know what these people were like. I saw a broad, dumpy woman with a wide face, wide cheek bones and wide-set eyes. Her fair hair was straight, parted in the middle and combed back so severely, her eyes seemed to be pulled upward at the corners. There was a vague resemblance to Catherine.

The man was about half a head taller than the woman, had coat-hanger shoulders and bony wrists hanging out of his jacket sleeves. He was squinting into the sun with a frown and his lips were pursed. He looked mean to me. I turned the page.

There was a man in priest's clothes; Father Vaughn? There
were several group pictures of nuns. I thumbed quickly through
the rest of the album and carefully set it next to me on the floor.

I opened the album I had given Lilly. It was filled entirely with
pictures from the upstate school. I remembered some of the ones
she had shown me and some of the names she'd mentioned.
Occasionally there was a date written on the black paper in white
ink.

Finally I reached the album that would hold the answer to all
my questions. There was no need to rush; I could linger indefinitely, or not go any further. Did I want to know more? Was it
better to accept what had happened without trying to understand
any better than I did? I hesitated, but not for long.

The first picture in the album almost made me laugh, it was so
familiar. The sepia print wedding picture. A woman looking very
much like Lilly, but at least ten years older, a tall woman, almost
the same height as her groom. Blond, marcelled waves on either
side of a rather heavily handsome face, a headband of flower buds
with a shoulder length veil attached. The gown was satin, shape-
less, and came just below the knee in a scalloped lace edge. She
had her hand tucked in her husband's elbow.

He wore a morning suit and a high collar with points that came
up under his chin, with a striped cravat. A good-looking man with
almost delicate features, large eyes that drooped at the corners, a
dashing large mustache whose corners drooped in line with the
eyes, a round chin.

The facing page must have been honeymoon pictures. They
were snapshots, faded and spotted, showing the couple in front
of an official looking building, leaning against a motor car, standing under a tree. They were in travel clothes, the woman in a
cloche hat, waistless suit, shoes with pointed toes. The man in
knickers, ribbed knee socks, black and white spectator shoes. He
wore his cap at a jaunty angle.

There was one large picture on the next page, a naked baby,
lying on its belly on a bearskin rug. The infant, perhaps six
months, was supporting itself on it's fat little arms looking into the
camera's eye with a happy smile. Like all babies, everything was
curves. It had a few curls in the middle of its head. I couldn't see

Lilly anywhere in this picture. It could have been any baby—the prototype baby of that day, lying naked on a bearskin rug.

The facing page held several snapshots of the baby clothed, in bonnets and lace dresses, sitting in a chair, in a carriage under a tree. The next page had snapshots of a toddler hanging on to the mother's skirt, being held by an obviously proud father, and then between mother and father. The child's face was hard to see. She squinted in the sun. The hair was a halo of fair curls. She wore a little military style coat with a double row of buttons. The leggings matched the coat.

The next pictures were of a girl of ten, Lilly, almost as I had seen her the first time. She was in what was obviously a new outfit—coat, purse, gloves, socks, and patent leather shoes. She looked into the camera stoically. There wasn't a hint of a smile, or of posing for the picture.

The last picture was a postcard scene of the Brussels City Hall which stood away from the page. It invited me to ease it out of its mounts to see if there was any information on the back. Held underneath with a bit of cellophane tape was a sheet of paper, carefully folded to fit the size and shape of the postcard. Gingerly, I picked off the tape, and opened the paper. It was an identification certificate in French, for one Lillian LeClerc, an orphan, parents unknown, left as a foundling with the Sisters of Saint Anne Orphanage in La Hulpe. Approximate birthdate, June 5, 1934, presumed place of birth, Brussels. There were some official seals and signatures, and that was all.

Reading the document I began to wonder about Lilly's real identity, and had to remind myself that at five she would remember her mother and father, that the LeClerc's knew who she was and kept track of her through the German occupation, and that other documents proved she was actually Lilly Janislowicz. The fact that I was able to doubt even for a moment pointed up how difficult it must have been for Lilly to accept her heritage, especially when she had other options open to her.

I slipped postcard and document into the album and turned the page. There were a few photographs of people with children whom I recognized from our own family portraits, but Lilly did not appear any more.

A pocket had been pasted into the back cover of the album and held a small packet of letters. All but one were addressed to 'My dear Brothers and Sisters.' They were written on blue note paper and not one was dated. They were arranged, it seemed, in rough chronological order, and had undoubtedly been saved for Lilly by the London aunties and uncles, then turned over to her when she came to the United States.

The handwriting was large and childishly round. The first one spoke of mundane things such as the cost of living, the difficulty making ends meet, a longing for the family, and requests that they write more frequently. The second, obviously a few years later, dealt with the growing uneasiness over the menace brewing in Germany and Eastern Europe, and repeated failed attempts to get papers for Leon that would permit the family to return to England. Esther pleaded with her relatives to 'do what they could,' to get her husband admitted on the strength of her citizenship. There were several letters in this vein, each more despairing than the previous one.

The last letter of this group no longer discussed the adults; it was a straight plea for the child.

It read, 'My dearest Sisters and Brothers, I am afraid there is no longer any hope for Leon and me to get out of here. It is only a matter of time until Belgium will be invaded and then—who knows what? Everywhere we turned we were stopped, so perhaps it is God's will. But our little Lilly must be saved. I beg you not to abandon my little flower. We have arranged with our good friends and neighbor to put her safely in a Catholic Home, where her identity will be concealed until, God willing, this nightmare will end. If we live to raise our little girl, I will bless God forever. But we cannot count on that and you must promise me you will find Lilly no matter how long it takes and raise her with our family where she belongs.'

Part of the letter was smudged as though tears had fallen on the ink. Were they Esther's tears, Lilly's tears, the brothers' and sisters' who had received the letter?

'I think of you all the time. I long for home. Do not forget my baby. My deepest love to all of you, Your sister, Esther.'

I sat for a long time with the letter in my lap, thinking of the hopeless plight of this woman, torn between loyalty to and love for her husband and the desire to see her only and beloved child safe and grown to adulthood. And then being unable to accomplish either safeguarding and supporting her husband or raising her child.

Yet compared to others, she was lucky going to the gas chamber, believing that her child was safe. Many mothers had their babies in their arms, and when they understood what was happening, prayed that their children would breathe deeply and die quickly.

There was one more letter. It was addressed to Lilly and read, 'My own sweet child, First of all you must understand that Papa and I love you above everything else, and our deepest sorrow is that we will not be able to watch you grow up. Such joy that would have been! But your aunties and uncles will love you as we would have and will raise you to be the wonderful girl you are. Remember only that we cherish you. You must forget the rest, God's blessings on you forever and ever. Your Mama and Papa.'

I was dry-eyed and emotionless. The demands of the story, unfolded for the first time in its entirety, went so far beyond the usual that I had no capacity for grief or horror or any strong feeling at all. It was like a circuit breaker that shuts down all the power with an overload so that the house doesn't burst into flames.

I felt down into the pocket in the album checking for anything overlooked. My fingers contacted a square of paper thrust into a corner. Carefully I worked it out and held the bit of paper folded several times into a two inch oblong. I unfolded it, smoothing out the deep creases against my knee. The message was handwritten in French in Lilly's neat, round school-girl script.

"*La Fin De La Journee*," it read. "The End Of The Day."

I translated as I went along, recognizing one of Baudelaire's poems.

Not caring about the fading light, Life—insolent and noisy wastes itself without reason Until night voluptuously reaches for the horizon, Consoling all—even hunger Concealing all—even shame. The Poet says to himself, "At Last! Both my spirit and my body ardently crave their rest; My heart brims over with dreams of dying, I shall lie down and sleep shrouded in your curtains, O refreshing darkness!"

I was looking at Lilly's 'key,' her escape from fear and shame and despair. She must have memorized the poem; some of the creases showed signs of tearing through the paper. Did she reread it when things overwhelmed her?

I recalled the night we sat in the yard after Yosuf left, the night I felt so impotent against her hopelessness. That was when she spoke of her key—the way out when every door appeared locked. There was no point in speculating what event or series of events might have changed her mind—might have kept her from what she did.

Very carefully I folded the poem and the letters along the same creases, and placed them back in the pocket. I put the false identification in the pocket with the letters. I replaced the post-card of City Hall and closed the album, to stroke the leather some more.

I imagined all the fingers that had smoothed this album in the same way. Lilly, her parents, my unknown aunt and uncle, the Le Clercs who bravely risked discovery to save Lilly's precious things for her—a whole chain of invisible fingers whose life fluids were incorporated into the leather, making it warm and pliable and soft, like a living substance.

I reached down, picked the two albums off the floor, stacked the three neatly in my lap, and got up to replace them in the open drawer. I went through the rest of Lilly's things, hoping, longing for a note or letter or message from her to complete the circle of her family. All I found were her school note books, beautifully organized, written in her fine clear handwriting. Math, science, history, French, Spanish, everything up-to-date and perfect. She might have been another *wunderkind* like Yosuf, or just another ordinary, nice girl, bringing joy and sorrow to the people around her, the people who cared about her.

She had said that she wanted to be with her parents. Was she now? Or was she burning in hell eternally, as the Catholics said, for the sin of suicide? I could never know and I wanted never to know. Because Lilly was incorporated into me for good. It was an involuntary memorial; one I would not have chosen. But no matter how long I live, or how many years elapse between the time of Lilly and the present, part of my center is Lilly, with everything else revolving around her.

I closed all the drawers, looked around the room checking one last time, smoothed the already wrinkle-less spread, and turned off the lamp and left.

After a one-year hiatus, I went to college and majored in library science, finding refuge when I graduated in the magnificent New York City library system as a reference librarian.

It was after my father died, during the period of *shiva*, the week of mourning when there is time to sit together and contemplate the life of the loved one, that Mama confided in me.

My father's illness dragged on for about five years after the diagnosis. I was twenty when we were told he had a malignancy in his colon, but I couldn't come to grips with the information. He had been in pain for months and I was sure they must have made a mistake. Papa was invincible; besides, I couldn't imagine a world without him.

I loved him not only out of a child's respect for a parent, but because he was a wonderful friend as well as my protector and guide. He'd always been there when I needed him. He couldn't desert me when I still had so many years to live.

He looked quite well at first, and between bouts of pain carried on very much as usual. After the surgery, he wouldn't hear of reducing his work hours although my mother pleaded with him to be reasonable. So, eager to put the dreadful knowledge out of my mind, I was able to forget about it much of the time.

Papa was stoical about himself and never complained to me. His deterioration was gradual, and until the end his loss of weight and vigor weren't startlingly apparent. When we were told nothing more could be done, Mama refused to hospitalize him. She turned their bedroom into a nursing area, with a cot for herself alongside the rented bed with guardrails that could be cranked up and down.

We filled the room with plants during the day and put them out in the hallway at night. Mama was with him almost constantly until I came home from work. I would sit down next to his bed, take up his frail hand in mine and kiss it. He'd open his eyes and smile at me. I'd smile back and start recounting stories and events of how my day had gone. He would close his eyes wearily, but I knew he was awake because when I stopped he would open his eyes again and smile.

When Mama returned to the room, I would go down and eat the food she had prepared, then come up to relieve her, urging her to eat something. She grew very thin during this period, which caused me additional anxiety.

There were better days when he was able to tap a small reservoir of energy and I would come home to find him sitting up in a chair. He was gaunt, however, and his pajamas and bathrobe flapped around his body. Even his house slippers seemed several sizes too large. The day before he died, he was up and cheerful, with more energy than we had seen in weeks. He questioned me closely, commented succinctly and appropriately, and then told me he had hoped to live to see my children.

"Papa," I said, "just get well and I promise to have at least a dozen for you."

"Saraleh," it had been a long time since he had used that diminutive pet name for me, "don't make that a condition for having children. You're a wonderful girl. You should make some man happy by being his wife and giving him children as lovely as you are."

Suddenly he was worn-out and asked to be helped into bed. Sometime during the night he died so quietly that my mother, who had learned to sleep with an ear cocked for any slight stirring, did not know it until she went to him in the morning. I heard her cry out and in my nightgown ran to their room.

There was a smile on my father's face; the lines of pain and stress had disappeared. It took me awhile to understand what had happened. Then I joined my mother at his side, weeping long, hard tears of grief for the irreplaceable, dearest one.

Uncle Chaim made the funeral arangements because Mama and I were beyond functioning. Only during the days of sitting *shiva* did we recover enough to begin the review of the happy and the sad times in our little family. One of the nodal points was when Lilly came into our lives.

Mama told me that often during the first year, she and my father discussed Lilly's arrival, especially as it concerned me. She said from the day we met Lilly at the ship terminal they questioned whether they had done the right thing to bring her here. Almost immediately they felt helpless, unable to break through the cold, almost palpable wall of enmity they felt surrounded this child.

When the weeks went by and Lilly still never smiled, spoke rarely and only in reply to being addressed directly, ate practically nothing, and in unguarded moments displayed a frightening depth of hostility, they began to discuss the possibility of sending her back. But to what? The relatives in London would have been hard pressed to keep her even if my parents had sent money for her needs, which they would have done gladly. To send her back to a Catholic institution or for adoption to a Gentile family was unthinkable, a sin against the memory of the parents who were consumed in the fire and had begged the family to save their little flower, Lilly.

My parents, caught in this quandary, delayed making any decision, hoping that time would work its healing powers on Lilly, and with my help, bring her over to us.

Here my mother broke down and cried, hysterical, wracking sobs, and I didn't know whether she cried for the loss of my father, for herself, me, Lilly, or a combination of all of us. I had never seen her like this, my attractive, modern mother, who with all the warmth of her personality had rarely showed me more than her eyes filling with tears over the many tragedies life brought. This kind of grieving was appropriate, however, for sitting *shiva*, on wooden crates, the curtains drawn and all the mirrors in the house covered. I felt at home with it, and regularly gave vent to my own attacks of grief. When the paroxysm of sobbing subsided and my mother wiped her eyes and nose, she began talking again. She recalled a night when I didn't eat and they suspected it had to do with Lilly. By then she was feeling guilty about finding it hard to like Lilly when she believed she had to love her as she loved me, or at least like a daughter.

"I felt I was some kind of monster, that I didn't have enough heart and sympathy to love this poor little girl who had suffered so much in her short life."

Torn between her love for me, fears for my well-being, and guilt over being unfeeling and unfair to such a needy child, my mother erred in favor of Lilly, pushing away the signals which might have been a warning in ordinary circumstances that things were not going well and were not improving with time. But eventually my parents were forced to acknowledge the size of the problem and went for advice to the rabbi.

I was fascinated with Mama's recounting of all this history, trying to play it back alongside my own impotence and hopeless confusion. To think that we had been running parallel to each other but had a wall of fear and uncertainty screening, isolating us from the comfort, reassurance and insight we might have shared by pooling our perceptions and doubts . . . . Whether things would have been different for Lilly or me will always be nothing but conjecture now. We cannot relive our lives.

The rabbi told my parents that survivors were wounded people; he had been hearing of many severe problems of adjustment.

"He told us we can do only the best we can and hope for the best, but that we must protect our own child and not make her a victim too. That's when Papa and I decided that at least you would have your own room again."

Tears welled in Mama's eyes and I put my arm around her. "Mama, you and Papa did the best you could and it was very good. You gave more than a home and food, you gave your love and concern and kindness. But even the best medicine doesn't cure when the person is too sick. Now is the time to stop blaming yourself for Lilly. As for me, there is no one in the world who's had better parents, or more love. I'm only sorry to find out so late how you and Papa were hurting yourselves over something beyond your control. It's too late for me to say this to Papa, but it's time you stopped regretting, Mama. I know from my own experience what a bad companion remorse is. We're only human; we did the best we could."

I held Mama in my arms to comfort her. Papa's approving presence seemed to enfold us as we leaned together drawing strength from each other.

Several months later our rabbi asked if I would record the stories of Holocaust survivors in the community. I spent a week of indecision, first attracted then repelled by the idea, but agreed at last as I knew I inevitably must.

Interviewing survivors is fearfully sad and draining work and I periodically need a rest of a few weeks before I can summon enough determination to go on. As I accumulate this data, I am continually amazed by the sane state of mind of most of the survivors I've interviewed. Why were they not driven irrevocably

raving mad? This is just one of the many things I do not understand about the Holocaust and its aftermath. I find it easier to
understand the course Lilly took, although I will never stop
regretting it and regularly find myself angrily arguing with her for
becoming her own and last enemy.

One day I may write about Lilly, what she was to me and what
she might have been if . . . things had been different.

Today I know what I really didn't comprehend as a child—that
hatred of Jews is just one of many the human family indulges in.
We are forever wiping each other out for some egoistic or material
benefit. We are even concentrating our attention on our planet,
as if it too is an enemy. Knowing this doesn't reassure me nor has
it made me more accepting of malignant prejudice against any
people. Yet as much as I sorrow over the abysmal plight of millions,
the suffering of my own people touches the deepest chord. And
if it didn't, could I feel for others?

If Lilly had plodded on, struggling against her despair to
accept life's reality, including the persistent drive against Jews
from Islam and Christianity, and from the new left and old right,
how would she have resolved her fears? If the idea that Jews are
now more than ever an endangered species chills me, how would
Lilly, her pessimism confirmed, have felt?

When I weigh the ponderous questions of irrational hatred
and the obsessions integral to nations and diverse peoples, I ask
myself, which way should Jews go? Do we fight to avoid extinction,
attempting to increase our dwindling numbers, or do we quietly
accept the world view of us and fade away? Fortunately, this is my
personal mental exercise and not a decision I have to make.

My somber thoughts of the world's problems contrast almost
teasingly with the love people give and take, the feel of sunshine
and water, the beauty of our planet, the surge of joy that fills me
when Life stirs my juices. Who knows what God's ultimate plan is
for us and the globe we inhabit?

Yet, when I turn my thoughts to the memory of one young girl
who touched my life with fingers of fire, the larger questions fade
and I'm left with only the smaller one. Could we have found the
way to each other and together created a small haven, a safe place
to huddle together braving the storm? But then, is this question
any smaller than the others?

At last I give up. I'm too sad, remembering, to think. Ah, Lilly, Lilly. I'm too sad to think.

GLOSSARY

Afikomin - A piece of matzoh hidden during the Seder. Its discovery by the youngest member of the group permits the ceremony to continue.

Ark - A special cabinet on the altar which houses the Torah scrolls.

Bar Mitzvah - A boy who at his thirteenth birthday celebrates becoming part of the adult religious congregation. Also colloquially refers to the ceremony.

Bima - The synagogue altar.

Challah(s) - The Sabbath bread, usualy braided.

Chanukah - The Festival of Lights commemorating the victory of the Maccabees over the Greek-Syrians. An eight day holiday usually in the month of December. The holiday symbol is an eight branch candlelabra called a Menorah.

Charoses - A paste of apples, nuts and wine used during a Seder to symbolize the mortar used by Hebrew slaves to build the pyramids.

Chumetz - Food stuff containing yeast and other substances forbidden during the week of Passover.

Diaspora - Jews who live in any part of the world *except* Israel are considered Diaspora or dispersed Jews.

Erev - The night before.

Goy - Singular form of Goyim, sometimes derogatory in intent.

Goyim - A Hebrew word meaning 'nations.' Has come to mean other nations, i.e. Gentiles.

Gut Yontif - Yiddish, meaning 'happy holiday.'

Hadassah - An international womens zionist organization.

Haftorah - Lessons from the Prophets, read by a Bar Mitzvah.

Kiddush - Literally, 'sanctification.' Also refers to a special meal after the Sabbath service.

Kosher - According to the rules of *Kashruth*, commandments relating to food and its preparation.

Leahleh - Yiddish, diminutive for Lilly.

Matzoh - Unleavened bread used throughout Passover.

Mezuzah - A decorative container which holds a special religious statement including the Sh'ma. It is placed on the entrance doorjambs of public buildings and private dwellings.

Minyan - The required number of ten adults before the Torah can be read.

Mitzvahs - Six hundred and thirteen commandments. The ten commandments are the best known. The word has come to be used as synonymous with good deeds.

Passover - The holiday that commemorates Moses leading the Hebrew slaves out of Egypt.

Pesach - Hebrew for Passover.

Plotz - Yiddish word meaning burst or split.

Rosh Hashanah - The holiday celebrating the New Year. Usually falls in the month of September.

Saraleh - Pet name, diminutive, meaning 'little Sarah.'

Seder - Literally, 'order,' the religious reading and meal celebrating Passover.

Sh'ma - The basic statement of Judaism, that there is One God.

Shabbat - The Hebrew sabbath which runs from sunset Friday to sunset Saturday.

Shiva - The prescribed ritual during the period of mourning.

Shofar - A ram's horn blown in synagogue to signify the end of Yom Kippur.

Shul - Yiddish word for synagogue.

Simhat Torah - The Torah is the first five books of the Jewish Bible. Simhat Torah marks the completon of the one-year cycle devoted to reading the Torah.

Sukkah - The hut built outside home or synagogue in which meals are taken during Sukkot.

Sukkot - (Tabernacles) A harvest holiday celebrated in the fall. Commemorates the Exodus.

Synagogue - A house of worship and study and a meeting place, and can be as simple as a modest storefront.

Torah - The first five books of the Jewish Bible (Pentateuch).

Yarmulkas - Skull caps worn by observant Jews in synagogues and at home in respect for God.

Yiddish - A German-based language which was the universal language of Eastern European Jewry. Before the Holocaust it had an extensive literature.

Yom Kippur - Concludes the New Year. It is a day of fasting and an exchange of apologies and forgiveness for transgressions against people and God's commandments (mitzvahs).